Checkpoint

by
Lisa Saffron

authorHOUSE®

AuthorHouse™ UK Ltd.
500 Avebury Boulevard
Central Milton Keynes, MK9 2BE
www.authorhouse.co.uk
Phone: 08001974150

This book is a work of fiction. People, places, events, and situations are the product of the author's imagination. Any resemblance to actual persons, living or dead, or historical events, is purely coincidental.

First published by AuthorHouse 2/11/2008

ISBN: 978-1-4343-5492-1 (sc)

Printed in the United States of America
Bloomington, Indiana

This book is printed on acid-free paper.

Acknowledgments

I am grateful to Monica Jones, Sally Collings, Judy Sherwood, Hala Abuateya, Vivi Jackson, and Sue Roe for commenting on the first draft; to Pameli Benham and Liz Welsh for their guidance and support, to Leah Green and Maha el-Taji for leading me on the roller-coaster ride of compassionate listening through Israel and Palestine and to Maria Kennedy, my partner, for being supportive and encouraging and level-headed through all my ups and downs.

PART ONE
October 2002

CHAPTER 1
Yigal

Boring. Boring. Boring. A year in the army and I end up at the most boring checkpoint ever. I want action, excitement, a hit of adrenalin. That's what I was trained for. But no, the only action at this checkpoint is up with the clouds. Hey, I take that back. Today even the clouds are boring. They hide the sky in a half-hearted kind of way, like they can't be bothered. Everywhere I look, there are places where the clouds get hazy and vague at the edges and the blue pokes through.

I'm not on my own in this deserted, bleak checkpoint. There's a girl with me. She's pretty or would be if she smiled once in a while. We'd never met before we got here even though we grew up less than 20 miles apart. We're gradually getting acquainted. There's no choice really. Most of the time, it's just the two of us here, stuck together like Siamese twins. You can't choose your mates when you're in the army.

Our first meeting was wild, explosive. We fought a lot. She was expecting a different posting and took it out on me. As if it were my fault we were here. She drove me crazy with her yelling and blaming and having to be right all the time. I had enough arguing from my kid sister, Orli. The best thing about going into the army was getting away from Orli and all that arguing. So I was really fed up to find myself with another argumentative girl.

We stopped arguing after a few weeks. Maybe it was only a few days. I can't keep track of the time. Now she hardly says a word. Most of the time, we lie on the hard, dusty concrete pathway and watch the clouds in silence.

At first, I felt relieved. I got into cloud watching too. Spent ages following clouds through their manoeuvres. I tried not to pay any attention to her. But it's kind of hard to ignore someone lying right next to you who's sending out hostile vibes. I can't stand the silence. I'd rather be arguing than not talking at all.

'Look,' I say. 'See that patch of blue. It's getting bigger. Do you see?'

She grunts. I wonder if she's as bored as me. We watch the clouds peel back from the blue patch, exposing more naked sky.

I remember the first time I flew in an airplane and saw clouds from above. I was seven years old. The tops of the clouds were so utterly amazing that tears came into my eyes. They were secret tears so my mom and little sister didn't see. If my dad had been with us, he would have smacked me on the back of my head. He hated it when any of us cried, especially my mom. I wanted the window seat all to myself so I could look at the clouds. But Orli kicked up a fuss, screaming and crying. She was four. She always got her way by screaming. Mom made us take turns in the window seat. When it was Orli's turn, she didn't even look out the window. She only wanted to sit there because I wanted it. I was so angry I sulked most of the way from Israel to Baltimore.

There's a strange churning in my gut and my eyes are stinging. I blink and look up at the sky. Grey clouds are plastering over the blue patches. Now it's a solid mass, like a lid on a coffin. I'm 19 years old and that fight with Orli still bugs me. How pathetic. I can't believe how much I miss my bratty little sister.

'I miss my father.' The words float by in a whisper. I wait for her to say more. The cloud is thinning out directly above us, hinting at blue sky on the other side. I want her to go on talking but I don't know what to say that won't set off another argument.

'He's a good man. He never hurt anyone.' Tears spill down her cheeks. The cloud has turned heavy and thick and a soft, dull rain begins. My eyes are stinging again. I look away. It's all right for girls to cry. Not for boys though.

'What's your father do for a living?' I'm not really interested. I just want her to stop crying. To my surprise, she answers. 'He hasn't worked since.. Not for a long time. He used to work in a grocery shop. He isn't well. Hasn't been well for years.'

'Oh. Too bad.' That was a conversation stopper. We watch the clouds again. I hope they lighten up soon. But they don't.

'My dad's an electrical engineer,' I say. She doesn't even glance at me. I don't get the impression she's in the least bit interested in what my dad does. That's okay. I'm not interested either. I'm not sure even my dad is all that interested. He never talks about his work. A few years ago, a teacher asked me what my dad did for a living. I can't remember why. I remember being embarrassed I didn't know. I went home and tried to get my mom to tell me but she said I should ask dad myself. Maybe she didn't know. More likely, she wanted me and dad to bond. My mom has a thing about us bonding. By age 16, I already knew bonding was out of the question. Still, I stood in the doorway of the living room when Dad was reading the newspaper and blurted it out. He frowned, like he always does when I say anything, like he's thinking what a stupid question. But he did answer. He said he was in charge of developing automatic test equipment and something else about investigating production faults. Then he changed the subject. The only time I saw him get real excited about his work was when he talked about his military service. He was in the Israeli air force working as a helicopter night vision field and lab technician and then he was in the reserves every year for a month. That stopped five years ago. Sometimes he talks about that and about his mates from the army. He still sees them but he never brings them home or takes us to meet them. Even my mom has never met them.

'So what's he like, your dad?' she says. But before I answer, she shrugs and rolls away from me. 'Oh forget it. I don't feel like talking about our families. Not with you.'

She's so damn rude. I could thump her but there's no point. I can't get away from her. Not for long anyway and not far. Anyway, how do you answer a question like that? What's my dad like? Well, he's my dad. We don't get on that well. We've got different personalities. He's angry and disapproving. I'm easy going. We like different things.

'Hey, I feel like talking, even if you don't,' I say to her back. I sit up and lean against a concrete pillar. 'I'll tell you what my dad's like. Here's a good example. Last year, he wanted to show how proud he was of me going into the army but he couldn't think what to do to celebrate. My mom made some stupid suggestions. As usual. She was always trying to get me and Dad to bond. But we could never find anything we both liked to do together. Mom said I should choose and Dad finally agreed. So I took him to… to a .' I crack up laughing. I must have been off my head to take my dad there.

She turns to face me and glares impatiently. 'Take him where? What's so funny?'

'I took him to a night club in Tel Aviv,' I say and can't speak for laughing. It was a disaster if the goal was father-son bonding. Still I enjoyed myself. There was a great DJ and I saw a few kids from school. I had a good time dancing and drinking. I say out loud, 'Dad was so out of place. Everyone was under 25 and there was my middle aged, nearly bald dad standing at the bar by himself, looking like a dirty old man. One time, he was surrounded by a group of girls pouring beer down his throat with beer pistols.' I laugh so hard I fall back against the concrete pillar and gasp for breath.

'That's disgusting.' She sits up straight and looks down her nose at me, as if I'm some kind of degenerate, low-life.

'Oh, what! Are you a killjoy like my father? Or super-religious? What's disgusting about it? Haven't you ever been to a night club?'

'No, certainly not.' She rolls her eyes, as if I'm an idiot even to ask.

'My dad had never been either. He acted as if it was an endurance test, an ordeal to get through, like in the army. Like he was being invaded by noise, attacked by toxic fumes from sweaty bodies and beer, forced into solitary confinement at the bar. All the way home, he sniped about the people at the club. Called them hedonistic and mindless. Said they didn't care about anybody but themselves, they didn't take anything seriously.'

I sigh. Even if I hadn't been drunk, I wouldn't have bothered arguing with him. It was too ridiculous. I've always stayed cool around my dad. I don't bother making fun of him and I don't let him wind me up. I figure Dad and I belong to separate worlds and that's the way it is. Orli, on the other hand, is like a caged pit-bull terrier. One poke by Dad and she's snarling and foaming at the mouth, ready to bite his head off. In a lot of ways, they're very similar to each other.

'Is that what you're like? Hedonistic and mindless?' She's still got a disapproving look on her face.

'No,' I say. 'Hey, I was having a good time. Being happy. Getting into the music. Why should I get all stressed out? But look, I'm not irresponsible. I've done what's expected of me. I joined the army. So I don't know what he was complaining about. He's so bitter and critical. Do you want to know what he said when we got home from the night club?'

She doesn't want to know but I tell her anyway. 'He said he hoped three years in the army would make me grow up. Well, it seems to have had the opposite effect.'

I glare at her accusingly and stomp off to the next concrete pillar. No, I don't want to grow up to be uptight like my dad. What I want is to grow up to be me. Thick, serious clouds cover up the blue patches in the sky. Everywhere I look, the clouds are stiff and final. No blue pokes through. Like my life.

CHAPTER 2
Ruth

For seven days, I sat. An entire week in October. On the first day, I noticed a low wooden bench had appeared in a corner of my living room. A herd of folding chairs had arrived to keep the bench company. I don't know how they came to take up residence in my living room.

For seven days, I sat on the low wooden bench and watched the chairs as they moved about the room, folded themselves up, unfolded themselves, were sat on, were empty.

For seven days, I sat on the low wooden bench cut off from the world as if I were down at the bottom of a well. Through the dark, murky haze, I could make out people moving around my living room. Some I recognised. Others were strangers.

For seven days, I sat on the low wooden bench and observed things as they floated by my field of vision - a paper plate with rice salad, a pair of wet eyes, a cup of undrinkable coffee, a face screwed up with embarrassment, legs in uniform, a bowl of cashew nuts, a hand with a turquoise wedding ring. Once I looked down and saw a dirty plastic knife and fork in my hand. Had I eaten something?

On the second day, I went into the toilet and counted 25 rolls of toilet paper stacked neatly in the bathtub. I counted them twice. I've never bought that many rolls of toilet paper. I suspected my mother-in-law. David's mother hoarded food and household goods, a legacy of war-time Ukraine. But when I went to ask her about the toilet paper, she was locked in a surreal conversation with David's father. I heard her say, 'Do I look like a coffee machine?' I didn't hang around to hear her husband's reply. He was a morose, uncommunicative man and seldom spoke.

Later that day, I caught a fleeting glimpse of a head with tightly curled brown hair. I half rose from the bench, convinced it was Yigal. But it was not my son. Whenever the front door opened, I looked up, expecting to see him dashing in, smiling and laughing, home on leave from military service.

Back on the bench, I talked to Rena about a particularly difficult boy in my class at the primary school where I teach. Only later did I pause to marvel at the topic of conversation. We'd lived next door to Rena for 16 years. In that time, I'd never once talked to her about my work. She wasn't interested in anyone but herself. A tray of candied almonds drifted by. I scooped them into my lap and ate them all without sharing one. Rena watched and unusually for her, made no comment.

In the evening, I was in the kitchen dishing moussaka onto ten paper plates laid out in a line. Back on the bench, I looked at the empty plate in my lap. Did I cook the moussaka? Did I eat any of it? A burst of young male voices blew in from the veranda where a group of Yigal's friends were gathered. That was just like Yigal to greet his friends before coming to say hello to his mother. Well, I wouldn't demean myself by pursuing him and embarrassing him in front of his friends. I made myself sit on the bench, as if I were busy with important things. At least he'd arrived.

I became aware of a comforting presence. My father was sitting next to me, reading a book. He patted my knee. How long had he been sitting there? When had he arrived in Israel? Snatches of conversation floated around me. Was it the same person saying the same thing hundreds of time or hundreds of people saying each phrase once? A notebook was thrust in my face by my 15 year old niece, Susie. 'Look, Aunt Ruth. Look what people have written in the book.' The writing on the page wiggled and squirmed out of focus.

On the third day, I heard an unfamiliar male voice say, 'You know what we say in the army, 'What doesn't kill you, strengthens you. What kills you, strengthens your mother.'' I nearly got off the bench to tell the man, whoever he was, it wasn't true. But I didn't have the energy.

On the fourth day, I heard Orli arguing loudly with someone. Annoyance and anxiety washed over me in equal measures. What was she on about now? Couldn't she ever act appropriately in company? This was hardly the time for her to fly off the handle. I noticed my nephew Tom sitting with me on the bench. He was holding my hand, not saying a word. I asked him to take Orli outside and calm her down. He went without an argument. How had he turned out so loving with a mother like my sister Shirley?

Later, Orli and Tom stood in front of the bench, looking down at me from a great height. They grabbed my arms and led me out of the house as if I were a toddler. As we walked around the block, Tom said, 'Hey Aunt Ruth, do you remember the time you came to Baltimore for the summer and you took us kids to Lake Roland for the day?'

'I remember,' Orli burst in.

'No,' I said. A vagueness, never far from my mind over the last week, blocked the memory. 'No, I can't remember. Which visit was it?'

'I was nine,' Tom said. 'It was the summer I started Little League. That's how I know. How can you remember it, Orli? You were only four.'

'So what? I do remember,' Orli insisted. 'I remember we walked along a path from a dam. I remember you said we might see Baltimore Orioles migrating. I remember Tanya fell over and hurt her knee. I remember Yigal got us all singing.'

'Yes, he did,' Tom said. 'We sang lullabies, Shabbat songs, songs from musicals, Israeli folk songs, rounds, campfire songs, corny songs.'

'If I were a rich man,' Orli shut her eyes and hunched her shoulders as she sang. Tom and I joined in. We linked arms and walked down the streets of Tsur Hadassah singing at the top of our lungs. It was only later I stopped to marvel at the thought of my 16 year old argumentative daughter singing in the street with her mother and her 21 year old cousin.

On the fifth day, the phone rang but by the time, I figured out I was supposed to get up and answer it, Rena had picked it up. My mother brought me a piece of apple strudel and insisted on explaining how she'd made it. I took a bite but tasted nothing. I wandered into the kitchen, intending to throw the strudel away. I saw David leaning against the fridge talking to Rena. The strudel curdled in my stomach and I backed out, unnoticed.

Back on the bench, I snoozed, my head bobbing up and down, my mouth falling open. In the moment of semi-wakefulness between dropping and lifting my head, I clearly heard Vivi's voice. She was calling me. Vivi, my best friend, my longest friend, my soul mate. The only person in the world I wanted to see at that moment. I jumped up, my heart pounding. She'd come all the way to Israel to see me. Even though I hadn't spoken to her for two years, I knew she would come when I needed her. The last time we'd seen each other, we'd had a screaming, sobbing, door-slamming argument. What idiots we were. I stood up suddenly and bumped into my sister, Adele, who was walking by. She hugged me tight. I pushed her away. My sisters and

I had never been in the habit of hugging. I wasn't about to start now.

'Adele,' I said quickly, hoping to forestall more unwelcome intimacy. 'Did Vivi and I fight a lot when we were teenagers?'

She shrugged. 'I don't know.' She pulled a used tissue out of her pocket and wiped her nose. Her eyes were bloodshot.

"C'mon Adele. Can't you remember anything?'

'You guys talked a lot. You were always together, always talking. About politics. Yeah, you used to have big arguments about politics.'

'No we didn't,' I said irritably. I don't remember big arguments with Vivi though I do remember how dogmatic she was. She always had to be right. Most of the time I let her be right but sometimes I'd get so wound up I didn't know what I was saying and I'd run home crying. Vivi always came after me right away and made up. She was good at making up. She wouldn't let me sulk. But we had a fight at Thanksgiving, two years ago, that time we were staying with my parents in Baltimore. She hadn't made up. I started sobbing, gulping air like a drowning fish. Adele put her arms out to hug me. We collided like two stiff boards and bounced apart. She patted my head.

'I'm sure you're not really crying about Vivi, Ruth. She's the last person you need around you right now. It's a good thing you two haven't made up. If she were here, she'd really put the boot in.'

I yanked my head away. 'No she wouldn't. And she is here.'

'Where?' Adele craned her neck to look round the crowded living room. 'Did you ask her to come?'

'No, but I heard her voice. I'm going to find her.'

I left Adele and wandered out to the veranda. I passed my husband talking intensely with a group of men. I didn't know any of them. I heard snatches of their conversation. '..shot him in the stomach... A boy in a playground... Maybe 12 or 13.' One of them, a man with a long beard and a knitted cap, noticed me and leapt out of the huddle. 'Hello Ruth. I'm Shlomo,' he said. He had kind eyes and a sweet smile. As soon as Shlomo spoke to me, the other men clammed up.

'What were you talking about?' I asked. My question dropped like a stone into the silence. David shifted anxiously from foot to foot and looked away. It was Shlomo who answered, 'Army talk. We were just catching up. We were all in the reserves together.' He nudged David who shrugged irritably. Shlomo continued, 'Ruth, this is Yosef, Eyal, Gil.' The men nodded at me. Gil, the youngest by several decades, reached over to shake my hand. 'I was Yigal's commanding officer,' he said. There was an awkward silence, broken by Shlomo. 'Since we finished reserve duty five years ago,' he said, 'well, we haven't seen as much of each other as we'd like.'

I'd never met my husband's army mates. He kept them to himself, jealously guarding his friendship with them like a poker player with his hand of cards. I was surprised he'd invited them to our house though his reluctance to introduce me didn't surprise me. He was shy and awkward in social situations. I turned to David.

'I heard Vivi's voice,' I said. 'Have you seen her?'

'No way is that bitch coming here,' he said. His voice was hoarse, scary. I stared at him in horror. My gut twisted with pain and I doubled over, gasping. Shlomo guided me back to the bench and handed me a glass of mint tea. I lost myself in its soothing taste, its total tea-ness. Nothing else mattered.

CHAPTER 3

Vivi

On the 7th of October 2002, I was on the plane to Israel. The Rocky Mountains were spread out below, winking up at me, bright sunshine exposing jagged peaks. I leaned my forehead against the glass and saw the mountains rolling into the distance as far as the view from the tiny window would allow. I thought of Buber. Whenever my cat wanted my attention, he would roll on his back, wave his paws in the air and expose his belly for me to stroke. I missed him already. What was I doing trapped on this airplane, leaving the safety of my home to stay in a conflict zone for a month?

All of a sudden, a hand shot by, narrowly missing my nose. It pulled down the blind and retreated. I blinked rapidly, my brain scrambling to register the change of scenery. The mountains were gone. The hand belonged to the middle-aged woman wedged into the seat next to mine, wearing headphones and staring fixedly at the screen in front of her. Her elbow was jutting into my territory.

'Excuse me,' I said, drawing out the second syllable to convey my annoyance.

No response. I studied her closely. She was wearing a navy polyester skirt and a chiffon blouse with a ruffle collar and elastic cuffs. A simple cross hung on a gold chain around her neck.

'Hey. What do you think you're doing?' I waved my hand in front of her face. She continued to stare at the screen as if I were invisible. I had an overpowering urge to kick her elbow off the armrest, rip the headphones off her smug, arrogant head and scream obscenities in her ear. Fortunately for her, I was so tightly jammed into the seat that my tantrum options were severely restricted. I ground my teeth and raised the blind.

The Rocky Mountains were still below us but I was only aware of my queasy stomach and pounding heart. If I couldn't concentrate on the view, I'd have to think about the purpose of my trip. And that I didn't want to do. The decision to go to a Palestinian village for a month was made two weeks before in response to an email calling for volunteers from abroad. After years of campaigning in Portland, I wanted to do something practical to help the Palestinian cause. I wanted to be there in person, to put myself on the line. But now I was on the way, I was beginning to wonder whether I'd been slightly impetuous. Was I really up for the task? What was I getting myself into?

The woman in the next seat launched another attack. This time I held tight to the blind. She retreated, again without speaking to me or looking at me. No partner for peace here. Shaking my head in amazement, I wondered what Buber would do if he were locked in a small space with an uncommunicative opponent. Of course. He would groom himself. The thought of Buber closing his eyes, twisting his neck to face his back, sticking out his tongue and vigorously licking between his shoulder blades cheered me up. I decided to try it for myself. I examined my finger nails, dug in my backpack for a comb, ran the comb through my hair, and wiped the crumbs off my new maroon sweatshirt bought specially for the trip from Nordstroms. I peeked at my adversary. She was still staring at the tiny screen, her shoulders hunched, her jaw clenched. There was something familiar about her. Who did she remind me of?

I'd have to do something more dramatic to get this woman's attention. Buber would do his sideways dance. He would arch his back, raise his tail into a daring bow and prance around his opponent. I wiggled in my seat, bumped the woman's elbow and banged against her knee. But I may as well have been a flea for all the notice I got.

That's when it came flooding back to me in waves of unwelcome memory. My friend Ruth! That's who she reminded me of. I hadn't been in touch with Ruth for two years. Like ice skaters gliding effortlessly over smooth ice, we'd skated arm in arm from the moment we met at the age of 12 until we graduated from college. After graduation we spent the summer together at a kibbutz in northern Israel. By the end of the summer, a crack had appeared in the solidly frozen lake of our friendship. That crack was Zionism. To my dismay, Ruth took advantage of her right to return as a Jew and made the decision to move to Israel for good. We stayed friends but the crack in the ice grew wider the more I learned about Israel's relations with the Palestinians. We skated on, awkwardly avoiding the crack by talking about everything else – partners, children, jobs, parents, friendships. Everything but politics. I tried to hang on but shortly after the start of the second Intifada, we had the fateful argument. The ice split open and I fell through to the freezing water below. Since then, I hadn't been able to crawl out. Our friendship was over. And now I was on my way to Israel not even intending to visit her.

Buber wouldn't have let a quarrel go on for years. He'd rather be happy than right. Of course, he never did anything he later regretted. If he wanted to be on good terms with me, he would seek me out, purr like a little engine, and offer me a dead mouse. It crossed my mind I could look Ruth up while I was in the country, make a peace offering of some sort. Maybe she didn't really mean the things she'd said during that argument. Surely my rational, thoughtful, compassionate, caring friend couldn't have turned into the bigoted, ignorant, hate-filled extremist that emerged during the argument. Maybe I should give her another chance. Maybe we could be friends again.

Encouraged by the thought of making up with Ruth, I tapped my neighbour on the shoulder. I didn't have a dead mouse but I did have a mint to offer her. She took off the headphones and examined the mint carefully.

'You don't have any Valium, do you?' she said. 'I'm terrified of flying. I've been willing the plane to stay in the air for hours and I don't know if I can go on.'

At last, someone to talk to. I smiled reassuringly back at her. 'No, I don't. I could use some Valium myself. Tell you what. Why don't I hold up the plane while you take a nap?'

She looked relieved but unconvinced. 'No, I'm too scared to sleep. Talk to me. That would help.'

'What about?' I said.

'I don't care. Anything. Just don't talk about plane crashes. Please. Tell me about your trip. What are you going to do in Israel?'

'I'm not going to Israel. I'm going to Palestine,' I said. Her eyes widened and her neck swivelled as she scanned the plane for help. Oh no! Why did I say that? Why is everything so complicated? Either she and I were headed for outright conflict or I would feel compelled to explain the entire history of the Middle East to her. Neither of which appealed to me.

There was a pause. She plastered a big smile on her face and said, 'I'm going to Israel on a Holy Land tour with my church. There's ten of us on the plane. Our pastor, see that bald man over there. He's leading the tour.'

'Will you see the Church of the Nativity?'

'Oh yes. Here's our itinerary.' Eagerly, she pulled out a small notebook from her purse and passed it to me.

'Look,' I said. 'It says here you're going to Bethlehem, Jericho and Gush Etzion. So you'll be in Palestine too.' I handed the notebook back to her. Gush Etzion? Why was a Christian going to an illegal Jewish settlement in the West Bank?

Her face reddened. 'No, no. You don't understand,' she said. 'We're going to Israel, to the Holy Land. There's my pastor. I'll get him to talk to you. I'm not very good at explaining things.'

'All the places you're going to are in the Palestinian National Authority, under Israeli military occupation. Those areas haven't been annexed by Israel.'

She caught her breath. 'Are you Muslim?' she whispered. She shifted in her seat, creating an inch of space between us, her eyes wild with anxiety.

'No. But you're not far off. I'm from another branch of the family, also descendants of Abraham.'

Her hands fluttered to stroke the cross around her neck. She craned her neck, looking for her pastor. I sighed. This was going to be a long tedious flight. I decided to take pity on her.

'I'm Jewish,' I said. 'Actually I'm thinking of visiting an old friend of mine. My high school buddy, Ruth. She lives in Tsur Hadassah, just west of Jerusalem in the Jerusalem mountains. My name's Vivi, by the way. Vivi Rubenstein.'

'Barbara.' She still looked wary. 'Where are you from Vivi?'

'Portland. And you?'

21

'St Maries, Idaho. Do you know it?'

No I didn't. An hour later, I was as familiar with the place as if I'd grown up there. Fortunately, her narrative didn't require my full attention. As she rattled on breathlessly about her church and her children, my mind drifted back to Ruth.

I met Ruth soon after my family moved to Baltimore. In the second week of junior high school, she invited me to sit with her at lunch time. Why she asked me, the shy, serious new girl, I'll never understand. In an agony of embarrassment, I sat tongue-tied, answering every question in monosyllables. I thought she was amazing. She was friendly and outgoing and popular. I wanted to be her. I wanted to be part of her lively, noisy Jewish family. In the Shapiro family, everyone talked at once. They interrupted each other. They didn't listen. Even the dog joined in. Ruth's two older sisters were always screaming with laughter. Her mother talked non-stop and every time I dropped by, her dad had another bad joke to tell me.

I was an only child. No pets. No brothers. No sisters. Just me and my parents, two dry academics who lectured me about the dangers of religion at dinner time and shushed me when I raised my voice. My parents belonged to a Reform synagogue which they attended twice a year in their stiff, suspicious way on the High Holy Days. The synagogue was a large modern building, the English sermon and prayers landing flat and sterile in the empty space.

The Shapiro's introduced me to Judaism with soul. They belonged to Beth Am, a conservative synagogue. They weren't embarrassingly different like the Hasidim and the Ultra-Orthodox. They were comfortably observant. By the time Ruth had her Bat Mitzvah, I was right there in the bosom of the Shapiro family, purring like a kitten at the teat.

Ruth took it all for granted. Her parents sent her to Jewish studies classes twice a week at an after-school *cheder*. Being obedient and well-behaved, she went as instructed and spent the time cheerfully chatting to her friends. She was delighted when I wanted to come too. But I didn't chat and throw paper airplanes at the other kids. I paid attention to the teachers. I wanted to learn everything I had missed.

I embraced Judaism with an all-or-nothing passion that swept Ruth along with me. Every Saturday, I met her at the Beth Am synagogue. I walked the two mile journey by myself, wearing a skirt, ironed blouse, tights and pumps. I badgered my bewildered parents into keeping kosher. I woke at six to study Hebrew. Without my enthusiasm, I think Ruth's Jewish practice would have faded into a casual, social activity like that of her sisters, Shirley and Adele. But my intensity and Ruth's agreeableness welded us into a devout, passionate pair.

'What about you? Do you have any?' Barbara's voice cut into my reverie.

'Sorry. I didn't catch what you said. Any what?'

'Any children?' Barbara was looking at me suspiciously.

'Oh, yes. One boy. Noah. He's 20. At university.'

'And what does your husband do?'

'A midwife,' I muttered hoping she hadn't heard.

'Did you say a midwife? How interesting. I've never heard of a male midwife. How does he like the work?'

I groaned. I was expecting questions about my husband from the Palestinians I'd be staying with. So I'd accepted the need to be evasive about my partner. But Barbara's reaction caught me off guard. Next time someone asked, I'd say my partner was a doctor. Thank God, Claire wasn't around to hear me lie.

'Yeah, it's okay. It's a job,' I said. 'Say Barbara, do you mind if I climb over you? I need to walk around for a bit.'

As I scrambled past, I wondered if I could bear another 12 hours with Barbara.

CHAPTER 4

Yigal

We've been lying flat on our backs, side by side, studying the clouds for a long time. An immense grey dinosaur-shaped cloud is stalking a tiny bird-shaped cloud. The dinosaur has wide-open jaws, ready to snap up the little bird. Beneath the dinosaur, there's a cloud bordering the horizon, grey with a pink trim. I am going out of my mind with boredom. I want to do something else, anything other than watch clouds. But my companion is in one of her moods. She's gazing up at the clouds as if there's nothing more important in the whole world.

I wander off, leaving her with the clouds. Lately, I've been doing some thinking. Trying to make sense of things. Sensitive things. Things I wouldn't normally talk about with girl friends or my mother or my American cousins. I know I shouldn't talk about them with girls. But she's here and I need to talk. I drift back the long way round. She's in the same position. I sit down next to her.

'Hey,' I say.

'Hey,' she says, not taking her eyes off the clouds.

I stare into the distance, take a deep breath and launch in, as if talking to myself. 'The first time I was on duty at a checkpoint, I was scared shitless.'

She scowls. She shoots a warning glance at me and quickly looks away. I take that as a sign to continue. 'Of course, I didn't admit that to anyone in my unit.'

This is a big admission for me to make and I'd like some acknowledgement. But she merely tuts. Her scowl darkens.

'There were a lot of Arabs, shouting and pushing, trying to get through. Men in suits on their way to work, old women carrying huge bags, mothers and fathers holding kids, pregnant women, all sorts.'

'I don't want to hear about it,' she says.

'I spoke politely to them. I was respectful. They smiled at me but they were false smiles, snide smiles. They had hatred in their eyes. They asked me how I was. I could hear the contempt in their voices. They mobbed me. They walked past without showing me their passes.' I hesitated and said it again. 'I was scared.'

'Huh,' she says.

'Gil rescued me. He was my first commanding officer. He fired his gun in the air and shouted at them to get in line and shut up. They did, real fast.' The dinosaur cloud has lost its jaws and has broken up into several smaller clouds.

'When everyone calmed down, Gil came over and slapped me on the back. He said, 'Listen kid, you've got to make the Arabs afraid of us. They have more reason to be frightened of us than we do of them. After all, it's up to you whether they get through the checkpoint or **not**."

'That's enough,' she says, sitting up and frowning.

I carry on. 'Then he grabbed a man out of the line, a middle-aged man, dressed in a suit, like a business man, ordered him to put his hands on his head and stand on the side. It was last July. The sun was blasting down. Gil sat on a cement block and took out a bottle of water. When he'd had a good long drink, he passed the bottle to me. I drank. Gil pulled out his…' I glance at her and decide the detail isn't necessary. 'He took a piss in full view of the man and the Arabs in the line. There were hundreds of them, all silent, watching us, waiting. It was creepy.'

'Would you shut up!' She turns her back to me.

I can't stop now. 'Gil and I ate our sandwiches. An hour went by. Two hours. After three hours, Gil said to me, 'It's up to you. You decide whether they go through and when.' I let them stew another half hour. Then I called them through. This time I didn't look them in the eye. And they didn't ask how I was.'

She's turned round and is staring at me. 'Please shut up,' she says. Her voice is weary. But I don't have any more to say. I feel flat. I wish she would say something more than shut up. We look at each other for the briefest moment.

'I didn't like doing it,' I say softly.

'Poor you,' she says. 'Why do you tell me about it? What do you want me to say?'

27

'I don't know. I was hoping… I guess I want you to … I don't know. It was hard for me. Can't you hear that?'

'How did I get stuck with a pathetic, cry-baby like you?' she says.

Which is not what I wanted to hear.

CHAPTER 5

Vivi

Once the plane left land and was over the Atlantic Ocean, I could no longer avoid Barbara by pretending interest in the view. I opened the Amos Oz novel I'd bought in a second-hand shop following advice from more experienced travellers not to carry any pro-Palestinian literature with me. I hoped the Oz book would allay suspicions by Israeli customs officers as well as being a good read for the long flight. However, I wasn't in the mood to read. Nor could I sleep. All I could do was think and the more I thought, the more uncomfortable I felt about going to Israel without seeing Ruth.

Suddenly a bald head loomed over me. Barbara warbled breathlessly in my ear. 'Vivi, this is Reverend Miller,' she said. 'He's leading our Holy Land Tour. I asked him to come over and have a chat with you. I just knew you'd want to meet him. Reverend, this is Vivi. She's a Jewess.' Her voice rose as she spoke, ending with a loud squeal.

I was trapped. With Barbara seated between me and the aisle and a large Reverend Miller dominating the entire width of the aisle, I didn't have a chance.

'Have you been to Israel before, Vivi?' Reverend Miller asked, leaning scandalously close to Barbara's face and pinning me to my seat with a much too interested look. Barbara tittered. He settled into position, resting one arm against the head rest of the seat in front and the other on Barbara's shoulder. She tittered again. My skin crawled with irritation.

'Yes, twice,' I said, frantically weighing up my range of evangelical-dispatch tactics and deciding none of them would work in this situation.

'Well, Vivi, I've been 12 times to your homeland. Exactly when were you there?'

'My home is the United States,' I said, more aggressively than was safe. He opened his mouth and I quickly jumped in. 'I was there in 1978 and again in 1987 to visit my friend Ruth.' That should keep you happy, I thought. Now go away and leave me in peace.

'Vivi, God bless you and your friend Ruth,' Reverend Miller said. 'We Christians of Idaho stand with you in these dark and dangerous times. It is an honour to meet you.' He plucked my hand from my lap and held it tightly in his sweaty palm. There was a surreal moment where we fought grimly for possession of my hand. He won. 'Vivi, you'll be glad to hear about our efforts to support Israel against the forces of evil. Islamic terrorism is a growing menace as I'm sure you know. Five years ago, our church adopted an Israeli settlement in Samaria.' His oily face lit up with pride and he looked intently at me. Horrified, I kept my mouth tightly shut, hoping my face wouldn't betray my true feelings.

'We raised more than $100,000,' Barbara interrupted.

'And Vivi, let me tell you about our efforts to help Jews from the former Soviet Union emigrate to Israel,' Reverend Miller continued.

'We raised $50,000 for Russian Jews to move to Israel,' Barbara said.

I scowled, thinking of the measly $3,000 my Justice for Palestine group had scraped together for a medical clinic in Gaza City. 'That's a lot of money,' I admitted. 'Yes, Vivi, we're proud of our humble efforts to fulfil the Biblical prophecy. It's God's will for the Jewish people to return to Israel. Our church has directly contributed to increasing the number of new immigrants at our settlement. Do you know the population has more than doubled in the last ten years? Perhaps you know of it? It's called Ma'ale Zahav.'

A chill went through me. Not only had I heard of Ma'ale Zahav, I was on my way to stay in the neighbouring Palestinian village of Beyt Nattif. Ma'ale Zahav was an illegal Jewish settlement in the occupied West Bank with a particularly vicious population. Thugs from Ma'ale Zahav had been carrying out pogroms against Beyt Nattif. Knowing they could expect no protection from the Israeli army and police, the villagers of Beyt Nattif had requested help from an international citizens peace keeping group. I had joined the group in the hope our presence would deter the settlers from further attacks.

I glared at Reverend Miller and yanked my hand out of his grip. While I was wondering whether it was my duty to present an alternative point of view, Barbara chipped in with a conspiratorial whisper.

'And do you know what happens then, Vivi? When all the Jews are gathered in the Holy Land, 144,000 Jews will repent and accept Christ as the Messiah. They'll join up with the army of the righteous for Armageddon. Then Christ will return. Isn't that so, Reverend?' Her final statement was muffled by Reverend Miller's jacket as he leaned against her mouth.

'Now, Vivi, let's not worry about the end-times right now. Our role is to support the Jewish people and to stand by Israel.'

End-times? Were they for real? I wiped my wet hand on my sweatshirt and shook my head. That did it. I was under no obligation to argue with people who were manifestly insane. Much as I disagreed with Jewish Zionists, at least their position had a kernel of logic. Fortunately, the arrival of dinner forced Reverend Miller back to his seat.

'Isn't he wonderful, Vivi?' Barbara said, unwrapping her tray of food. I grunted. Wonderful was not the word that sprang to my mind.

'You know, I'm so glad you had the chance to speak to him.' My scowl deepened. I focussed on my food, wondering how someone so boringly normal could believe in Armageddon.

'He's a true leader,' she continued. 'He works tirelessly for the State of Israel. Tirelessly. I only wish I had half his energy and clarity.' She chewed with an irritating complacency. Any sympathy I had for her vanished. I wanted to shake her. I took a breath and launched in before my good sense could talk me out of it.

'Barbara, are you aware your church is supporting terrorists?'

She stopped chewing and stared at me uneasily, her mouth open.

'What do you really know about Ma'ale Zahav, Barbara? Did you know Ma'ale Zahav was built on land stolen from the Palestinian village of Beyt Nattif? Did you know that? Ma'ale Zahav is an illegal settlement. It is against international law for occupiers to build settlements on the land they're occupying. Did you know that? Thugs from Ma'ale Zahav come into Beyt Nattif all the time. They vandalise property, stop farmers from tending their olive trees and beat up anyone they get their hands on. Did you know that? Did you know in July, they kicked a boy so badly he was in a coma and died a few weeks later? Do you even know that boy's name?'

While I paused to draw breath, Barbara reached over and patted my hand. 'It's shocking what those Arab terrorists do. How can any civilised person attack a child! After dinner I'll get the Reverend back. He can explain it all. I get muddled up but he, well, he knows all the facts. Look, I think they gave you the wrong meal. I'm sure that's not kosher food. Do you want me to call the stewardess and tell her?'

'Ahmed,' I shrieked. 'His name was Ahmed. He was 16 years old.'

Now it was my turn to put on the headphones and stare fixedly at the screen, ignoring Barbara's attempts to get my attention. My non-kosher meal curdled angrily in my stomach. I wondered uneasily whether Ruth would be on the same side as these *meshuganeh* Christian Zionists. Suddenly I felt alone and friendless. Maybe it wasn't such a good idea to visit Ruth after all.

CHAPTER 6

Ruth

Back on the bench, I cradled the mint tea between my hands and let the curls of steam soothe my wounded feelings. David's outburst had left me reeling. How dare he call Vivi a bitch and say she isn't welcome at our home! Vivi is my friend, not his. I'm the only one who can welcome or reject her. I knew David didn't like Vivi but I hadn't realised he felt that strongly about her.

Shlomo sat down on a chair opposite me. Holding his face between his hands, he slowly raked his fingers through his bushy sideburns and thick moustache. When his fingers reached the tip of his long shaggy beard, he spoke softly. 'How are you, Ruth?' he asked. His smile was kind and his voice was warm. How different from David! The only similarity between them was the bald tops of their heads. And even that exposed a fundamental difference. Shlomo's bald top was covered by a colourful knitted cap while David's was bare.

Shlomo looked a lot like my long-dead Hasidic grandfather. When I was a little girl, my grandfather used to carry me into the *shul* and dance wild, joyous dances with the other black-coated, fur-hatted men. The memory made me feel at ease with Shlomo. Smiling back at him, I said, 'Did you hear what David called Vivi? She's my friend. I need her now. Why is he so hostile?'

Shlomo leaned towards me and stroked his beard again. 'Look around you Ruth. Your family and your true friends are all here for you. Why do you need Vivi? David told me she ended your friendship a couple of years ago. He said Vivi is one of those self-hating, Israel-bashing American Jews who sympathise with the Arab terrorists. She's the type who criticises Israel but doesn't have the courage to live here and face the fear of being blown up in a suicide bombing. I'm not surprised David's hostile towards her. He's only trying to protect you. He was proud of you for cutting her out of your life. Why don't you forget about her now? She's scum, Ruth. She's not worth it.' His voice was no longer warm but harsh and loud. It pounded into my head. Carefully I handed him the still warm cup of tea and staggered into the bedroom. There I collapsed on the bed and fell into a deep sleep.

Hours later, I woke shaking and drenched. I mopped my forehead with my sleeve, trying to ward off the vivid images that flashed through my mind. In my dream, I was in a lake, fully clothed, treading frantically to keep my head above the surface. It was dark. The water was icy cold. The lake was vast. I could barely make out the shoreline. My glasses had fallen off and everything was blurred. In the distance I saw a rowboat with a solitary figure in it rowing around in a haphazard way. There was something familiar about the figure but the dream was fading rapidly. I sat up and realised I'd been lying across the bed in my clothes, covered with a heavy blanket. No wonder I was sweating. I wondered who'd put the blanket over me. Probably my mother. I was sure David wouldn't have done it. I groped around for my glasses and found them on the other side of the room on top of the bookcase instead of on the bedside table where I usually kept them. I could no longer remember how I came to be in the water or whether the person in the row boat was on their way to rescue me or had thrown me overboard and was rowing away from me. All I was aware of was an overpowering sense of abandonment. I wanted that person in the row boat to come and get me, to make everything all right.

Unable to bear the feeling a minute longer, I leapt out of bed and ran into the bathroom. I ripped off my clothes and stepped into the shower. Instead of washing the dream away, the warm water had the opposite effect. With a jolt, I remembered who the person in the row boat was. It was Vivi. She was rowing all over the lake looking for me but she couldn't see me in the dark.

Yes, that was it. The message of the dream was clear. The argument had gone on long enough. It was time to make up. If Vivi wouldn't or couldn't call me, I would have to do it. Energetically I dried myself and danced into my bathrobe. The frightening gloom of the night had brightened by several degrees. Even though, by right and by tradition, it should be Vivi who made the first move, I would do it this time. Never before had an argument between us gone on this long. The previous record was only two days. That was when we were 17. We'd planned to see *Last Tango in Paris* at the Johns Hopkins film club until Mike Levine asked me to go out with him that same night. I wasn't going to turn down a date with the cutest boy in the senior class, especially when I'd had my eye on him for weeks. To my surprise, Vivi was furious. She didn't find boys in the least bit interesting and couldn't see why I would prefer to go out with Mike Levine, a boy I hardly knew, than with her, my best friend. She said some mean things about Mike Levine, which I later discovered were true, and some mean things about me, which she later admitted were untrue. I went ahead with the date but it was a disaster. Mike had only one thing on his mind and that thing was sex. Being a good Jewish girl, I didn't even kiss boys on a first date. Afterwards, I locked myself in my bedroom and cried my eyes out, pining for Vivi. It took her two whole days, two unbearably long days, to stop being mad at me. At the end of the two days, a Carole King album was left propped against my bedroom door with a note saying, 'Sorry. If you play the first song on the second side, it tells you what to do. Love, Vivi.' I knew the album by heart and didn't have to play the song to know what to do. Unable to bear the agony another minute, I called her. To my intense relief, she came right over, making a big show of knocking at my door.

I checked my watch. It was three in the morning. If I phoned now, it would be five the afternoon before in Portland. I stood with my hand hovering over the telephone, my heart beating wildly. Do it now, I told myself. I picked up the phone but still hesitated. What if Vivi really did mean to end our friendship? After all, she hadn't sent me any messages in two years. I put the phone down and sank to the floor. What if Shlomo and David were right about Vivi? Maybe Vivi really did mean the things she'd said during that argument. Maybe my rational, thoughtful, compassionate, caring friend had turned into a self-hating Jew, an Israel-bashing, hate-filled extremist. Maybe we could never be friends again.

I jumped to my feet and stood glaring at the phone. What did Shlomo and David know about Vivi anyway? The truth was David had taken a dislike to Vivi as soon as he knew about her existence. It wasn't over politics because Vivi and I had stopped talking about politics long before I married David. It was jealousy, pure and simple. David hated me having a best girl friend. He hated me confiding in her. In long letters and even longer phone calls, there were never any secrets between me and Vivi. I told her everything about my life with David. I told her about our sex life, about our arguments, about the way he treated the children, about his hostility towards my family, everything. David has never been the type to talk about his feelings so he couldn't understand why I needed to talk about mine. Soon after we got married, even before the children were born, he demanded I stop communicating with Vivi. Of course, I didn't. That would have been like asking a zebra to remove its stripes.

It never occurred to me to stop my friendship with Vivi just because I was married and living 10,000 miles away. She was my best friend since we were 12 years old. From the time we met in junior high school until we graduated from college, we were inseparable. For ten years, we talked non-stop. That's a lot of hot air, as my father used to say. My older sisters, Shirley and Adele, would roll their eyes and tease me, 'What do you two talk about all the time?' As if they didn't talk themselves. They talked about boys and music and clothes all the time. Vivi and I talked about important things – we talked about Judaism and God and Israel, about racial harmony and integration, about over-population and the environment, about the Vietnam War and the inadequacies of the school system. It was Vivi who talked me out of running away when Shirley and Adele ganged up against me and shredded my ego to bits.

It was Vivi I talked to about boys. All through high school and college, I had boyfriends. Compared to my friendship with Vivi, they were disappointing as friends. Mike Levine was the worst but even Daniel Kaufman, the shy soon-to-be orthodontist I almost married, wasn't a friend the way Vivi and I were friends. By the time I met David, I'd come to accept I would never meet a man who could also be a friend. I scaled down my expectations of marriage and assumed any husband would realise he couldn't have his cake and eat it. If he didn't want intimacy with me, he didn't have to have it but it wasn't fair for him to resent the intimacy I had with my girl friend. The way I saw it, instead of being jealous of Vivi, David should have been grateful to her. Without Vivi to talk to all those years, the marriage would have ended long ago. It struck me, not for the first time, that in some ways, Vivi was more important to me than David.

I took a few deep breaths and picked up the phone again. David's jealousy was his problem, not mine. If he didn't want me to be friends with Vivi, he'd have to be a friend to me. Talk to me. Tell me what's going on his head. Stop being so angry and start relating to me, his wife.

I dialled Vivi's number. No one answered. With a mixture of relief and anguish, I put the phone down and went back to bed.

CHAPTER 7

Vivi

Barbara was still clutching my hand when the plane came to a stop at Ben Gurion airport. As soon as she inhaled, I retrieved my crumpled hand and took a few deep breaths. I needed to pull myself together to get through Israeli customs. I'd been warned that people intending to enter the West Bank to support Palestinians could be refused entry. Some activists had been sent home on the next plane. I rummaged in my backpack to find my fake itinerary and remind myself of my cover story. While I was occupied, Barbara shouted good-bye and turned her attention to the task of gathering the members of her church group. She was still counting heads and clucking like a mother hen when they were all swept away into the jostling, shoving crowd.

Alone in the belly of the beast, with only my anger for company, I pushed past the armed soldiers and the noisy, inconsiderate people. Why should I have to lie to enter this country? I fumed. How could my actions be interpreted as supporting terrorists? No, I wouldn't sneak in as if ashamed of myself. I would tell the customs official exactly why I'd come here and what I thought of Israel's behaviour.

The customs official was a young woman with the long black hair, dark eyes and olive skin of an Arab. I gazed at her as she studied my passport. I guessed she was a Mizrahi Jew, a descendant of one of the Jewish communities from the Middle Eastern countries. 'Vivienne Rubenstein?' she said, giving me a shy, welcoming smile. Automatically, I smiled back. She greeted me as if I were one of the family, as if she were delighted I would come all the way from Portland, Oregon to visit Israel in these troubled times. Forgetting my cover story, I told her my plans were to visit my high school friend Ruth Shapiro in Tsur Hadassah. 'Have a good trip,' she said warmly. Before I could gather my wits about me, she'd stamped my passport and I was in.

I stuffed the fake itinerary in my backpack and considered what to do next. Why not go straight to Ruth's? I wasn't expected at the Palestinian village of Beyt Nattif for another two days. I found a pay phone and started to dial. I'd phoned so many times over the years that I knew her number by heart. Or should have. But my mind had seized up. I couldn't remember the last three digits. Staring blankly at the floor, I wondered if calling Ruth was the best thing to do. What if Ruth hung up on me? What if she really didn't want to see me ever again? Don't be silly,

I thought. This is my friend Ruth. I know her like the back of my hand. Of course, she'll want to see me. I tried again. Again the number eluded me. This time, I asked myself if I really wanted to see Ruth again. Did I really know her that well? What if she had become a hate-filled bigot? Not possible, I told myself firmly. I tried again. This time I remembered.

'*Mah?*' It was a woman's voice but not Ruth's.

'Hello. *Shalom.* Um. Uh. Is Ruth there?' I asked.

'Eh?' she said.

'Can I speak to Ruth? It's Vivi.' My heart was thumping. Maybe I shouldn't have told her my name. I was about to hang up when a different woman came on the phone.

'Yes?' she said abruptly.

'Could I talk to Ruth?'

'Between four and seven.' She hung up. A shiver went through me. I couldn't imagine what was going on. If it had been David who answered, I wouldn't have been surprised. Many times in the past, he'd lied to me and told me Ruth wasn't home when she was. Weariness overcame me. I'd have to deal with it later after a night's sleep. I set off on the journey to Jerusalem, too tired to make sense of the strange phone call.

In the morning, I carefully dialled Ruth's number, in case I'd got the wrong number the day before. Another unfamiliar female voice answered, still with an Israeli accent but speaking English.

'Could I speak to Ruth Shapiro please?' I said. 'It's Vivi and I'm in Israel.'

'No. Come by between 11 and three,' she said and hung up. Something odd was going on. Still, she didn't tell me to stay away. So at ten, I called a taxi to take me to Tsur Hadassah.

The scent of pines mingled with the jet lag to lull me into a false sense of wellbeing as we drove into Tsur Hadassah. As we passed through the Jerusalem Mountains, I remembered my first visit to this beautiful area 15 years before. Ruth and David had moved to Tsur Hadassah 16 years ago in 1986. In those days, Ruth used to phone me every week to chat. One day, she called in great excitement.

'Vivi, you won't believe it. We found the perfect place. You know I've been desperate to get out of the city. It doesn't bother David but I really don't want to bring the kids up in Jerusalem. I want somewhere with clean air and a calmer pace of life. Well, I've found it. It's in the mountains west of Jerusalem. A place called Tsur Hadassah. David will be able to commute to Jerusalem in less than half an hour. It's ideal for us.'

'What side of the Green Line is it on?'

'Oh Vivi, can't you be happy for me? Why do you see something sinister in everything? For your peace of mind, it's in Israel proper. We aren't settlers.'

'Is it really all countryside? No developments? No villages?'

'That's right. There are only ten other families living there. It's totally off the beaten track. We're moving in a month. Come visit us when we're settled.'

A year later, I packed my bags and my five-year-old son Noah and took Ruth up on her invitation. I slept late the first two days but by the third, I was back to my usual routine. Always an early riser, I was up at dawn, dressing for my morning run when I heard what sounded like a muezzin calling the faithful to prayer. I stopped, my tracksuit trousers halfway up my legs and listened. I heard dogs barking, a rooster crowing, and yes, there it was again, the unmistakeable sound of the call to prayer blasting out from a loudspeaker. I wondered if it was possible for sound to travel the twelve miles from Bethlehem. Hopping to the window while pulling up my trousers, I put my ear to the glass and listened hard. It sounded like it was right across the road.

No one else was awake so I slipped quietly out the front door. Too curious to waste time stretching, I jogged towards the sound of the muezzin. From Ruth's house to the main road was no more than a block. I crossed the traffic-free main road, and jogged carefully across a rocky slope. At the crest of the hill, I stopped still and stared in wonder. I was looking down at a good-sized Palestinian village in a green and cultivated valley. The minaret was the tallest building, standing like a rocket at one end of the village. I picked my way down the slope, crossed some indifferent barbed wire and was soon passing low stone walls, grape vines, fields of cucumber, orchards of olive trees, a donkey tethered just out of reach of lush green vegetation, a large squat building with a basket ball hoop in a playground and houses. Hundreds of houses.

This was clearly a well-established village, not a recent settlement.

For a brief moment, I wondered if I had inadvertently entered a time-warp and been transported to some time before 1948 when hundreds of little Palestinian villages lay dotted around the countryside. But the style of architecture of the houses was more recent. They seemed to have been built in the sixties or seventies. Still I couldn't shake the feeling of unreality. The call of the muezzin, the soft early morning light, the cultivated orderliness all contributed to a sense of magical peacefulness.

An old man stepped out from a field carrying a hoe over his shoulder. He took a step back when he saw me. I suspected he wasn't used to seeing joggers. I greeted him in the only Arabic words I knew, '*Salamu aleikum.*'

A smile creased his face. '*Aleikum as-salam wa rahmatu allahi wa barakatuh.*' I didn't get any of that but I picked up the welcoming tone. 'Do you speak English?' I asked.

He shrugged expansively, pursing his lips and raising his arms in the air. I took that as a no. He nodded towards my tracksuit and trainers and mimed running in place. I nodded vigorously, smiling encouragement. He mimed lifting weights and doing push-ups. I shook my head no but he'd got into it by then and carried on with his charade of keep-fit exercises. I was beginning to feel uncomfortable. Was he making fun of me? Finally, he picked up his hoe, pointed to the field where he'd just come from and pretended to work the ground. He straightened up, bent his arm at a right angle and showed me his muscles. I nodded weakly, my smile grown stiff on my face. OK, OK, I thought. I get it. He roared with laughter.

'Amreekan?' He pointed to me.

I didn't know what he meant

'Amreekan?' He paused, tilted his head and looked at me questioningly. Before he could embark on another corny charade, I waved good-bye and headed back to Ruth's the way I'd come.

Everyone was up when I arrived back. The children, still in their pyjamas, and David, dressed for work, were seated around the kitchen table. Ruth was attending to a frying pan, in a frenzy of pancake production. She tossed a pancake onto Noah's plate and another onto four year old Yigal's. Yigal poked three holes in his pancake and put it on his face, wearing it like a mask. He stuck his tongue through one of the holes and growled at Orli. She retaliated by throwing her pancake, sticky with maple syrup, at him. Yigal threw himself off his chair, giggling manically. David snapped at them both in Hebrew. Chastened, they settled down on their chairs, kicking each other surreptitiously under the table.

'How was your jog?' Ruth asked. 'Where did you go?' She turned back to the frying pan.

'It was very interesting.' I looked at Ruth and waited until her attention wandered back to me.

'I didn't go far, just over the main road.' She nodded, distracted. 'Ruth, I thought you said this area was practically uninhabited. No developments. No villages.'

'That's right. Though in the last year, ten more families have moved in down the road. I'll show you their houses. They're really nice. Orli, let me wash your hands. Have you had enough, honey? I think we've started a trend. More and more families are moving here from the city. Noah, sweetie, would you like another pancake?'

'Ruth, I came across a village while I was out jogging. Not a few families but hundreds of families. A big village. Been there quite a while by the look of it.'

Ruth looked at me blankly. 'What do you mean, a village? There are no villages around here.'

Why was she quibbling about semantics? More irritably than I intended, I said, 'There are about a thousand people living less than a thousand feet from your front door in a village, a town, a hamlet, a human habitation, whatever you want to call it. I walked all around it. I saw the school and the houses. I had a chat with an old man. I'm not making it up.'

David looked at me as if I were stupid. 'That's an Arab village,' he said.

Ruth gave me her full attention. 'You went into an Arab village? On your own? Anything could have happened to you. Did anyone threaten you?'

'You are an idiot,' David said, shaking his head in disbelief. At the front door, he turned back to Ruth. 'Could you explain the situation to your friend? I'm off to work. Bye, everyone.' Orli ran to David, arms raised, to give him a kiss but Yigal and Noah were already absorbed in a mountain of Lego pieces on the living room floor.

Ruth looked at me, chewing her lips. 'Vivi, you know what it was like living in Baltimore? There were certain neighbourhoods we didn't go to. Like, the inner city where the blacks were. If we had to drive through, we rolled up our windows and locked the doors. You know what I mean, don't you? Well, it's sort of like that here.' She trailed off, unnerved by my stare.

'God, you've sure changed Ruth. That's how your parents used to talk.'

Ruth stood up. 'That Arab village happens to be on the other side of the Green Line. We're not on their land and they are not my problem. They get on with their lives and we get on with ours. Anyway. Enough of all that. You haven't had a pancake. Do you want one?'

The subject was closed. And remained closed ever since. I never found out if Ruth even knew the name of the village across the road. My horror at learning the story of Wadi Foquin was one of the reasons I got involved in solidarity work. Soon after I returned from my trip to visit Ruth, I found out Wadi Foquin was one of the more than 400 Palestinian villages forcibly evacuated in 1948. In 1953, the Israeli army dynamited most of the town but by a most unusual fluke in Israeli occupation politics, the refugees were allowed back to rebuild in 1972. However, the good times were short lived. Soon the nearby illegal settlement of Beitar Illit encroached on the villagers' land and polluted their crops with sewage. With the security wall being built close by, life had become increasingly hard in the village.

As the taxi reached Tsur Hadassah, I wondered if Ruth was any more clued up about her next door neighbours than she was 15 years ago. I promised myself I wouldn't bring it up when I saw her, at least not as the first topic of conversation. But I was already churning when we passed the road to the village and there was not even a sign indicating its existence. Once again, I wondered if making up with Ruth was such a good idea. Did I really want to be friends with someone able to close her eyes to such appalling injustice right on her doorstep?

I decided to ask the taxi driver to wait outside Ruth's home. Just in case.

CHAPTER 8

Ruth

I'd only been asleep an hour when I was woken by another dream. Again I was in the middle of a large lake but this time I was in a rowboat with David and Yigal. The paint was peeling. The planks were rotten and there were gaping holes in the bottom. Icy, black water was pouring in. I was clutching the sides of the rowboat which was splintering and breaking off in my hands.

I looked over at David lying beside me in the bed. He was scowling. Even in sleep, even in the midst of a family tragedy, he was guarded and distrustful. I kicked him hard. He grunted and opened his eyes.

'Stop it,' he said and rolled over to lie with his back to me.

I crossed my arms over my belly and frowned into the darkness. I knew there was no point talking with him but I always tried. And I was always disappointed. David consistently refused to open up to me. 'So why are you crying to me about it?' Vivi would say, irritated with my hysterical phone calls. 'You knew he wasn't the lovey-dovey type when you married him.' She never understood why I kept hoping he'd change. Still I knew even Vivi would expect David to comfort me now.

In the dream, David behaved just as I expected him to. He was rowing the rotten rowboat as hard as he could. His face was red. 'Hurry up,' he shouted at me and Yigal. 'Bail out the water. The boat's leaking and we're going to drown.' There was only one bucket. Yigal took the bucket and filled it with exaggerated slow movements. As he poured the water over the side, he was laughing. He seemed to treat our desperate situation as a big joke. David was furious. He threw himself at Yigal and they both fell into the water. Yigal was shrieking with laughter. He splashed about as if he were having a great time. He shouted to David, 'Chill out, Dad. You can't drown in the Dead Sea. Look, we're floating.'

I glanced over at David's stubborn back. How dare he ignore me? I poked him hard. He didn't respond. Just like in the dream. He always misjudged the situation. And he'd never understood his own son. I wondered whether to call Vivi again. No, she was sick and tired of hearing me moan about David. I got up and wandered around the house. Eventually I fell asleep on the sofa in the living room.

When I next woke, sunlight was pouring into the living room. A fly buzzed drowsily against the window. A patch of sunlight lit up the crumbs on the carpet. I closed my eyes and drifted mindlessly back towards sleep. It all came flooding back to me. Instantly, the square patch of sunlight vanished as if it had been nothing more than an illusion. I could still hear buzzing. With great effort, I sat up and listened carefully. It was more a murmur than a buzz. The sound drew me like a magnet. I followed it to the open window. There on the veranda, I saw David with Gil and Shlomo. They were huddled close together, talking quietly. That's typical of David, I thought. He'll talk with his army mates but not with his own wife. He had no right keeping secrets from me. I crouched on the floor and listened.

Gil was speaking. 'Just like we did after the attack on Ein Arik when four soldiers were killed. Remember that? Our squad commander sent us on a revenge action to kill four Palestinian policemen. Somewhere. Any policemen. Four of them, like they took out four of ours. We hiked to a checkpoint. A long hike. Didn't get there til four in the morning. We waited til they woke up. They came out to open up the checkpoint. That's when we opened fire.'

There were appreciative murmurs from David and Shlomo.

'It was my first mission,' Gil continued. 'And you know what! I liked it. We got up and fired. We hit two of theirs. One in the back. One in the shoulder. One ran off. I shot that one in the head. One guy crawled into a shed. We threw a grenade into the shed. Sprayed it with bullets. It exploded and caught fire. We chased another policeman. Got him in the back. He went down. Three or four of our guys kept shooting at his body. Punching holes in it. It was the first time we'd been in this kind of combat situation. We'd trained for it. We knew what to do. And we performed flawlessly.' Gil's voice was low but animated.

'Did any of you get injured?' I recognised Shlomo's voice.

'Not one. Anyway they weren't armed. They never fired back at us.'

The whispered voices had a soporific effect. In my half-asleep state, I heard David say, 'Was Yigal with you?' I sat up, alert and listening hard.

'No, not that time,' Gil said. 'But on others. He was with me when we went patrolling the refugee camps in armoured vehicles. We cruised around close to the buildings. Driving past schools. Past people's homes. Kids would throw rocks at us. They tried to climb onto the tanks and take our machine guns. Kamikaze style. It was wild.'

'Always kids, isn't that so?' Shlomo said.

'Yeah, like eight or nine years old. And some teenagers. They didn't have weapons. Stones, rocks, concrete bits, that kind of thing. We always came out on top. We had the machine guns after all. Like the incident I was telling you about yesterday. There was a huge crowd of boys, maybe a hundred of them, in a playground at a school. They picked up rocks and came toward us. Their teachers got them inside. But there were a few boys who were totally out of control. One boy in particular would not give in. He was a big brute of a boy, a real thug. He was heading straight for our tank. He could have been a suicide bomber, for all we knew.' He lowered his voice to a whisper. ' . shot him in the stomach.'

His voice was barely audible and I wasn't sure I'd heard him. Automatically, I pressed my ear against the wall. At the same time, I was overwhelmed by tiredness. My eyes closed and my head sank against my knees.

'You said there was no investigation so it couldn't have been a big deal,' Shlomo said. 'Anyway, I've been in situations like that. You don't have a choice. You have to shoot or you've had it. If you'd gone into the playground, the other boys would have come out or fired at you from the windows. It would have been too dangerous.'

Gil said. 'Yeah. We were told to put the area under curfew, to prevent a riot. We drove around announcing the curfew, making sure everybody stayed inside. An ambulance came for the boy. We made it wait.'

'Of course. What else could you do? They use ambulances to carry weapons and terrorists.' That was David's voice. 'You can't even let an ambulance through. They have only themselves to blame.' His voice got louder. 'Orli, where have you been?'

I didn't hear her reply. I imagined her giving him her narrowed-eyes sneer, the kind that always left me quivering with rage, my hands itching to throttle her.

'Orli, do not walk away when I'm talking to you,' David said. I cringed on his behalf. The more parental his tone, the more stubborn Orli would become. David could provoke Orli into all-out combat from nothing. She just had to give him that look and he'd be off. I scrambled to my feet as she flew in through the door and slammed it behind her. Seconds later, David burst in. 'Don't you dare slam that door in my face.' He stopped within an inch of her and screamed into her face. Orli stood her ground and screamed back.

'Calm down. Stop it, both of you.' My pathetic pleading had no effect. They kept right on at full volume. To make things worse, the room was rapidly filling up. My mother who doesn't know when to stay out of it did her best to intervene. But soon she threw up her hands in exasperated frustration and left them to it. Tom tried to wriggle in between David and Orli without success. My father, oblivious as ever to subtle undertones in behaviour, said something to Adele who rounded on him in a fury. They yelled at each other, increasing the noise to unbearable levels. Just when I thought the tension couldn't get any worse, Orli pushed David in the chest so hard he staggered backwards, falling against his mother who had just walked in the door carrying a steaming casserole dish. The dish and mother went flying, both making loud sharp noises as they landed. Above the din, Orli was shrieking, 'You want me to die, don't you? You don't care if I live or die, do you? I hate you.' She hurtled out the front door, crashing into Rena on her way in, and ran down the drive. As suddenly as it started, it stopped.

The slam of the door reverberated in the hushed room. A cough was delicately suppressed, gazes averted. David's mother, muttering under her breath, climbed onto the sofa. A chair creaked as someone shifted their weight. A throat was cleared. My mouth felt dry. The metallic taste of embarrassment filled the room.

My father stood up, picked up a glass of juice, and tapped it with a spoon. I wondered if he was about to propose a toast. 'Let me tell you a story,' he said to no one in particular. 'I won't say if it's true or if it's made up. Let's just say it's apocryphal. The correspondent for the British Broadcasting Corporation, she is in her air conditioned hotel in the Gaza Strip. Her phone rings. She picks it up. A voice she doesn't recognise, not her usual contact, says, 'I'm calling on behalf of the military wing of Hamas. Those bloodthirsty Israeli pigs have just massacred hundreds of Palestinian women and children. If you go to this hospital just inside the Israeli border, you will see the surviving casualties.' Within minutes, she's off to the designated hospital. Now she can prove to the world, once and for all, just how evil Israel is. At the hospital, she collars an Israeli doctor and demands to see the Palestinian casualties brought in after the massacre. The doctor shrugs. He doesn't know what she's talking about…'

'Dad,' Shirley said. 'Get to the point.'

My father nodded serenely, unfazed by the interruption. 'The correspondent gets really angry and says, 'OK, tell me how many Arab patients you have here today.' The doctor says, 'I guess there are a few hundred.'' My father took a breath.

'I bet he's forgotten the punch line,' Adele said to my mother and Shirley. All three snickered unkindly.

'Convinced she's onto something, the correspondent exclaims, 'Ah ha. So you don't deny it now!' She heads for the emergency room and marches in. What does she see? Lots of empty beds and a few surprised patients. Turning to the doctor, she says 'So where are you hiding the hundreds of Arab patients you told me about?' The bewildered doctor says to her, 'They're in our new state-of-the-art maternity ward further down the hall. Come, I'll show you.''

My father looked around, smiling proudly. There's still silence but it's a lighter silence than before. Rena picked up the broken casserole dish and carried it dripping into the kitchen.

'Is that it, Grandpa?' Tom asked. 'Is that the end of the story?'

'Grandpa, why did they put the casualties in the maternity ward?' Susie asked.

'Is that story supposed to be funny?' asked Shirley.

'Jacob, what do you know about telling jokes?' My mother emerged from the kitchen with a dustpan and brush. 'Now here's a joke. Listen everybody. Three prisoners are about to be executed. They are each asked what they wish to have for their last meal. The first one, a Chinese, says he wants won ton soup. He is served won ton soup and *phut*, he is executed. The next one ..'

'But why did they put the casualties in the maternity ward?' Susie's plaintive voice cut in.

'The first one is Italian, not Chinese,' my father said. 'The Italian asked for pepperoni pizza, not won ton soup! Where did you get that from? You made that up.'

'Chinese, Italian, what's the difference?' My mother shrugged, waving the dustpan and brush in the air. 'The next one is a Frenchman. He asks for filet mignon. And so, he is served filet mignon. And he too is promptly executed.' She mimed a sawing motion at her neck. 'All right, Jacob? Do I have your permission to continue? All right. The third prisoner is a Jew. And he,' she looked slowly around the room for dramatic effect. 'He requests ..'

'Now she has forgotten the punch line,' my father said, draining his glass and smirking. My mother shot him a filthy look.

'He requests a plate of strawberries,' Her voice squeaked with excitement. 'Yes, strawberries. And he is told, 'But they are out of season!' You hear that? They're out of season. And what does the Jew say to that?' She looked around to make sure everybody was listening. 'He shrugs.' My mother hoiked her shoulders up to her ears and raised the dustpan and brush in the air. 'He says…'

'Spit it out already,' my father said irritably.

'He says, 'So, nu, I'll wait.' Get it? So nu, I'll wait.' My mother burst out laughing. My father groaned. A few smiles flitted across a few faces, a few eyes rolled, and a few quick guffaws erupted out of a few mouths. And like wild fire, it caught. The little guffaws sparked bigger guffaws until everyone was rolling with laughter. Even David chuckled quietly to himself. Eventually people dried their eyes, shook their heads and wandered into the kitchen to fill a plate with food. Conversations started. For a brief, blessed minute, I relaxed, and enjoyed the party.

CHAPTER 9

Yigal

After my painful confession and humiliating response, I'm lying on the dusty ground as far away as possible from my tormentor. I gaze at the clouds without seeing them. I wonder what possessed me to bare my soul to this hostile and unsympathetic girl. That was a mistake I'm not likely to make again.

I wish there was somebody else to talk to. Anybody would do. But the place is deserted. No one has been through this checkpoint for weeks. Why are we here, I wonder, not for the first time. Being at this checkpoint is totally pointless, a complete waste of everyone's time. I am in great danger of going mad with the boredom.

I hear him before I see him. There's the unmistakeable sound of a football being kicked against a wall. I look around. A small boy, maybe 12 or 13, is kicking a football, weaving in and out between the concrete barriers and the barbed wire. He's got on the blue shirt and blue trousers

I've seen Palestinian children wearing to school. His black hair is cut short and his ears stick out. Other than that, there's nothing remarkable about this kid. He doesn't greet me or say a word. I gesture to him to kick the football to me. His face lights up with delight. We kick to each other. He's good, better than me.

When I've had enough, I fling myself down at the base of a concrete pillar. The boy joins me.

'Yigal,' I say, pointing to myself. 'You?'

'Hassan.' He rubs his stomach, picks at his shirt and talks a blue streak. 'Last year, Palestine came second in our group in the world cup elimination. We went to Kuwait and played in the West Asian Games. We went to Syria and played in the second West Asian Championship. I'd like to play with the Alaqsa club. They got to the second round in the Asian cup championship. You know who my favourite player is? It's Ronaldo. I like him better than David Beckham. I'd give anything to see Ronaldo play. Did you know, he was only 16 when he scored twice in a 3-0 victory over Moreirense?'

'Whoa Hassan. Slow down. Say, you're really into football, aren't you?'

He nods and babbles on. 'I wanted to play for the Palestine Football Association. I was training at a sports club. The coach said I had potential. If I'd have got on the team, I could have played in the world cup. I could have travelled and seen the world.'

He stands up, brushes himself off and says, 'Did you know Ronaldo was only eight when he was first scouted? I've got to go. I'll come and play with you tomorrow.'

I nod and watch him run off in the direction he came from. It's only as he disappears around a barren hill that I wonder where he lives. There isn't a town anywhere near here, at least not as far as I know. Travelling through the Negev, I've seen Bedouin children by the side of a road in an apparently empty desert. No human habitation for miles around. Maybe this boy is a Bedouin. Somehow I doubt it but I don't really know much about Palestinians. I've never met any, not to talk to anyway. Oh well, they're like a different species. Mysterious and weird.

CHAPTER 10

Vivi

'When we get to Tsur Hadassah, could you wait? I might not be staying long.'

The taxi driver, a scrawny, grey-haired man with a lined, weather-beaten face, looked at me in the rear view mirror. 'That's a long way to go on the off-chance,' he said.

I shrugged. It was too complicated to explain to a stranger.

'Been here before?' he asked.

'Yeah. 15 years ago. I'm sure it's changed a lot since then.'

'You're not kidding. Have you heard about the latest zoning plan for Jerusalem? They're going to annex Tsur Hadassah. Build it up to 30,000 people. It'll be the end of all this open natural space.' He waved his hands towards the pine forests around us. 'There'll be massive environmental damage. A tragedy. That's what it is.' He shook his head in disgust.

'Why would Tsur Hadassah be annexed to Jerusalem? It's so far away,' I said.

'Demographics, that's why! Got to keep the 70-30 Jewish-Arab ratio. You know what I think? I think it would make a lot more sense just to expel the Arabs from East Jerusalem. You'd still keep the ratio but without destroying the environment here.'

I sighed. It would make even more sense to forget about the 70-30 ratio, I thought but was too distracted about the imminent meeting with Ruth to argue with him.

I'd convinced myself Ruth would be glad to see me. But David was another matter. We'd only met once, 15 years before when I came to stay in Tsur Hadassah. Although I tried real hard to be friendly to my best friend's husband during that visit, we were only ever a hair's length away from all-out warfare. He was the kind of Israeli whose arrogant belligerence made him the perfect recruiting agent for Hamas. I couldn't figure out what Ruth saw in him. I thought she would come to her senses and leave him but she showed no signs of doing so.

As I got out of the taxi, I noticed the mass of brilliantly purple bougainvillea flowing over Ruth's veranda, the cars lining the street, the steel blue of the sky, the clusters of sombre people and the murmur of voices. They must be having some kind of meeting, I thought. But before I could even speculate about the meaning of it, David was by my side and my elbow was in his grip. Without a word, he marched me down the drive and along the road until their house was no longer in sight. Still grasping my elbow, he put his mouth to my ear and said, 'What are you doing here? Ruth never wants to see you again.'

'Let go of me,' I said. I meant it to sound assertive and authoritative but it came out as a mouse-like squeak.

'You are not welcome here. You will go away. Now.'

'David,' I said. 'OK. I won't come on your property. I can meet Ruth somewhere else. Just give her a note from me. OK?' I was struggling to keep the wobble out of my voice. I didn't like to admit I was finding David somewhat scary. He had a peculiar smile on his face and a vice-like grip on my arm. He released my arm while I rummaged in my purse for a sheet of hotel stationery and a pen. Before I'd written a word, he'd glanced at the name of the hotel, snatched the paper out of my hand and deliberately ripped it into little pieces. The pieces fell to the road.

'David, what is going on? How can you carry a grudge about a stupid argument Ruth and I had two years ago? You weren't even there.'

'There are three men on guard duty outside my house.' He grabbed my elbow again and dragged me back along the road until I could just see the house. 'Look. Do you see them?'

I did indeed see three middle-aged men standing in a group at the bottom of the drive. They weren't in uniform and didn't look particularly threatening.

'Do you see them?' David yanked my arm. Pain shot up to my shoulder. I wasn't sure how to change the subject but I couldn't bring myself to say yes.

'David, you can't keep us apart forever. It's up to Ruth whether she wants to see me. What are you going to do, put a guard around her wherever she goes? It's not going to work. Come on. This isn't the way.'

'She's finished with you. She doesn't want to see you. Ever. Now get out of here.'

I tried to make eye contact and wished I hadn't. When I looked into his eyes, I saw hatred. It was all I could do to keep calm and not scream from pain. He was strong. I wondered if he was going to break my arm. He tightened his grip until I could no longer stand.

'Let go of me.' I was having trouble speaking through the pain. He twisted my arm until I was crouched on the road. I tried to breathe into the pain, the way I'd learned for childbirth. That was 20 years ago and I hadn't had an opportunity to practise it since. Not that it had worked at the time. This felt a lot worse. At least with childbirth, you know you're going to have a wonderful reward when the pain stops. This pain didn't seem to be bringing any signs of reward.

David forced me down onto the road so that my face was on the gravel and my arm was twisted up my back. I wondered if he had ever treated Ruth like this. Would Ruth have admitted it to me if he had?

Still gripping my arm, he knelt over me and said, 'You Will Not Come To My House. You Will Not See My Wife. You Will Go Away And You Will Leave This Country. You Are Not Wanted Here. Do You Understand?' He started his speech in a clipped monotone, each word clearly enunciated for emphasis. But by the end, the words were spiked with hysteria. An image of my son in a two-year old's tantrum flashed through my mind. I knew from experience you don't reason with a tantrum. I waited, silently, hoping he'd calm himself down before he did me a lasting injury. He grunted with frustration, let go of my arm and disappeared.

By the time I'd struggled to a sitting position, the taxi driver was leaning over me, wheezing. 'Hey lady,' he said, as he awkwardly helped me to stand up. 'I can see why you wanted me to stay around. Your friend sure wasn't very welcoming.' It took all my will power to walk the 50 yards to the car. The taxi driver shuffled beside me, shaking his head and looking anxiously behind. I crawled into the back seat and lay down. That settled it. Whatever generous impulse I'd had to make up with Ruth was dead and gone. As long as she was with David, we could never be friends.

CHAPTER 11
Ruth

The next night another disturbing dream woke me. I lay rigidly in bed, staring wide-eyed into the darkness. My heart beat like a caged animal trying to escape. This dream showed no signs of fading. It remained solid and real, each detail etched in my mind. I threw off the blanket and stumbled into the kitchen, straight to the fridge, my first refuge in times of distress. Inside, a piece of cheesecake called out to me, 'Eat me. Everything will be all right when you eat me.' As I reached in, I heard an ambulance wail in the distance. I shuddered and slammed the fridge door shut.

There was an ambulance in the dream. An ambulance waiting on the edge of a playground. Maybe I was still dreaming. Or maybe it wasn't a dream and was really happening. I held my breath. The clock ticked loudly in the night silence. Snatches of the dream flashed through my mind. Yigal and David playing football. Both of them laughing, running about, kicking the football at each other. It was in a strange playground, not anywhere I've been. Somewhere dry and dusty with no equipment. Yigal was laughing so hard he'd fallen over and was rolling around on the ground. Clutching his sides. Being goofy as he often was. David was smiling. He was enjoying himself. I was watching from the side and feeling pleased. I'd managed to get the two of them together for quality time.

But the dream was shrouded in apprehension. Was the feeling of dread due to regret that I'd failed to get them together and now it was too late? Was it the thought of all the wasted years of tension with me in the middle desperately trying to make them bond? I'd wanted David to show some affection towards Yigal, to demonstrate his pride in his son. But the excursions I'd organised were nearly all disasters. I'd buy two tickets to a play or a football match or a film. They would go, reluctantly, late, not dressed appropriately. And they'd always come back bad-tempered and sulking, not talking to each other, less bonded than before.

Maybe it was jealousy. In the dream, they were both having a great time. The sun was shining but I felt cold and unloved, excluded. Another snatch of dream flashed through my mind. I couldn't remember the sequence. Was it just after they'd played together or had other events happened in between? I was holding a machine gun. It felt heavy and awkward, a burden. It was mine but I couldn't bear to hold it. I didn't want anything to do with it. I called David over and handed him my gun. He took it, turned around, aimed the gun at Yigal and fired. Blood came out of Yigal's stomach. It poured onto the dust. But he was still rolling around on the ground, laughing. In the dream I felt no surprise, no shock, no interest even. It was as if I'd asked David to shoot Yigal.

I needed that cheesecake badly. So badly that I didn't bother getting a knife and fork and plate. I reached into the fridge, broke off a sizeable chunk of cheesecake and stuffed it into my mouth. Luckily it was just a dream. A silly incomprehensible dream that didn't mean anything.

In the dream, a tank had appeared, driven by David. It was weaving drunkenly around the playground. Yigal was next to him, holding a machine gun, shooting in all directions. They were both laughing. I felt irritated and disapproving. I wanted him to drive the tank in a straight line, to be orderly. David kept driving the tank around the playground, circling a boy lying bleeding on the ground. I didn't recognise the boy. He was holding a football. An ambulance was waiting at the edge of the playground. That's when I woke up.

Out of the corner of my eye, I caught a glimpse of someone in the doorway. 'Yigal?' I called out. My voice, hoarse and loud in the silent house, frightened me. My heart beat wildly. My breath came in short gasps. I felt myself floating in a bubble, unanchored. 'It's okay,' I said aloud. 'I'm just having an anxiety attack.' Naming it only made me more frightened. Frantically, I tried to remember the coping techniques a psychologist had once taught me. My mind was blank. It had been so long ago, just after I met David and made the decision to marry him and live in Israel. The techniques had worked. The attacks came to an end and had never returned. Until now.

There was someone in the living room. I forced myself to go nearer. Reaching for the light switch, I hesitated. There sitting on the brown leather sofa, a booted foot resting on a khaki-clad knee, was Yigal.

I didn't dare look directly at him. 'Breathe,' I said to myself. 'I've got to breathe.' I couldn't remember what kind of breathing I was supposed to do. I felt dizzy. My fingertips tingled. I made myself look in the direction of the sofa. Yes, he was there, smiling at me. I took a deep breath in and let it out slowly. No, he wasn't. He was gone.

When I was ten, my mother took me and my sisters to Broadway to see 'Fiddler on the Roof'. On the way to the theatre, we'd walked through Times Square. I'd been mesmerised by the neon lights flashing their disjointed and mindless messages at me. I couldn't take my eyes off them. Shirley and Adele had shouted at me to come but I was rooted to the spot, my mouth hanging open. Finally, they'd each grabbed an arm and dragged me down the road.

A boy bleeding to death in a playground. An ambulance waiting in the background. 'He shot him in the stomach.' Whispers overheard. Now they flashed like neon lights in my mind. And I knew it was Yigal who shot the boy. The cheesecake stuck in my throat. My fingers and toes tingled. I'm really going around the bend, I thought. This is absurd. Definitely a sign of stress and mental instability. I've got to get a grip. I've got to call Vivi.

This time I didn't hesitate. I grabbed the phone and dialled. At Claire's cheery greeting, I burst into tears and stood clutching the phone while I tried in vain to bring the choking and sobbing under control. With a superhuman effort, I forced Vivi's name out of my throat.

'Who's that?' Claire asked, her voice squeaking with alarm. 'What happened to Vivi? Who are you?'

'It's Ruth,' I cried in between sobs. 'I want to speak to Vivi.'

'Ruth? What did you say? What about Vivi? What's wrong? What happened to Vivi? Tell me. Is she all right?'

She was speaking too fast. I tried again. 'Vivi! Is Vivi there?' I was beginning to feel dizzy. Claire's hysteria was not helping.

'What do you mean?' Claire was shouting even louder. 'What did you say? Isn't Vivi there with you? Ruth, please. Take a deep breath and slow down. I can't figure out what you're saying.'

'I want to speak to Vivi. I want to speak to Vivi.' What was the matter with Claire? Why couldn't she understand me? Why didn't she just go and get Vivi? I slumped onto the floor. I felt queasy. Specks of light flickered before my eyes. Breathe, I told myself. To the count of four out through the mouth. To the count of two in through the nose. But my nose was blocked from crying. While I struggled with this dilemma, Claire bleated faintly from my lap where I'd dropped the phone. When I was calm enough to try again, I said slowly, 'Claire, I'm sorry. I need to talk to Vivi. Can I speak with her?'

'Ruth, you've called Portland. How can she be back in Portland already? She only left three days ago.'

Breathe in, one, two. Breathe out, one, two, three, four. 'Claire. Look. We haven't talked for two years. How am I supposed to know where she is?'

'Vivi's in Israel, Ruth. I got an email today saying she was on her way to see you.'

'On her way to see me?'

'Yeah. Didn't she get there? She said she called your house several times and was told to come over.'

'Vivi is in Israel to see me?'

'Oh no she's not.' David was towering over me, pulling his bathrobe over his shoulder, his glasses hanging lopsided on his face. 'She's not coming here. I won't have her in my house. Who are you talking to?'

Before I could reply, David had snatched the phone and was shouting into it. 'Who's that?'

'Claire? Oh yeah. Claire,' He shuddered with disgust. 'What is Vivi doing in Israel? She didn't come to see Ruth, did she?' There was an ominous silence as he listened to whatever Claire was saying. I struggled to my feet, straining to hear. He said, 'Tell Vivi to stay away from Ruth. Ruth does not want to see her ever again.' With one decisive movement, he hung up the phone and steered me back into the bedroom.

'Vivi came all this way to see me. I do want to see her.'

In a calm, almost satisfied voice, David said, 'I don't think you do. Vivi didn't come to Israel to see you. She's here with a so-called solidarity group supporting Arab terrorists at a village called Beyt Nattif in Samaria.'

'I don't believe that,' I said. But I did. It was the kind of thing I could imagine Vivi doing. Though I'm sure she would have used other words to describe what she was up to, it came to the same thing. She was on the other side, on the side against us, against everything I stood for, against everything my son and husband had fought for. No, I couldn't see Vivi ever again. Any desire I'd had to make up was gone. Our friendship was well and truly over.

CHAPTER 12

Vivi

'Wake up,' the taxi driver shouted beeping his horn. 'We're nearly at Ecce Homo.' Groggily, I struggled to a sitting position. My arm throbbed as the taxi hurtled along the cobbled Via Dolorosa. A group of Japanese pilgrims staggering under a five foot long cross plastered themselves against the wall to let us pass.

'Why the hell are you staying in the Muslim quarter?' he asked. 'I could recommend a hundred better hotels in West Jerusalem.' He screeched to a halt and demanded a sum for the journey that would easily cover the cost of a new car. I paid, cursing myself for not asking how much before we set off. No sooner was I out of the taxi than he was gone, backing up the narrow lane in a tyre-squealing retreat.

Across the street, a bearded middle-aged man stood in an open doorway. He wore a multi-coloured cap and a floor-length black robe with gold trim. Except for the wristwatch and the button-down shirt typical of modern office workers, he could have stepped out of the 17th century. He smiled a greeting and invited me with a nod to come over.

'Are you Vivi?' a woman with a broad Yorkshire accent called. Two European women and a man were striding up the lane, waving large oval bread rings. 'We're your comrades for the next month. I'm Jude. I'm from Sheffield. This is Carol from London and this blond midget is Nils. He's from Stockholm.' The midget was more than six foot tall. He grinned and hid behind his bread ring.

'We were expecting to see you this morning. What happened to you?' Carol said, giving me a hard disapproving look. I decided not to mention Ruth. Carol looked like the kind of comrade who might misinterpret my friendship with Ruth as consorting with the enemy.

'I had a run-in with an angry man. I think my arm might be broken.' My voice wobbled and I was close to tears. Jude came to my rescue. She worked for the ambulance service and had come prepared. She escorted me to my room and examined my arm which wasn't broken, only sprained. She wrapped it in a sling and gave me pain killers. Once she settled me in bed, she left me alone, saying she was going to talk to the Sufi sheikh across the road.

That night, I dreamed a man came into my room. He cleared his throat, tapped a microphone and began chanting. The chanting mingled with pain and nausea to become an avalanche of noise. It grew louder and more persistent until I woke. I wasn't dreaming after all. It was 4.30 in the morning and the muezzin was calling the faithful to prayer. The pain killers had worn off and I'd missed dinner.

I staggered out of bed and groped my way to the rooftop courtyard. The minaret, lit by a row of garish green electric lights, was no more than a stone's throw away over a clutter of courtyards, stone buildings and domed roofs, ghostly in the dawn darkness. I watched breathless with joy as sunrise drew the Old City into life. From over the hillside to my left, the sun set the sky alight, painting a strip of pink beneath the silhouetted clouds. It played over the Dome of the Rock which glinted back in an ecstasy of gold. I heard birds chirping, a man talking on a cell phone, church singing, a rooster crowing and distant sounds of traffic. I smelled the sweet aroma of bread baking. As the sun rose higher, there emerged a wild jumble of ancient buildings, domes, stone walls, arches, railings, churches, mosques, courtyards, solar water panels, satellite dishes and a single Israeli flag flying over a tower enclosed by barbed wire. A miniature garbage truck moved slowly beneath me, unfazed by steps and the narrowness of the lane.

I closed my eyes, spread my arms and surrendered myself to the magic of Jerusalem. I was in a place where people had lived and loved and fought and died for thousands of years, where whatever happened today had already happened in the past. It was a place more alive and more real than anywhere I'd been before. And I was part of it, whatever it was. Part of history, part of a people struggling to heal itself, part of something bigger than myself. A small part, to be sure, but not an insignificant part. In the cool October morning, alone on a roof in the Old City, I felt at peace, alive to the moment, fully present. If only Ruth were here with me, I would be complete.

After breakfast, Jude, Nils and I followed Carol up the Via Dolorosa and out through the Lions Gate. 'I was here last year. I know what to do,' Carol said as she hailed a taxi. But when she commanded the driver to take us to Beyt Nattif, he looked at her as if she were crazy and drove off. As did three more taxi drivers. While Carol argued with a fourth uncooperative taxi driver, I noticed a battered yellow taxi cab with Palestinian license plates across the street. The driver agreed to take us as far as the Qalandiya checkpoint. I stifled the urge to jump in the cab and leave Carol to make her own way. Instead I waved my comrades over and said, 'I've sorted it. Let's go.' We piled into the taxi and sped off.

An hour later we approached the most chaotic, noisy traffic jam I'd ever seen. The taxi driver stopped the car and said, 'You walk across. Get a taxi at the other side.' Carol gave me a filthy look. Yellow taxis and vans were parked at odd angles, their drivers leaning against their cars or wandering around kicking stones. There was a long stationary line of cars and trucks. People on foot bustled about in all directions.

We joined the throngs of people shuffling between concrete barriers to stand in a holding pen surrounded by a chain linked fence topped with barbed wire. Jude bought dates and thick Arabic coffee at one of the stalls and offered them to the people around us. Nils tried out the few words of Arabic he knew but no one understood what he was saying and he soon gave up, red-faced with embarrassment. Carol cornered a couple of university students and proceeded to lecture them about the situation. Each time she mentioned The Jews, which was frequent and piercing, I winced and slipped further away. When her voice no longer reached me, I tied on a head scarf and stood in the crowd, breathing deeply.

Gradually, I let myself become aware of the people around me. Beside me, an old woman squatted wearily on a bag stuffed with clothes. A student shuffled from foot to foot, reading a textbook he held open in his hands. Three young boys in school uniform mimed the act of throwing stones at a young soldier on the other side of the fence. The soldier pointed his gun at them. The boys jeered and stuck their tongues out. The soldier walked away, turned back, stuck his tongue out and quickly withdrew it. A stout middle-aged business man talked on his cell phone. 'They can't keep this up forever,' a woman wearing a purple and black striped knee-length coat was saying to Jude. 'The Israelis are a divided people. Eventually they'll destroy themselves. And we will still be here. They're afraid of us. So we are the powerful ones. Please, have a *kibbeh*.' She rummaged in a black leather hand bag and thrust some small brown balls at Jude. Seeing Jude's agony at the possibility of eating meat, I quickly stepped in and accepted for both of us.

Two hours later, we came face to face with a pimply-faced Israeli soldier holding a real machine gun. Before showing him her passport, Carol said something to the soldier in a loud accusatory voice. I cringed, waiting for the soldier to turn his gun on her. A young woman with a toddler on one hip, a large plastic bag on the other, and two small children and three more stuffed plastic bags by her side ranted in Arabic. The toddler wailed. A middle-aged man snapped his cell phone shut and shouted in English, 'Go on. We've waited long enough.' When Carol finally produced her passport, the soldier said 'have a nice day' with a tight hurt look on his face.

When it was my turn, the soldier kept his gaze down. Silently, I handed him my passport. This boy could have been Ruth's son. Yigal must be in the army now. The argument with Ruth meant I also lost touch with Yigal. The last time I saw Yigal was when he was 16 and Noah was 17. I'd driven the boys from Portland to San Francisco, camping along the way. We arrived in San Francisco in time for the start of the Gay Pride march. Standing on the sidewalk on Castro Street, Yigal and I cheered as drag queens and biker dykes marched past. Noah rolled his eyes, bored.

'Are you going to tell your dad we brought you to Gay Pride?' I asked.

Yigal stared at me, wide-eyed and open-mouthed. 'Are you kidding? He doesn't even know I'm with you. Dad thinks I'm in Baltimore with my cousins. He doesn't know Mom is coming out to meet us next week.'

'He's not too keen on me, is he?'

'You can say that again. Never mind. I like you, Auntie Vivi.' He gave me a reassuring hug. 'Don't worry about my dad. If I spent all my time wanting him to like me, I'd always be disappointed. Look how unhappy my mom is. She's always nagging at my dad to spend more time at home, do stuff with us kids.'

'Well, I'd be disappointed if my dad didn't do stuff with me,' Noah said. Noah's father was a friend of mine who'd agreed to be an actively involved dad even though we never lived in the same house. Noah had spent a weekend a month with his dad and long vacations together.

Yigal slapped Noah playfully on the back. 'You're lucky. When my dad spends time with me, we fight. We don't get on. I'm just not his type. He's got a lot of anger in him. He's a macho man. I'm not.'

'C'mon Yigal,' Noah said. 'You'll be going into the army in a couple of years. You've got to start being more macho. Let's join the parade.'

And they skipped off the sidewalk into the parade, roaring and beating their chests like gorillas. They stood smartly to attention and marched in unison, stiff backed and straight faced, with a contingent of burly men wearing pink tutus and twirling pink parasols. As they passed, Yigal turned and saluted me.

That was my last memory of Yigal. It clashed uneasily in my mind with an image of Yigal as a soldier – Yigal holding a machine gun as if it were a guitar; Yigal in a helicopter dropping a bomb on a residential neighbourhood where a suspected terrorist lived; Yigal in a bulldozer demolishing a house with five generations of one family inside; Yigal at a checkpoint refusing to let a pregnant woman pass until she gave birth in public on the rocky ground, forcing a middle-aged businessman to crawl on his belly, strip searching an elderly man shaking with Parkinson's; Yigal shooting live bullets at a crowd of boys no older than ten. Tears welled up in my eyes and spilled down my cheeks. The soldier, handing me my passport, looked at me in surprise. 'I'm so sorry. So sorry,' I said and rushed past.

CHAPTER 13

Vivi

With each minute of the journey, the gulf between me and Ruth widened. By the time we arrived in Beyt Nattif, six hours after leaving Jerusalem, the gulf seemed impassable. I had entered a parallel universe and could no longer see or hear Ruth across the divide.

And soon I was too busy to think about Ruth. The four of us were scattered around the village, each staying with a different family. Wahid, a slight man with curly grey hair, a grey moustache and a short white beard, was my host. He brought me to his home and settled me in a large living room. There were cushions lining three of the walls, a plastic sheet covering the floor, a large TV and video player, a tapestry of Jerusalem with Arabic text and a life-size framed photo of a teenage boy on the wall. No sooner had I sat down, when four young girls ran into the room. Giggling and shoving, they fought each other to be the one to sit next to me. Anxiously, I pointed to the sling on my arm.

'What happened?' Wahid asked.

'My welcome to Israel,' I said. 'Someone was not happy about me being here.' Wahid sighed. He said something in Arabic to the girls. They stopped wriggling and nodded sorrowfully at me. The littlest one, a bright-eyed girl about five years old, pointed to the photo on the wall.

'My son, Ahmed,' Wahid said. 'In May, he was beaten by the settlers. He died two weeks later.' He stood facing the photo, his arms hanging heavily by his side, his head bowed. 'The murderers were not caught. Not even arrested.' His voice dwindled to a whisper. 'He was sixteen. Only sixteen years old.' The little girl wrapped her arms around her father. 'This is Habiba. She misses her brother very much. We are all devastated.'

Ahmed gazed straight into the camera, unsmiling, with what seemed to me to be a puzzled expression. I sensed him looking at me, asking why. Why do your people hate us? Why did they kill me? My skin felt cold and clammy.

'I'm sorry,' I said. The words hung uselessly in the air. Wahid didn't respond. I searched my mind for something else to say. An image of Noah lying dead in a coffin came to me. I closed my eyes to push it away. I decided I had to say something, however inadequate it might be. 'I too have a son.' Tears threatened to choke me. 'If Noah were killed, I don't know how I could bear it. It's too horrible.'

Wahid lifted his head and smiled at me. 'Do you have a photo of your son?' he asked. 'Let us see.'

As I showed the photos of Noah, a door opened down the tiled hallway and the smell of onions frying and meat cooking wafted out. A woman, with thick black hair tied back in a pony tail, carried a tray with a steaming pot of mint tea and a plate of baklava into the living room.

'This is my wife, Zainab,' Wahid said smiling at her tenderly. 'She does not speak English.'

I smiled at Zainab and passed her a photo of Noah standing on a beach in Oregon. She put the tray on the floor, studied the photo in silence and went back to the kitchen, drooping like a wilted flower. The girls followed her quietly, stroking her arms protectively. Left alone with Wahid, I wondered whether Zainab resented me coming into her home. Here I was, an American woman monopolising her English-speaking husband, a mother with a living son.

The four of us internationals had been invited to protect the village from attacks by settlers from the neighbouring Israeli settlement, Ma'ale Zahav. I'd assumed we'd be told what to do when we arrived. But I soon discovered the villagers were just as clueless as we were on how to achieve this aim. Carol, however, had come prepared with a plan which she unveiled to us the next morning. To be identifiable as foreigners, she ordered us to wear silly hats. Nils was to patrol the streets of the village on foot, wearing a striped baseball cap with a propeller on top. Jude and I were to pick olives in yellow bicycle reflector belts and matching head bands sprouting pink and white fluffy ears. Carol set herself the task of patrolling the perimeter of the village. She wore a jacket emblazoned with the words 'End the Occupation' and a Santa Claus hat. Such was Carol's authoritative manner that none of us argued with her ridiculous plan.

When our meeting was over, Habiba led me to her uncle's olive grove where the rest of the family were already busy with the olive harvest. Like a monkey, she clambered up a tree and sprinkled olives and leaves onto the ground. Her three older sisters sat cross-legged on a white cloth beneath the tree, deftly picking out the olives and putting them in a large sack. Wahid urged me to join the sorters on the ground but I didn't want to be a drain on my hosts and decided I should do the picking. Shrugging, he produced a step-ladder and watched anxiously as I climbed to the top rung. I ran my hands gingerly through the leaves in search of the hard green olives. I didn't dare move too fast or reach too far. The step ladder, resting lightly on the uneven rocky ground, wobbled with every move I made. I grabbed the thin branches to steady myself, sending a shower of leaves onto the girls. They looked up and giggled at my clumsy efforts. Pain shot through my injured arm.

Carefully, I lowered myself down the ladder. Wahid looked relieved. 'Come, you pick olives tomorrow. Today I show you around. You see what we're up against. Where are the others?'

We found Nils by the school, conspicuous even without his propeller hat by the mob of little boys jostling for his attention and fighting each other for possession of his hat. He abandoned his post without much persuading. As soon as Jude saw us, she handed the headband with the fluffy ears to her retinue of giggling children and left. Carol was nowhere to be seen.

Wahid led us through the olive groves up a steep hill. At the top, no more than a quarter of a mile away, was a walled town. It was built like a medieval fortress, and it gleamed a harsh white in the sunlight. He leaned against a tree, his hands stroking the coarse twisted trunk. 'I was born in Beyt Nattif in 1964,' he said. 'My parents were born in Beyt Nattif. My grandparents, also born in Beyt Nattif. Their parents, born in Beyt Nattif. For centuries, my family is in Beyt Nattif. There are a thousand people in our village. We are farmers. We keep sheep, grow vegetables, tend olive trees.'

'Since I was two, we lived under Israeli occupation. That was okay until 1985. Then Israelis come and make a camp on the hill there.' He pointed to the fortress. 'On our land, on land with our olive trees.'

'Did they buy the land from you?' Nils asked.

'No. No. No. They take. They tell us nothing.'

'Aren't there land deeds or something?' Nils asked. 'Don't they have to prove ownership?'

'Who has land deeds?' Wahid shrugged irritably. 'We go to talk to them. We don't know Hebrew. They don't speak Arabic. I am the only one from the village speaking English. They say to us, 'this is our land now, not yours. You haven't done anything with it.' And they tore down our olive trees. The trees I planted with my father and my grandfather. To us, the trees are like family. And they cried, the trees cried. We could hear them crying and it broke our hearts.' Wahid wiped away a tear and looked down at the rocky ground.

'What could we do?' he continued more calmly. 'We talk about it in the village council but we know nothing. Who could we turn to? How can we protest? We have no choice. We have to accept them.'

'But I don't understand,' Nils said plaintively. 'Why couldn't you go to the police, the courts? Why didn't you complain?'

Wahid stared blankly at Nils. 'The police? The Israeli police? When the Israeli army is there protecting them? You must understand. This is not like Sweden where you have laws for every citizen. We are not Israeli citizens. We are living under Israeli military occupation.'

Nils opened his mouth to protest but Jude interrupted, digging Nils with her elbow, 'How big is that settlement? It looks enormous.'

'Many many thousands of people. Maybe 20,000. In 1994, they started building on a big scale. They grew quickly. They steal our water supply. They dump their sewage in our valley where we grow our vegetables. They have spotlights that shine on us all night. They built a road to their front gate. Only Israeli cars can drive on this road. The men are armed. They patrol these hills. They shoot at us.'

Wahid rubbed his hands over his face and struggled to control his trembling voice. He shook his head, as if he couldn't believe this was happening. I looked towards Ma'ale Zahav, my face burning with outrage and shame.

'Wahid, not all Jews are like those in Ma'ale Zahav,' I said, my heart beating wildly. I wanted to tell him I was Jewish but my mouth was too dry to get the words out.

Jude spoke indignantly, 'And not all Palestinians are suicide bombers. But Vivi, if those Jews in Ma'ale Zahav are just fringe extremists, why don't Jewish leaders in Israel and throughout the world denounce them? Instead, most Jews in America and Britain support them, send them money, encourage them. I've never heard of Jews criticising Israel.'

'Yes, we do,' I said. 'Not all Jews support the State of Israel.' Jude looked sceptical.

'I have no quarrel with all Jews,' Wahid said. 'I have a problem with those people who stole our land. Our land is where we grow our food that we live off of. Our land is our identity. They have stolen our identity. And then last May…'

He stopped speaking and turned away. 'I get my brother's car. Show you something else.' We trailed after him down the hill.

'A Samara,' Nils said with delight when he saw the brother's once-white car. He jumped into the front where he sank into the soft seat. 'I haven't seen one of these for ten years. They're Russian, basic but sturdy. No gimmicky luxuries.' In the back seat, Jude and I perched on a hard cloth-covered bench and soon discovered which gimmicky luxuries the car didn't have. I wasn't worried about the lack of electric windows or power steering but I wouldn't have minded shock absorbers and an airbag.

For the first ten minutes, there was a tense silence punctuated only by our stifled groans as we bounced on the hard bench. Wahid drove as if he expected an ambush by armed bandits at every turn in the road. He balanced on the edge of the seat, right against the steering wheel, his gaze darting from one side of the track to the other. Just as dangerous as trigger-happy Israelis were the car-sized craters that appeared in the track at frequent intervals and which required Wahid's total concentration. Water had eroded deep ruts in the track causing the car to vault from side to side.

In a rocky uninhabited area, Wahid rammed on the brakes and jumped out. The rubble from a ruined village was visible on either side of the track. A few olive trees, gnarled and unkempt, bravely made a stand amongst the heaps of stone and debris.

'This was the village of Dayr al-Shaykh,' Wahid said. 'Before the Naqba, there were 200, 220 people living here. They were no threat to anyone. No one wanted their land. But in 1948, Jewish soldiers came into the village and rounded everyone up. In front of children, babies, old people, women, men, the entire village, they shot two young men dead. They pointed their guns at the crowd and said they'd kill anyone who didn't get out immediately. Of course, everyone fled. They took nothing with them.

Some families took refuge in Beyt Nattif. After a few weeks, several of the men decided to see if it was safe to go back to Dayr al-Shaykh. What they found put them in a state of shock. Every single house and building had been destroyed. All their possessions had been burned and broken up. Most of the olive trees had been uprooted. This is all that's left.' He knelt down, brought a handful of soil to his lips and kissed it, murmuring softly in Arabic. We bowed our heads and stood in silence. May they rest in peace, I thought. The wind whistled by. I shivered. I felt cold and desolate in the weak October light.

The rest of October passed quickly and to my relief, uneventfully. It seemed as if we'd accomplished our mission. There were no attacks on the village. I settled into everyday life, becoming part of the family. I perfected my olive picking technique, surpassing Habiba in stamina if not in speed and agility. I acquired enough words of Arabic to discuss the weather and the names of food. I taught Wahid's daughters a few English phrases and some American songs. And, most rewarding of all, I made friends with Zainab. Determined to break through her reserve, I followed her around, helping in the kitchen and praising her cooking. I knew I'd succeeded the day she took my hand and led me into the living room. She stood in front of the photo of her son, and wept grey silent tears, still holding my hand. I was glad I didn't speak better Arabic. Words would only have got in the way.

The illusion of success was shattered two days before we were due to leave. At 2.30 in the morning, I was woken by the sound of glass breaking. I put my glasses on and pulled myself slowly up to the window, shivers of fear tingling up my spine. Not more than twenty feet away, clearly visible in the bright moonlight, were three dark figures wearing balaclavas, dark bomber jackets and jeans. They were smashing the windows of the house across the road with baseball bats. Glass was everywhere. I grabbed my backpack to find my camera and catch them in a photo.

The attackers turned towards Wahid's house and saw me through the window. 'That's her,' one said in Hebrew. I stopped in shock. There was something familiar about his voice but I couldn't place it. I searched harder for the camera. The zip stuck, clothes went flying and my toiletry bag burst open, spilling deodorant and hair brush and toothpaste over the floor. I found the camera and peered hopelessly at the miniature symbols and knobs. All at once, as if in slow motion, a baseball bat struck the window, the glass shattered, the camera flash went off, a scream came out of my mouth and the attackers fled into the night.

From upstairs, I heard a high-pitched girl's voice screaming. I raced up the stairs and into the girls' bedroom, Wahid and Zainab close on my heels. Habiba was leaning out the window, shouting. All four girls threw themselves into their parents' arms, sobbing hysterically.

Downstairs, the living room filled with alarmed neighbours. With Wahid translating, my account was anxiously analysed as if it were a complicated puzzle. The digital camera I'd used was examined but no amount of fiddling with the picture revealed anything other than the reflection of the flash. Three pieces of the puzzle were particularly worrying as they didn't fit the profile of any previous attacks. First of all, the attackers had never worn balaclavas before. Secondly, they'd never come at night. Thirdly, they seemed to be looking for me. I was less sure about this as it seemed likely I misheard the Hebrew. And the mysteriously familiar voice still flitted at the back of my mind, like a butterfly not wanting to be caught.

CHAPTER 14

Ruth

The shock waves of Vivi's betrayal reverberated in my mind. I couldn't let it go. Since the events of the 2nd October, I had been in torment. I needed Vivi more than anyone in the world. Yet, she was lost to me, gone to support our enemies. Sitting on the bench, I thought back to that moment when my life was blasted apart and left hanging at a crazy angle, like a door knocked off its hinges.

At five o'clock on the 2nd October, I was in the kitchen preparing dinner. I was trying to follow a complicated recipe. I had to hold the cookbook up close to my face to see the words. I was disturbed by this, thinking it was too soon for me to need bifocals. David got them last year and I know it's a normal sign of middle age, but I wasn't ready for middle age. I chopped up onion, cucumber and tomatoes. I put the onions in the frying pan.

The phone rang. It was Orli. 'Mom. I'm going to a meeting tonight. I'll stay with friends after. See you tomorrow.' My stomach clenched into a tight knot. That meant another night of worry, imagining a suicide bomber in the café or bus she'd be on.

'Oh, no you're not,' I jumped in. 'You've been out every night for the last two weeks. You act as if this is a hotel. You get home and eat dinner with us. Be here by seven at the latest.'

Despite the assertive words, I could hear the whine in my voice. I was powerless and she knew it. Not surprisingly she hung up, after a breezy, 'Oh, I'll be home tomorrow. Gotta go.'

I felt a wave of longing for my firstborn, my beloved Yigal. Yigal had never been as wilful and rude as Orli. I missed his laughter, his goofiness, his easy-going nature, the way he tossed his head to get the hair out of his face, the look of adoration in his eyes when he saw me. When I was with Yigal, I felt alive and loved.

I made myself sit down at the table to do some preparation. I was trying not to cry. A strong smell of burning filled the kitchen. I jumped up and ran to grab the frying pan off the cooker. The onions were charred. I dumped the frying pan into the sink and turned on the tap. Steam and smoke and sizzling sounds filled the room.

I closed my eyes and imagined Yigal next to me, caressing me on the cheek. I shivered, got out another onion and chopped. Tears streamed down my cheeks. I gave myself a good talking to, 'What's the matter with you? How pathetic to miss your son so much. It's not like you'll never see him again. He will come home on leave. Anyway, children grow up and leave home. You have to get used to it.'

Although Yigal had been in the army for a year, I still hadn't come to terms with his absence. I knew it was my problem, not his. He was more than ready to join up. For him, the army was like an extension of high school, a place to be with his friends. Yigal was a sociable boy. He was having a good time with his friends. He wasn't missing me like I was missing him.

I turned on the radio. 'This is the news at five o'clock on Wednesday the 2nd of October. An IDF soldier was killed this evening when a female suicide bomber with explosives strapped to her body attempted to cross a checkpoint in Samaria. While search procedures were being implemented at a post by the crossing, the bomber detonated the explosives, killing herself and the soldier.'

My skin turned clammy. I could hardly breathe. I rocked back and forth, saying 'Not Yigal. Let it not be Yigal.' Every time a soldier was killed, I was gripped with a stomach-churning, mind-numbing fear that only lifted when I discovered the soldier killed was not Yigal. This time, the fear did not lift.

CHAPTER 15

Yigal

There are no clouds in the sky right now. I watch, waiting for one to blow in. But no matter how hard I stare or how long I wait, there's nothing but empty blue sky, going on and on forever into nothingness. Just as it was the day I came here from the other world, the day I first met the girl sitting beside me.

I was at a different checkpoint then. Early in the afternoon, I was left on my own for half an hour. Gil, my commanding officer, had taken two others from our unit a short distance away. There was nothing for me to do. I scanned the sky, looking for clouds, when I saw a girl about my age coming towards me. She was on her own. I couldn't take my gaze off her. She was stunning, not like any of the Palestinian girls I'd seen before, certainly not at checkpoints. Her loose black hair bounced on her shoulders. She was wearing hoop earrings, a padded blue leather jacket and tight-fitting grey trousers. She marched towards me, confident and graceful. She looked into my eyes. I smiled at her. In Hebrew I said, 'When I get off duty, let's meet for a drink.' It was a joke. But I meant it. She was a good looker and I would take her out. If things were different. She didn't seem to think I was funny. She didn't smile. She had a determined look on her face. She reached inside her jacket. I held out my hand, ready to check her pass.

I heard a shriek like the breaking of a thousand glasses. I saw jagged shards of light inside my head. Then silence. I couldn't focus. I didn't know where I was. I groped my way through a dense white fog.

When I got my bearings, I realised I was looking down on a scene of devastation. Gil and the rest of my unit were combing the ground around the checkpoint picking up a bloody arm, a severed torso, a fragment of skull. What was left of my body and the girl's.

What really amazed me was how light I was. As if I'd been lugging a heavy sack around for the last 19 years and all of a sudden I'd dropped it. I don't remember feeling my body was a burden when I was alive. I was always comfortable in my body. But it sure was incredible to be so light.

Without a body, I found I could be wherever my thoughts took me. I thought of home and right away, I was there. My mother was in the kitchen, doing all the hundreds of things she does at five p.m. on a Wednesday afternoon. Whizzing about. Everything half done. She had that tight face on. Like she was trying really hard to get it right and she didn't think she'd manage. If I'd been back in my body, I'd have grabbed her round the waist and danced the hora with her.

The phone rang and Mom whined and shouted. When she hung up, she looked like she was about to cry. That's how I knew it was Orli who'd called. My mother is a wimp. And Orli is a bully. I used to hit her when we were little. But I had to change tactics when she grabbed a frying pan off the cooker and bashed me over the head with it. That's when she was six. Since then, I've limited myself to verbal teasing and quick dodging.

I wanted to hug my mom, to tell her everything's all right. But without my body, I couldn't get through to her. And I guess from her point of view, things were not all right. I came up close and caressed her on the cheek.

There was a news bulletin on the radio. A girl suicide bomber at a checkpoint. A soldier killed. No names. Mom stopped what she was doing and closed her eyes. Gripping the counter top, she rocked back and forth and whispered, 'Oh please. Not Yigal. Make it not be Yigal.'

That's when everything misted over. It was as if I'd been blown into the centre of a thick grey cloud. When the mist cleared, I found myself at this checkpoint. It looked like an army checkpoint but I knew I was in the Other World because there was no wind, no birds or insects, no people, no traffic sounds in the distance. Real life checkpoints are noisy and chaotic with people and cars and trucks and taxis and carts swarming all over the place in an endless, bad-tempered muddle. The

Palestinians are not orderly people. We have to yell at them to get in line.

But at this place, it was just me and concrete. There were concrete pathways, dusty dry and cluttered with spirals of barbed wire. Concrete barriers arranged like dominoes. Concrete fence posts holding up wire mesh fences. Concrete pyramids pointing to a blue cloudless sky. A concrete cylindrical building squatted on top of a barren, rocky mound, its slit-like windows facing down onto the concrete world below. I patted one of the pyramids and was surprised by its rough texture and rock-hard solidness.

I kicked half-heartedly at a rock. It scuttled off and landed in the barbed wire with a lonely, hollow sound. I kicked at another rock. This time I put more energy into it. The rock flew into one of the concrete pillars with a satisfying crack. I scooped up some gravel and threw it into the air. It fell down around me like rain.

When I stopped, there was nothing, no activity, no sound. I panicked and ran in and out of the concrete pillars, back and forth along the concrete pathway, around and around the concrete pyramids. I shouted and cursed, my screams disappearing into nothingness no matter how loudly I yelled. The scenery never changed. I couldn't get out of the concrete checkpoint.

I'd been running round the same pillar for hours when suddenly a girl appeared in front of me. She had black hair tied back in a pony tail. Her clothes were drab and unstylish but her eyes were bright and lively. She didn't seem like a ghost but I didn't pat her to make sure. When she smiled at me, I didn't smile back. What was there to smile about?

'So, how long have you been here?' she asked. When I didn't answer, she laughed. 'That's a stupid question, isn't it? I don't know how long I've been here so how can you know how long you've been here.'

'I think I just got here,' I said. Something about her was bothering me. Maybe it was her good mood. It didn't seem right in the circumstances. Or maybe it was because she looked vaguely familiar and I couldn't figure out who she was. I patted the concrete pyramid again, just to check it was still the same. 'Have we met before?' I asked hesitantly.

She took a step back, screwed up her face as if she was thinking hard and looked me over from head to toe. I followed her gaze as far up as my neck. I was no longer wearing my uniform but had on a green T-shirt, jeans and sandals. When she'd finished her examination, she shrugged and said, 'I don't recognise you. But, yeah, you look familiar. Say, aren't you the boy shot dead by the soldiers at the demonstration in Nablus? You were with me in the mini-bus? That's you, right?'

I stared at her, feeling uneasy.

'My name's Aisha,' she said. 'Aisha Awad. Oh, I know. You're one of the martyrs from the Church of the Nativity siege in Bethlehem. Aren't you?'

The last time I was in Bethlehem, I was on a school trip to Rachel's Tomb. Then it hit me. I reeled back in shock as a tsunami of recognition washed over me. She was the girl at the checkpoint, the one who exploded her bomb as I checked her pass. What the hell was she doing here? This was too weird. It was way out, far beyond anything I could ever have imagined. But there was no doubt about it. I pulled myself together, narrowed my eyes and said, 'I'm off duty now. So what do you say to a drink?'

Aisha leapt into the air, her face a mask of disbelief and horror. 'You! You're a Jew. You're that soldier at the checkpoint.'

'I was.' I wondered if I could shoot her into a different Other World but my gun was nowhere to be seen.

'What are YOU doing here?' She wasn't in such a good mood any more.

'I'm here because of you. It wasn't my idea.'

'Oh yeah. If you didn't want to end up here, you wouldn't have joined the Israeli army.'

Smart aleck, I thought. 'We wouldn't have to have an army if you and your terrorist friends didn't keep blowing us up.'

'We wouldn't have to blow you up if you didn't keep taking our land, killing our children, demolishing our houses, uprooting our olive trees, stealing our water, denying our human rights...'

'We wouldn't have to do any of those things if you were willing to make peace.'

'We would be willing to live in peace if you were. You are occupying our land.'

'It's our land.'

'No, it's ours.'

'It's ours.'

'We were here first.'

'No, we were. Like 2000 years ago.'

'We are here now.'

Aisha and I were nose to nose, eyeball to eyeball. It was my turn but I didn't say anything. I wasn't stuck for a good come-back but I was distracted by an unexpected sensation lower down. I was getting turned on by this girl. And that was way too weird for me to deal with. For one thing, we're sworn enemies. For another, we're both dead.

I stepped back. 'Look, I think there's been a mistake. I should be in the Jewish World-to-Come, waiting for the Messiah. You should be in the Muslim heaven, having sex with 72 virgins.'

'Ha. Ha. Very funny. You sure are ignorant. And stupid.'

I ignored her. 'I've got to find someone to sort this mess out. Who's in charge here?'

Aisha slumped against a pillar, wrapped her arms around her legs and dropped her head onto her knees. I walked away thinking hard. Since I'd been able to be with my mom by thinking about home, I reasoned all I had to do to get out was to think about something else. I dredged up thoughts about my dad - Dad at the dinner table mocking Mom's cooking, Dad yelling at Orli for staying out late, Dad refusing to come to a dance performance at school because he thought I was a sissy to be dancing. I let them all go. Frantically I searched for one memory of me and Dad having a good time together.

The only one I could come up with was Dad beaming with pride when I walked in the front door wearing my uniform. But if it weren't for that uniform, I'd be alive now. So I didn't dwell on that.

I closed my eyes and tried again to think about anything other than Aisha. The harder I tried not to think about her, the more I did think about her. Finally I gave up. I opened my eyes. Aisha was right next to me, curled up on the dusty concrete pathway.

I ran. I ran in a straight line, away from her. I ran and ran, but I kept passing the same concrete structures. When I stopped, I heard muffled sobbing. Without looking, I ran, this time even faster than before. It didn't matter how far or how fast I ran. I was still in the same concrete checkpoint. And Aisha was still with me, sitting on the ground crying.

'Go away,' I said. 'Leave me alone. Stop following me around.'

She didn't look up at me. 'I can't.' I could barely hear her.

'I said, go away.'

'I said, I can't.'

'Why not?' I stamped my feet and paced like a caged lion. I wanted to have a tantrum but it wasn't my way. Orli was the expert on tantrums in my family. I used to secretly provoke her until she lost it. She'd look around for a comfortable spot before she flung herself screaming and kicking on the floor. It was gratifying for me but it didn't do her any good. If I let myself have a full-scale tantrum, it would only give Aisha the satisfaction of seeing me as a loser.

'I don't know why. Wherever I am, you're always there.' Aisha's voice was flat, matter of fact, almost resigned.

That's when it sunk in for real. Aisha and I were stuck together in this concrete Other World. We couldn't get away from each other. Furious, I flung myself down on the other side of the pillar, my back to her. No, this was not fair. It didn't make sense. I could see why Aisha should be here but I didn't do anything wrong. I was the victim.

I clutched my head and thought hard. There must be a way out. I was determined to find it.

PART TWO
October 2003

CHAPTER 16

Ruth

It was the first anniversary of Yigal's death. I sat alone in his bedroom and waited. I waited for him to show himself. I just wanted a sign, any sign. There had been nothing all year, not since that fleeting vision I'd had a few days after the funeral. I had convinced myself he would appear today. So I waited and watched and listened. A car drove by. Down the hall in the kitchen, the fridge hummed. The clock on the shelf ticked. A bird chattered outside the window. Each sound was discrete, dropping into the silence like a stone into a pond, the ripples lapping against my brain.

I looked at the photos of Yigal I'd placed behind the *yahrzeit* candle, willing the images to come alive. But the photos remained what they had always been, ink splotches on paper. When I could no longer bear the deception, I focussed my attention on the candle. Maybe Yigal's spirit was in the flame, waving to me. The flame flickered but I didn't sense Yigal there. Overwhelmed by the emptiness, I passed out, my head dropping forward. Instantly I jerked awake. My heart was pounding. Had I missed him?

I was alone with lifeless things, trying to find Yigal in the guitar resting against the wall, the magazines in the bookshelf, the navy blue cotton bedspread on the bed. I walked around his room, trailing my hands along the chest of drawers, the wardrobe, the bookshelf. I opened his drawers and pulled out his clothes, burying my face in a pile of shirts, drinking in the faint or imagined smell of his body. I lay on the bed and stared up at the ceiling. Was he looking down at me through the crack in the paint? I rolled off the bed and lay on the floor on my stomach. The lino felt reassuringly solid under the palms of my hands but I still felt alone. I rested my cheek on the smooth lino. In my line of vision were the round scuffed legs of the chest of drawers we'd bought on a tense family shopping trip to Tel Aviv when Yigal was ten years old. It was memorable because it was the last time the four of us went shopping together.

I turned my head to the right and could see under his bed. I saw a carpet of dust balls, a baseball bat and something dark crumpled up against the far wall. I had kept Yigal's room just as it was when he was killed. Every day I came into his room and sat on the bed. Every day I looked at his things and saw the same furniture, the same few possessions. But until this day, I had never looked under the bed, never seen the dust growing in the dark space, like mushrooms on a decaying log. A lot of dust can accumulate in a year. 'You are dust and to dust you shall return.' I closed my eyes. I had been kicked out of the Garden of Eden and like Eve, I didn't know what I'd done to deserve it.

When I opened my eyes, I consciously ignored the dust and focused on the dark object against the wall. Vaguely, I wondered what it could be. Yigal had always kept his room tidy. He wasn't like Orli who stuffed things under her bed rather than deal with them. I took hold of the bat and used it to drag the dark something away from the wall. By the time I'd got it within arm's distance, it was no longer dark but fluffy grey. I shook it, filling the room with clouds of fine dust. In between sneezes, I held it up to the light. It's nothing more than a piece of black cloth with holes in it, my rational brain declared. But my gut recognised it as a balaclava and sent out a sharp distress call. At that moment, the shutters came down. I only just managed to get onto the bed before I fell into a coma-like sleep.

I woke shivering and uneasy, in the middle of a gut-wrenching thought about the balaclava. There was something wrong about the balaclava and the baseball bat. I couldn't picture Yigal with either of them. He had never played baseball and what possible reason would he have for a balaclava? Yet they were hidden under his bed. My brain, like a rusty engine left unused for a year, creaked into first gear.

If it wasn't Yigal's, maybe it was Orli's. But I couldn't imagine what Orli would be doing with a baseball bat and a balaclava. Even if she had such objects, she would have hidden them more successfully in her own bedroom. Orli's room was an impassable jungle, a perfect environment for small objects to disappear in. Years ago, I had given up the struggle to make her tidy her room. I didn't have the energy to fight with her or to do it myself. I figured it was her business and she had to face the consequences. If she couldn't find her homework or her favourite top, that was her problem. I had enough problems of my own.

That left only one possibility – David. I wished my brain would seize up and grind to a halt. Instead, it shifted into third gear and raced through my memory bank searching for a hit with the keywords David, baseball bat and balaclava. The search engine retrieved an email from Vivi. She had sent me the email last December when she clearly didn't know about Yigal's death. When the email arrived, I'd scanned it quickly, hoping for some kind words. But it was a long and angry harangue about Palestinians and the occupation. My first impulse was to delete it. Vivi was out of my life for good. She'd come to Israel to support the people who'd murdered my son and she hadn't even tried to visit me.

But the next day after a sleepless night, I regretted deleting the email. It implied a finality to our friendship that was too painful to contemplate. I printed it and stuffed it in a drawer in the kitchen. I don't know why I kept it. I never seriously thought I would reread it. Now I went to find it.

'*Saturday 14 December 2002 20:23*

Dear Ruth,

Do you know what's going on in your own country? How can you live an ordinary life while millions of

Palestinians are suffering under this endless and brutal occupation just miles from your home? How can you not know what's going on? What happened to your values, your principles? Have you become so insular that you no longer care about justice and truth? And you send your beloved son to oppress these people. What kind of person have you become?'

My gut clenched and my breathing turned jagged. No wonder I deleted it. I skimmed quickly over three pages of diatribe about attacks on some insignificant Palestinian village I'd never heard of until the words balaclava and baseball bats leapt out and grabbed me by the throat.

'It really bothered me that the settlers wore balaclavas and used baseball bats when they attacked. It made me think they knew an international peacekeeper was here and they wanted to hide their identities. That shows a scary new development in these attacks.'

I clutched my throat to stop the nausea and threw the paper onto the table. But my gaze was drawn back to the email and I couldn't stop myself reading on.

'Why haven't you been in touch with me? You know I came to see you at the beginning of October. Claire said when you phoned, she told you I was in Israel and I was coming to see you. Didn't you wonder why I never showed up? Maybe David didn't tell you what he did to me when I came to your house. He attacked me and I don't mean just verbally. He twisted my arm until it nearly broke and he threatened me. I was in agony for weeks. And you never even got in touch with me to see if I was all right. Why are you married to that thug?

How can you live with such a man? He's a low-life hoodlum, a violent, aggressive man.'

Shocked, I reread this paragraph. No, I hadn't read this bit when I first got the email. I never knew Vivi had come to see me. David had never said anything about meeting Vivi. I sat down at the kitchen table, trembling, my breath shallow and laboured. Was it true? Would Vivi lie to me? I couldn't believe it. For all her faults, Vivi would not make up something like that. Would David?

'David! Hello! Anyone home?' Rena called from the front door. She appeared in the kitchen and looked at me with an expression I couldn't read. 'Oh hi Ruth. Are you alone? Where's David? Um. And Orli? Are you all right? Have you been to work today?'

It was just like Rena to barge in uninvited and ask stupid questions. Was I all right? Of course not. Why would I be all right? Did she even need to ask? And why would she think I would go to work on the anniversary of Yigal's death?

'Want me to make you some coffee? Here, I brought you a coconut cake.' She thrust a freshly baked cake on the table and hovered, bouncing from foot to foot. I kept staring at Vivi's email hoping she would go away. I hadn't felt close to Rena since Yigal's death. Actually, I hadn't felt close to anyone. Still, I needed to unburden myself and Rena was the only one present. And we had been neighbours for years. Surely she'd understand what I was going through. Anyway, there was nothing I could do about it.

'I found a balaclava and a bat under Yigal's bed,' I said. 'They belong to David. He beat up Vivi when she came to see me during the *shiva* and I think he attacked the Palestinian village where she was staying.'

She drew in a sharp breath and said, 'Did David tell you that?'

'No, I just read an email from Vivi she sent last December.'

Rena shrugged. She opened cupboards and banged cups and plates onto the table. 'Where's the sugar?' she asked. I pointed vaguely in the direction of the counter and picked at the cake. I hated coconut. Why didn't she make a chocolate cake? I pushed the cake across the table. David would appreciate the cake. He loved coconut.

'David knew I wanted to see Vivi,' I said to Rena's back. 'But he drove her away. He beat her up. He must have followed her to this Beyt Nattif place in the Territories with that Shlomo friend of his and ..'

'So what?' Rena snapped suddenly and turned to face me. 'What do you think David should have done? Just after Yigal was killed, she shows up on her way to help our enemies. You know how he hated your so-called friend and how worried he was about her influence over you. To have that woman, that vicious, gloating toad, come right to your house at a time like that. It's more than anyone should have to bear. What's the big deal? It was just a little act of defiance to let her know she's not welcome here. It's not like he killed anyone or even really hurt her. Why are you looking at me like that?'

'You knew? All along, you knew?'

'It's not like you were still friends. You told me you'd had a fight and hadn't talked to each other for years. What's the big deal?'

'You don't think it's a big deal for my husband to beat up my friend?' I said, standing up and taking a step towards Rena. But to my surprise, Rena didn't back down.

'Have you ever thought you're not the only one who lost a son to a suicide-bomber?' she said, speaking loudly and fast into my face. 'You've cut David off. You've acted as if… I don't know, as if Yigal's death was your own tragedy. As if David doesn't count. What kind of comfort have you given David this last year? He's your husband for God's sake. And you're going on about this evil woman as if she's more important than David. Ever since we moved in next door almost ten years ago, you've complained about David. You always criticise him. You've never had a good word to say about him. The first time we met, you were crying because David had yelled at Yigal. You never understood him. And I always took your side. Until…' Abruptly she ground to a halt and looked at the floor, clamping her mouth shut.

As if it were coming from someone else, I heard a voice asking, 'Until what?'

'Where is the sugar? I can't find it. Oh, here it is. Why don't you keep it where people can find it?'

'Until what?'

'Until he came to me… he was crying… said he was so lonely… so misunderstood.' She didn't look me in the eye and she sounded hesitant, her voice fading to a whisper. My scalp tingled. I was learning much more about David than I could take in. And about Rena. I smelled betrayal. Anger bubbled up in my gut and was dangerously close to the surface.

'When Was That?' I said, each word a bullet shot from my gut straight at her.

She dumped three spoonfuls of sugar into her coffee and stirred, spilling coffee onto the table. We watched a trickle of brown liquid slide down the cup. The clock ticked, a loud clanging noise.

'When Was That, Rena?'

She hesitated before spitting it out. 'When you and Orli were in Baltimore last November. You left David here on his own for three weeks.' Rena glared at me and made eye contact, briefly. What an arrogant, self-righteous bitch, I thought. I wouldn't have gone to Baltimore to stay with my family if David and I had been getting on. I turned to them in desperation and in vain, as it turned out, because of the tension that had erupted into full-scale war between me and David after Yigal was killed.

'And when David came to you crying, you encouraged him to sort things out with me, his wife, didn't you Rena?'

'Of course I did and he tried. God, he tried. Time after time, he tried. But you, you made no effort. You sneered at him and criticised everything he proposed. You did nothing to try to understand him. You're just a victim and a nag, a taker. You're full of self-pity but you aren't prepared to give anything back to him. You're pathetic, Ruth. That's what you are. And I'm sorry to say this to you on Yigal's *yahrzeit* but if David's too sensitive to say it to your face, well I will.' She sat back, with her arms folded across her chest.

I was speechless. I couldn't remember one incident in the last ten months when David had tried to sort things out with me. But the accusations were all too familiar. They were David's words. Words that David had been using against me since the children were little. Words that hurt but had become such a fundamental part of our marital landscape I'd come to believe they were normal.

'Is something going on between you and my husband?' My mouth was dry and it was almost impossible to get the words out.

'Surely you know already. Or are you completely blind as well as self-centred?'

My fingers and toes were tingling with shock. No, I didn't know already. Since Yigal's death, I had been oblivious to everything but the chasm in my heart. Even though I'd gone to work, done the housework, cooked meals, talked to people, got on with life, really I was just going through the motions. Inside, I was precariously balanced on a thin rope stretched across a dark, indifferent abyss. If I didn't put all my effort into staying on that rope, I would drop into nothingness.

So yes, Rena was right. I was completely blind to anyone but myself. With an effort, I wrenched my attention away from the chasm and onto Rena. Her face was red and flushed, like she was about to cry. Her legs were crossed and her arms were folded across her chest. An image flashed into my mind – of Rena next to me on the rope, the two of us dangling over the abyss, fighting a life-and-death battle to keep from falling into oblivion. There wasn't room for both of us. I needed to say something to get her off my lifeline.

I took a deep breath and paused, struck dumb by the sight of her shoes. She had on running shoes - dirty, worn Hi-Tec running shoes. It wasn't Rena's style to wear anything but heels, even around the house. The cogs in my brain whirred and clunked. So that's how they did it. She went running with David, on those innocent jogs that allowed him a legitimate excuse to be away from the house for hours. And I had never suspected. Why would I? I leaned towards Rena and spoke firmly and softly. 'When I've had enough of David sneaking around behind my back and lying to everyone, including you, you stupid idiot, and beating up my friends and behaving like a low-life hooligan, I'll let you know. Until then, you can jog back out of my home. Now get out and take that disgusting cake with you.'

I stood up majestically, my nose in the air. As I escorted her off the premises, I noticed the rope felt a tiny bit more stable and the abyss a tiny bit lighter. And at the corner of my mind, I sensed a smile. Yigal's smile.

CHAPTER 17
Yigal

Today there are only two clouds in the sky. As I watch, they drift towards each other, merge into one and drift off locked together. Aisha has been sitting on the concrete pillar, glowering. I guess she's been chewing over the same thoughts as me because all of a sudden she jumps down and says, 'OK, if we can't get away from each other, you come with me. I want to show you something.' I don't like her high-handed manner and my first impulse is to say no. But I'm curious and I wonder what she plans to show me. So I'm hooked and I find myself following her where her thoughts take her. That seems to be how it works around here.

Her thoughts take us to a narrow unpaved road in a crowded neighbourhood. Water runs through the middle of the road. There are lots of people about, all Palestinians. They're wading through the puddles because there aren't any sidewalks. Weeds grow by the side of the road. The street is lined with walls made of concrete blocks and chicken wire fences. Houses made of unfinished concrete are jumbled on top of each other. Scattered above the houses I see grey cylindrical water tanks squatting on platforms. There are bullet holes in many of the water tanks. The place is dilapidated. It wouldn't get any prizes for best kept town. I shrug to myself. All that money from the United Nations and they choose to live in squalor.

Aisha is moving quickly through the lane, glancing at the walls. She seems to be looking for something in particular. She doesn't pay any attention to the many wall murals we pass. Under one window, there's a crude landscape of two tents in the desert beneath a blue sky. You can tell it's not just a painting of scenery by the words UN and 1948 printed on the tents. Further along the road, we pass a 20 foot high drawing of a young boy. In the background are a mass of pink flowers. A black and white ribbon zig zags from the top of the picture around the boy's shoulders to the bottom of the wall where there's a black rectangle with English and Arabic words. The caption reads, 'the martyr of chilhood and sufering'. I snigger. That's what I call over the top, definitely not my taste in art. 'Hey you,' I call to her. 'Whoever wrote this can't spell. Who's this kid anyway?' But she's already turned a corner and doesn't answer. When I catch up with her, she's absorbed in the graffiti and posters pasted over the peeling paint and half-finished plaster.

'See,' she says, pointing to a brand new poster. 'That's me.'

It is her. It's a good photo of her. She's looking directly at the camera, unsmiling, her hair tied back, her mouth a straight line. She's wearing magenta lipstick and her eyes are outlined in black. It could be a photo of a model or a dancer if she weren't carrying a machine gun across her chest.

Seeing an Arabic inscription under the photo, I sneer. 'Oh, let me guess what this says. All hail Aisha Awad – the girl who blew herself up because she couldn't get a boyfriend!'

Aisha raises her chin in the air and looks down her nose at me. Turning back to the poster, she reads slowly and ceremoniously as if addressing a crowd of cheering supporters, 'Aisha Awad – the woman martyr whose heroic deeds stamped fear and horror on the face of the Zionist enemy. How beautiful you were when you raised the humiliated nation to Paradise.' Aisha's eyes are shining. She's practically swooning in front of the poster. She leans forward and kisses the photo of herself.

I snort. 'So is this what you wanted? Are you pleased with yourself now?' I can't believe I've been killed for this. She's clearly a psychopath. I try desperately to think myself out of this hell-hole but my anger against Aisha is so strong my thoughts are stuck. I can't get away.

Smiling, Aisha goes down an alley, up a flight of stairs, through a front door and into a living room. Reluctantly I follow her. It's a good-sized living room but cluttered with chairs and sofas. The walls are decorated with green plastic plants, family photos, prayer beads, inscriptions, pictures of Jerusalem, a large framed photo of Yasser Arafat and embroidered wall hangings. A red curtain covers an archway. I can hear shouting from another room in the house. The shouting gets louder and closer, until suddenly a teenage boy, about fourteen, flies through the red curtain, closely followed by a stout middle-aged woman.

'That's Osama, my brother. That's my mother,' Aisha says. She doesn't translate but I soon pick up the gist of their conversation. Osama is holding a crumpled poster, waving it wildly at his mother. He's standing by the front door with one hand on the door knob, facing his mother and shouting loudly. He seems to be accusing her of something. This kid looks like trouble to me. I've seen Orli yell at Dad before but not with the ferociousness Osama uses. I wouldn't want to meet him in a dark alley.

His mother is just as loud. And just as scary. She doesn't burst into tears or run away like my mother would. She keeps on at Osama, pumping her arms up and down for emphasis, fire shooting out of her eyes, squaring up to him, telling him what for. Then she grabs the poster out of his hand. I catch a fleeting glimpse of the photo of Aisha before her unsmiling face is ripped in two and thrown to the floor.

I look over at Aisha. Her shoulders are slumped. Her eyes are wide, her mouth slack-jawed. She is shaking. I'd say her bubble has definitely burst now. Aisha won't be getting Mother's approval for her heroic deed. I allow myself a moment of gleeful satisfaction.

Mother turns to an arm chair in a dark corner of the living room. Peering into the gloom, I make out the shape of a man slumped in the chair. His face is haggard. It looks as if it is the most enormous effort for him to look up. Mother begins haranguing him but without noticeable effect. He seems to have become one with the chair. I don't know what she's saying. Maybe she's pleading with him to get off his backside and beat the shit out of Osama. When the man doesn't even lift his head, Osama butts in with more shouting, makes an unmistakeable gesture of contempt and shoots out the door. Great! Another suicide bomber is born.

Mother throws her hands in the air and collapses on a sofa. She weeps, rocking back and forth, covering her face with her hands. It's heart breaking watching her. Aisha is still frozen to the spot. The man sinks deeper into his chair. Eventually, Mother mops her face with a cloth and gets herself under control. She picks up a scrap book lying open on the sofa and flips through it. Aisha hovers next to her. I creep closer and look over her shoulder. The scrap book contains newspaper clippings about female suicide bombers. 'I made it a month ago,' Aisha says to me, stroking a picture of a heavily veiled woman with only her eyes showing. In large letters, Aisha has written 'Wafa Idris – first Palestinian woman martyr. January 27, 2002.' Aisha begins reading one of the articles.

'She decided to end her fresh young life at a moment of a profound sense of oppression such as no people had suffered as the Palestinians do. But before that, she decided her death

would reverberate so as to draw attention to the tragedy created by the Israelis, with their airplanes and tanks against a defenceless people. The inhuman Israeli policy has made the entire Palestinian people into human bombs...'

Her mother flips the page over and Aisha begins reading another article to me: *'Wafa revealed the meaning of the Palestinian personality; she revealed the heroism of the Palestinian woman and turned from a living creature walking on the Earth to a symbol that went down in history, the trace of which cannot be eradicated.'*

Before she can finish, her mother has turned to a new page. *'Wafa Idris did not sit in the coffee shops of rage to which our intellectuals are addicted, becoming procurers, and the writers who sell themselves for a shekel or a dollar. She did not go out to demonstrations....'*

Mother is having trouble breathing. She grunts, grabs the scrap book in both hands and rips until every page is in shreds. I get the impression she does not share Aisha's admiration of Wafa Idris.

Aisha is crying, 'Mama. Please don't cry. Mama. Please don't be angry with me. I wanted you to be proud of me. You're always going on demonstrations and protesting against the Zionist oppressors. I was following your footsteps. I thought you'd understand. Especially after Papa was beaten up by the Israeli soldiers. Please stop. When they came into our house and beat him in front of us, something snapped in me. They're inhuman. They only understand the language of violence. You preach non-violence but their minds are closed. You'll never get anywhere. The international community doesn't care about us. There's no point asking the world for help. The bomb is all the world listens to. I did it for you and Papa, for Osama and Fazia. I did it for Palestine.'

What a vain, egotistical sick girl Aisha is. I've seen enough. I've got to get out of here. Get back to my own family even though I know now I'm never going to be able to talk with my mother again.

CHAPTER 18
Ruth

The house seemed different once Rena left. It buzzed and hummed. Dull, ordinary objects, which moments earlier had made up the unobserved backdrop of my life, now gleamed and shimmered. Their colours and textures danced out at me. Everything was in movement. My breath chafed cold and sharp as it rushed through my nose and into my lungs. All my senses were on fire. It was as if I were waking up from a long, deep sleep.

I know exactly when I fell into that mind-numbing sleep. It was just after I heard Yigal had been killed. I didn't cry when I heard the news. I sat. It was out of character for me. I am someone who cries easily, all the time. I cry when David yells at me. I cry every time I see 'Fiddler on the Roof'. I cry when Orli's rude to me. I cry when I sing *Hatikva*. I cry when the car breaks down, when I can't get through to the bank, when the toilet overflows. I cry when a Jewish child is killed by a Palestinian terrorist. I didn't cry when I heard Yigal had been blown up by a suicide bomber.

I sat on the kitchen floor. The phone rang, stopped, rang again. I didn't answer it. Rena appeared and stood looking at me with a sad, fearful face. Her mouth moved but the words never reached me through the fog in my brain. She put a cup of coffee on the floor next to me and sat at the table, crying. The Chief Rabbi of the Israeli Defence Force came by. He spoke to Rena and left. Rena phoned everyone in my address book trying to track down David and Orli.

No, I didn't cry when I heard Yigal was killed. I had no time to cry. In my mind, I was there with Yigal when the bomb exploded. I saw his body blown apart. With my eyes closed, I could see it vividly and clearly. I covered my face with my hands. There was no escape from the gory details. I watched it again. And again. And again. I couldn't stop it.

The image shifted. Instead of Yigal, it was Arabs being blown up by bombs. And it was me throwing the bombs, blowing up Arabs, any Arab, all Arabs. Arab women. Arab children. Arab homes. Arab olive trees. Arab villages. Arab mosques. I roared, 'See how you like it, you cowards. You terrorists. You want bombs. I'll give you bombs.'

But the revenge energy was short-lived. Soon nausea and desolation flooded in, pinning me to the floor. Rena held me while I wailed plaintively, over and over again, 'Children are not supposed to die before their parents. Children are not supposed to be blown up by bombs.'

Then the self-blame. How could I have let Yigal join the army? He was still a boy. He had his whole life in front of him. He should have been at university, not in the army. My nieces and nephews in the States aren't in this situation. It was my idea to make *aliyah*, to leave my comfortable life in Baltimore and live in Israel. This was my passion, my path in life. What right did I have to impose my choices on my children? Why do we make our children into soldiers, force them to defend us so we can live our selfish, materialistic lives? Why wasn't I on military duty at the checkpoint? My life is meaningless now without Yigal. Why did I ever move to Israel? All sorts of confused thoughts went through my head. I wasn't rational. I didn't know what I was thinking.

That's when my brain short-circuited and turned off, releasing me from further torment. And I was only just waking up now, a year later. So Rena was right in a way. I had not been there for David. With a shock, I suddenly remembered it hadn't been me who first broke the news to David. It had been Rena.

That day a year ago, Rena was still with me when David finally arrived home. He marched across the living room into the kitchen and frowned at us from the doorway. 'It's midnight,' he said, as if we were naughty children and he'd caught us out after curfew.

I remember staring at him, wondering where he'd been all evening. He never told me where he was going or when he'd be back. I assumed he'd been with Shlomo and his other army mates. I'd never met them until the *shiva* but I had a sense they were a bad influence on him. I had hoped he would stop seeing them when he finished his reserve military service five years ago. But they kept in touch. After Yigal's death, David spent even more time away from home. Sometimes he told me he was with Shlomo. Occasionally I over-heard him organising their get-togethers. This surprised me. In all our 22 years of marriage, he'd never initiated any social engagements that included me. He didn't socialise with co-workers from the engineering firm where he worked or with other married couples. When the children were little, I invited couples over for dinner parties. But David used to pick arguments about the stupidest things and would criticise me in front of our guests. I gave up socialising as a couple. There was no point trying to change him. I gritted my teeth, determined to accept him as he was even though David wouldn't accept me as I was. When I went out on my own with my woman friends, he picked fights with me. I drew a deep breath, sandpaper scraping against raw skin. The picture I'd had in my mind, of me with my friend Rena and David with his army friends, had just been ripped to shreds. And I couldn't bring myself to put up the new picture.

It was no surprise when David arrived home the night of Yigal's death and laid into me. 'What are you two looking so guilty about?' David said. 'Been gossiping about your husbands again? Been tearing us apart and finding fault? As usual? Oh yeah, I know what you're like.'

I stood there, unable to speak, rolling my thumb around inside my fist. Rena stepped in. 'David. Please. Listen.'

But he didn't stop. 'My god. What's happened to this kitchen? Can't you even be bothered to clean up? You're a real slut, Ruth. You really are. What do you do all day when I'm working? No, don't answer. I can see. You sit around and drink coffee with your friends.'

Still I stood there mute, looking at him as if seeing him after a separation of many years. His features were familiar – stocky build, blue eyes behind wire-rim glasses, a wide nose, thin lips. But when had the bald patch chased his hair to such a small space above his ears? When had the last vestiges of his hair turned grey? Had he always been so chubby? His anger was certainly familiar.

I realised a part of me didn't want to tell him about Yigal. Maybe the telling would make it final or maybe I wanted to spare him suffering but even in my blanked-out state, I knew the true reason was I didn't want to deal with his grief. I didn't want to have to comfort him or contain his rage or take care of him in any way. I wanted him to be there for me. And that wasn't going to happen. Tender-mindedness had never been part of David's repertoire. I had accepted that about him years ago.

That's when Rena burst out with it. With a puzzled glance at me, she said, 'Yigal's been killed. A suicide bomber at the checkpoint.' David clutched his heart. 'Oh. No,' he whispered. He stood stock still. Then, almost immediately, he wept. Great, gasping sobs, shook his body. I was shocked. I had never seen him cry before.

If I'd gone to him them, if I'd wrapped him up in my arms, if we'd wept together, then maybe we could have healed the gulf between us. But I didn't and the gulf got bigger and bigger until Rena came along to fill it. That night, instead of reaching out to David, I let my mind go blank and my stomach take over. I hadn't eaten since lunch time. Leaving him sobbing in the doorway, I turned my back and rummaged in the fridge for something instant to eat. I was so focussed on the task of spreading cream cheese on a bagel I didn't notice when David had stopped sobbing and was glaring at me.

'How can you eat at a time like this?' he said, his voice trembling with rage. 'Our son is dead. Don't you have any feelings? What kind of inhuman mother are you?'

I looked guiltily at the bagel but my hunger won out. The bagel jumped into my mouth. David lurched towards me, grabbed the bagel and threw it across the room.

'You only care about yourself,' he shouted. 'You never think about anyone but you. You just do what you want regardless. You don't care that your son is dead.'

'David, I'm sorry. I wasn't thinking.' I wasn't sorry. It was an automatic response, the kind of thing I had got in the habit of saying to head off David's attacks. But this time, it didn't work.

'You spend the entire evening chatting to your friends. How could you? When Yigal is dead. Where is Orli? You don't care about her, do you? You just forgot about Orli.

You forgot about me. Why didn't you let me know instead of leaving me to find out when I got home?'

Guilt and hunger left my stomach twisting with nausea. 'I'm really sorry,' I said but I was looking around for the bagel.

'I tried to phone you,' Rena said. David ignored her. 'You're not sorry,' he said to me. 'You look down on me. You're a spoiled princess. That's what you are.'

At any other time, I would have been crying and pleading for forgiveness by now but that night, I was cold inside. I really didn't care. Still, I knew my lines and I trotted them out in an insincere monotone. 'Please forgive me, David. I don't look down on you. Please don't attack me. I am sorry.'

'Stop your snivelling. It's too late for all that.' He raised his fist as if he was about to hit me. Instead, he looked at Rena and ran out of the house. I crumpled onto the sofa and fell asleep.

I sighed, thinking back to that night a year ago. No, I didn't handle it well at all. I'd missed my chance, not only that night, but several times through-out the year. Maybe Rena was right that David had tried and I had rejected him. I remembered another occasion when I could have, but didn't, reach out to comfort him. It happened exactly a month later, the first month's anniversary of Yigal's death.

When David returned from his jog that Saturday afternoon, he called from the shower, 'He's got six kids. They live in a community in Gush Etzion.'

'Who?' I asked, picking up the sweaty running clothes he'd dropped on the floor.

'Shlomo,' David sounded irritable, as if I hadn't been paying attention. 'He's been trying to persuade me to move out of Tsur Hadassah and join them there. And I'm tempted. There's plenty of housing. New houses are going up all the time. We could get tax breaks and mortgage benefits. It's close to Jerusalem. It's safe. There are roads and tunnels that bypass Bethlehem and Beit Jala. I think we should go out and see it.'

'Doesn't Shlomo live an ultra-orthodox community? Since when are you religious?'

'We don't have to live in his community. There are lots of communities in Gush Etzion.'

'I thought they're all extremist settlers, David. I'm not sure I want anything to do with them. Aren't they living on land that will eventually be given to a Palestinian state?'

'Not that land. Gush Etzion will never be part of a Palestinian state. Everyone knows that. In any final status negotiations, Gush Etzion will stay in Israel. Believe me, Ruth. I know what I'm talking about.'

I didn't want to argue with him so I kept quiet. 'Let's go today, just for a visit. OK?' He said it so nicely I agreed. I was ridiculously pleased David wanted to be with me, no matter what it was we'd be doing.

'I'll call Orli on her cell phone and we'll go get her,' David said.

'Don't be too heavy with her, David. Just be matter of fact. This morning, she suddenly flared up and took off.

I don't know where she went. She's been doing that a lot lately.'

David grunted. I thought Orli might not answer but she did. 'Orli,' David said. 'Ruth and I are going to visit Shlomo and his family. We want you to come with us. Where are you?' David's face turned white. 'You're what!?' he said. 'Stay there. We're coming right now.' He put the phone down.

'Where is she?' I asked, feeling sick with anxiety.

David took a deep breath. 'She's at the checkpoint where Yigal was… where Yigal… at the checkpoint.'

I gasped. 'Oh no. I never thought she would think of going there.'

'We've got to get her. Right now.'

'I can't face it, David. I can't go there.'

David opened his mouth to speak but no words came out. He stood there, his mouth hanging open and his arms hanging by his side, looking vulnerable and frightened. I should have hugged him then but I didn't. Instead, I turned away and marched out to the car, my whole being focussed on rescuing my daughter.

Another opportunity missed, I thought to myself. I paced wildly around the house. I couldn't stay still. In Yigal's room, the balaclava and baseball bat were on the bed where I'd left them. Anger washed over me. Compared to David's crimes, my two missed opportunities were nothing. What difference would it have made if I had hugged David? How many times in the 22 years of our marriage had I pandered to David's needs, listened to him, comforted him, looked after him, serviced him? And when had he ever noticed me? When had he ever considered my needs?

I slipped the balaclava over my head and seized the bat. Then I stalked the corridor, tossing the bat from hand to hand, feeling its solidity and hard smooth surface. I stopped in front of the hall mirror. The image that looked back at me was ruthless and menacing, capable of any kind of violence. I stood tall with narrowed eyes, a warrior on a revenge mission. The rope across the chasm widened into a concrete path and I strode confidently onward. Then I sat by the front door and waited for David to come home.

CHAPTER 19
Vivi

'Vivi, you're back!' Claire called from the bedroom as I blew in from the wet, windy night. Frantic to tell Claire about my evening, I struggled out of my rain gear, flung the dripping clothes over the banisters and dashed upstairs. But Claire had more pressing news.

'Vivi, guess what?' she said, bouncing off the bed and grinning excitedly at me. 'Snowy owls have been sighted on the Columbia River.'

I waited. She kept grinning. Finally I said, 'So nu, I can't guess. What's so exciting?'

'I told you. Two Snowy Owls have been seen on the Columbia River by the ocean.' Claire twirled around the bedroom.

'Oh,' I said. 'Is that it? That's .. um ... that's interesting. Listen Claire, I've got to tell you about the meeting I went to tonight. Two guys from Amnesty International spoke. They'd been to Jenin after the Israeli invasion last

April. They told about houses being demolished, soldiers occupying homes, people under curfew not allowed out to get food, assassinations by Israeli snipers. One guy, only 23, had been looking out his window and was shot in the heart and...'

'Snowy owls, Vivi. They've been sighted. At the river beach by the coast.' Claire had a stubborn look in her eyes.

'Claire, I'm telling you it's terrible what's going on. The Israeli army is on a rampage, shooting children, killing civilians. There are no sanctions on their behaviour. We've got to do something.'

Claire grabbed my shoulders and held me at arm's length. 'You're ranting, Vivi. Ever since you got back from Israel, you've been obsessed. You need to relax. Let's go away for the weekend, check out the Snowy Owls. We can stay at your parents' beach house in Cannon Beach.'

'You're not listening to me. They even kill people from the United Nations. This British guy, Iain Hook. He worked for UNRWA. He was trying to arrange the safe passage of children and their parents from a UN compound. The Israelis shot him. And then they didn't let the ambulance...'

'Vivi, call your parents tomorrow and see if it's okay for us to stay there. They won't have rented it out to anyone in December. Will you do that?'

'Listen to me Claire. I'm trying to tell you what's going on. Do you know what the international response is? It's not to help the people of Jenin but to quibble over whether it was a massacre or not.'

'Vivi, stop it. Please. Leave it for a few days. Come with me to see the Snowy Owls.'

'I'd love to see the Snowy Owls,' I said, not entirely sincerely. 'Unfortunately, I can't this weekend. On Saturday, I'm doing a street stall for the Justice for Palestinians Campaign from noon till three. Then in the evening, there's a public meeting with a film about the siege of the Church of the Nativity. I said I'd collect tickets at the door. On Sunday, my choir is singing carols outside the evangelical church on Burnside Street. Tell me what you think of my updated version.' I cleared my throat and sang, 'O little town of Bethlehem, Your people have to crawl, Separated from school and work, By Israel's ghetto wall. The occupation must now wilt, It's illegal and a sin; Their senseless wall must not be built; Palestine will win.'

Claire groaned and rolled her eyes. 'I prefer the original. Why don't you leave the carol singing to the Christians? Don't you have enough to do provoking Jewish Zionists without aggravating Christian Zionists?'

'Did you know American Christian Zionists are into this crazy notion of the Rapture. I told you about the people I met on the plane going over. They need to have their eyes opened.'

'Vivi,' Claire said. 'You don't have to be campaigning 24 seven. I'm worried about you. You're on the edge. If you're not careful, you're going to burn out and have a breakdown. Take a weekend off and come with me to the coast. See the

Snowy Owls. They're beautiful birds. It's unusual for them to come this far south. Come on. Please.'

'Claire, you don't understand. Things are getting worse and worse over there. I can't just turn my back and walk away.'

Claire stamped her foot. 'If you have a breakdown, you won't be any good to anyone.'

I never had understood Claire's lack of concern. She could hear about atrocities and injustice without feeling she had to do something about them. We certainly had different temperaments. I tried again. 'The children of Beyt Nattif have never seen the Mediterranean Sea even though they live less than 20 miles away. How can I go to the beach and have a good time when Palestinians are suffering every day under this occupation? It doesn't feel right.'

'What good is your guilt? How does it help the Palestinians if you drive yourself into the ground?' Claire's voice was loud and high pitched.

'Okay, okay,' I said. 'But I feel dreadful about letting people down. And I'm not giving up the actions I've planned for the following weekend.'

'You better not have anything planned,' Claire said, eyes narrowed. 'We're going to stay with my parents that weekend, don't you remember? I told you to put it in your diary.'

Claire was childishly excited about seeing the Snowy Owls and didn't seem to appreciate that the gale force winds and sheets of rain were likely to make a sighting uncomfortable, if not impossible. During the drive to the coast, I marvelled at our different priorities. I couldn't understand what person in their right mind would choose to spend their time sitting outside in a storm looking at birds. How can anyone put birds above human beings? I stared glumly at the grey road, the incessant rain and the windscreen wipers, clunking back and forth in an irritating way. Claire poked me hard. 'Come on. Enjoy yourself. There are terrible things happening all over the world and there's bugger all you or I can do about any of them. That's the reality. What is the point of tormenting ourselves about something we have no influence over? While you're focussing on Israel, people are getting away with all sorts of terrible deeds in Afghanistan, East Africa, Iraq, China, Thailand, Indonesia, Russia, England…'

'What atrocities are happening in England?' I asked, drawn in against my will.

'I don't know the details,' Claire said cheerfully. 'But you can bet your bottom dollar, there's somebody being given a hard time in England. Hey, here's the state park. Look out for signs to the South Jetty.'

Along the open, flat river beach, there was no shelter from the wind and rain. I felt miserable and uncomfortable. While I laboured head down over the grass-covered dunes, Claire bounded ahead like a puppy.

'Look, there's the owl,' she cried, pointing into the storm and handing me the binoculars. My glasses steamed up when I tried to look through them. How anyone could see a white bird on a white beach in a grey rain was beyond me. But a lull in the wind suddenly brought the Snowy Owl into focus. I caught my breath, amazed. The owl was majestic in its snowy white feathers with its pattern of black wavy lines. It looked like it was wearing an elegant cloak and stylish boots.

'They live in the northern tundra and only come as far south as Oregon when the lemming population crashes,' Claire shouted above the wind. Yet despite the catastrophe that forced the owl to leave its home in search of food, I was struck by its calm expression, as if it were at peace with its fate. It accepted whatever happened. It probably didn't even think of the loss of the lemmings as a catastrophe. It flew south until it found a new home and got on with life.

I gave the binoculars back to Claire and watched her as she gazed adoringly at the owl. Water dripped down her face. Strands of hair had escaped from her hat and plastered her eyes and cheeks. Her nose was red and her lips were chapped but the expression in her eyes mirrored that of the Snowy Owl's. She was absorbed in watching, not needing anything else in order to be happy.

My parents' beach house had been empty for more than a month. Despite the sensational view of Haystack Rock, my parents prefer Acapulco to Cannon Beach in the winter. I drifted from room to room turning on lights and heaters, bringing the house alive. Claire reclaimed the kitchen.

In the basement den, I glanced guiltily at the computer. I wanted to check my emails but I didn't want another argument with Claire. Still, she was busy cooking dinner and shouldn't object to my absence for half an hour. On the other hand, she would be furious if she knew I was reading news bulletins about Palestine on our weekend away. However, the urge to check them was overwhelming. Like an addict in need of a fix, I had no choice. I had to turn on the computer. I quietly closed the door and sat on the edge of the chair, my attention on the screen. With my heel tapping impatiently on the floor, I waited for the emails to appear.

There were 85 messages for me. I felt overwhelmed, even invaded, but also flattered and excited. Somebody out there wanted to communicate with me. After deleting the ads for 'V I a g r a', 'cheap mediactions' and virus warnings that are bound to be hoaxes, I still had 62 left. I saved the long chatty email from my father to read when I had a free afternoon and quickly scanned the three emails from my mother – two snide jokes about Bush and a series of meaningless 'how-to-be-happy' sound-bites from the Dalai Lama. That left 58 emails, all about the Middle East. Ever since I realised how biased the mainstream news media was in its reporting of Israel, I relied only on first hand accounts. I took a deep breath and opened the emails.

The first is from B'Tselem: *'For the past four months, Israel has imposed a full curfew on hundreds of thousands of Palestinians in the Occupied Territories. This curfew constitutes collective punishment, and as such is in contravention of international law…'* Someone had gone to a lot of trouble to compile the evidence and write it up. Silently, I promised

B'Tselem I would read the report in full when I had more time. Respectfully, I moved it to a folder marked Palestine: To Read.

The next was from the Palestine Human Rights Monitoring Group. *'Not Safe Even in Their Homes: 3 Gaza Children Shot to Death This Week by Israeli Soldiers. 11 year old Nadda Maddi of Rafah was shot to death by Israeli soldiers on Thursday at noon. She was standing inside her home, near the window, when she was fatally shot in the chest.'* I closed my eyes in pain and reverently saved the email to read later.

The third email was from a British woman with the International Solidarity Movement: *'I'm in the Balatta refugee camp near Nablus in the West Bank. I can see F16 fighter planes flying over the camp. Altogether Israel has 237 of these F16 planes, with 105 more on order from Boeing. Each plane costs about $35 million.'* Thank you for this valuable information. I kept the email. I deleted the next email with regret: *'Your presence is needed in Palestine….The International Solidarity Movement is urgently trying to get international volunteers to come to the Occupied Palestinian Territories to stand with Palestinians against attacks on their very existence. Join us December 15, 2002 – January 15, 2003. For more information …'*

I hurried through a series of emails calling on me to do something. Write a letter to your congressman. Support the disinvestment campaign in Caterpillar. Attend a rally. Send money. Email President Bush. Boycott Israeli goods. Fax Ariel Sharon. Send more money. Sign a petition. Write to the newspapers. Organise a public meeting. Show a film. Read this report. Find out more. A chorus of voices shouted at me from the emails, saying, 'It's up to you, Vivi Rubenstein. Can you stand by and do nothing while Israel is crushing the Palestinians? Vivi Rubenstein, now is the time to take action. It's urgent. It's desperate. Things are getting worse.' Despite my shallow breathing and sweaty palms, I didn't even dare blink. These weren't words on a screen but Wahid and Zainab and Habiba calling out to me for help.

And then I thought about David and Ruth. David twisting my arm up my back while telling me to stay away from his wife. Ruth, cooking pancakes and telling me the plight of the Palestinians in next-door Wadi Foquin was not her problem. Energised by rage and desperation, I typed a long email to her, not stopping until I'd told her everything about my trip to Beyt Nattif and about how David had greeted me when I came to see her two months before. Without rereading it, I clicked 'send' and sat back with my eyes closed.

A new message had arrived while I was typing to Ruth. It was from an unnamed person in Gaza City. There was no heading: '*We are being bombed NOW. Bombs are falling NOW. I can see them and hear them outside my window. I see dead people. I see body parts. They are killing us. HELP us now. My relatives are being killed in front of my eyes. This is happening NOW.*' I gasped and pushed myself away from the computer. Burying my head in my hands, I wept.

That's when Claire walked in. 'I've been calling you and looking all over for you,' she said. 'Dinner's ready. For Christ's sake, what's the matter now?'

I pointed wordlessly to the computer. She read the first line of the email and erupted in a high-pitched rage. 'Is this where you've been for the last hour? Tormenting yourself? This is self harm. You're a voyeur to other people's suffering and for what?' While she screamed, she leaned over, snatched the mouse and deleted the emails.

'No,' I shouted, grabbing her arm. 'Don't. If you delete the emails, it's like deleting the people. It's saying I see your suffering and I don't care. No, I've got to keep the emails.'

'Vivi, this is the way to madness.'

'Stop please, Claire, don't delete them. I can't bear it. I might have to withdraw gradually. Don't make me go cold turkey.'

'This is not doing you any good and I know for a fact, it's not doing the Palestinians any good. Look at you. You're a nervous wreck. You're hysterical.'

'I can't bear it,' I sobbed. 'While we were watching the Snowy Owl, Palestinians were being killed. That man was looking out his window and seeing body parts of his relatives on the ground. Doesn't that affect you? I can imagine him, a human being like you and me, cowering in his home typing frantically onto his computer while bombs are falling all around him. He knows the international community won't listen to him because he, like all Palestinians, has been labelled a terrorist. His desperate cry for help comes to me in Cannon Beach where we've come to watch Snowy

Owls. Doesn't that do your head in? How can you come to
terms with that? How can I sleep at night knowing what
I know?'

Claire hugged me and held me tight. 'Calm down.
Shhh. You can choose not to read these emails. Let's eat
dinner.'

Exhausted, I let myself be led into the living room where
Claire settled me on the couch with a blanket and a bowl of
carrot soup. Eventually the sound of the wind and the rain
battering the house and the din of the ocean soothed me.
Claire said quietly, 'I'm sorry I yelled at you. I don't know
what to do when you get like this. I care about you and it
seems to me you're on some kind of self-destructive path
and I can't understand what it's about. I feel frustrated and
alarmed. I hate it when you get hysterical and intense and
single minded. I lose you then.'

'It's so confusing,' I said.

'What is?'

'Israel. I know there are bad guys and good guys in this
conflict. There's right and wrong. But it's not so clear-cut.
Ruth isn't one of the bad guys. David clearly is but then
again, maybe there's more to him than meets the eye. Why
would Ruth stay with him if he was a total baddie? Then
again, why don't people like Ruth see what's going on right
under their noses? Ruth's living there in the midst of it all.
Yet she can distance herself and say it's not her problem.
And all these years, I've wanted to talk to her and tell her
what I know and what I've seen and I can't speak to her.
She put up this enormous barrier to hearing anything

about what Israel's really about. I feel so frustrated. I don't know how to fix it.'

Claire laughed. 'Well if you don't know how to fix it, then there's no hope for the Middle East. Don't you think Wahid and Zainab and Ruth and David are all part of the solution? They're the ones that have to fix it. All you can do from outside is bear witness and help them towards reconciliation. But don't burn yourself out with pointless guilt. And do it with love. You'll have a lot more impact if you're coming from a good place.'

'I wish I knew how to do that,' I said. I stared out the window into the dark. The wind had died down. 'While I'm figuring it out, let's go watch the Snowy Owls tomorrow as soon as it's light.'

For the rest of the weekend, I didn't turn on the computer. Instead we walked along the sandy beach to Haystack Rock and back again and stood in the cold, admiring the Snowy Owls. It was a relief to have nothing in my head other than the roar of the ocean and the sight of a beautiful bird.

CHAPTER 20

Yigal

We haven't spoken to each other since we got back from the visit to Aisha's family. We're sitting under a heavy overcast sky on opposite sides of one of the many concrete pillars dotted around the Other World Checkpoint. I don't know what she's thinking but I'm thinking about the world I was in when she exploded her bomb. I'm thinking about how strange it is to be one moment in a world that feels real and solid and the next moment, you're in a totally different world. And that totally different world feels even more real and solid than the first one. And because I'm thinking so hard about that moment, I find myself back in the living world checkpoint, face to face with my sister Orli.

'You're not allowed here. This is a Palestinian controlled area.' The soldier is someone I've never met before. He frowns as he hands Orli's Israeli passport back to her. He seems annoyed and impatient. Orli shrinks into herself.

She hesitates, then whispers, 'Is this the place where Corporal Yigal Shapiro was killed on the 2nd October?'

He looks at her suspiciously. 'Who are you?'

'Orli Shapiro. Yigal is…was…is my brother.' She's not her usual confident self. Her voice is barely audible. The soldier reaches out and touches her lightly on the shoulder. 'Oh shit. I'm sorry.' His eyes fill with tears. 'Orli, I'm really sorry about your brother. Look, uh, I don't think you should be here on your own. I'll call my commander. Come with me.' He puts his arm around her and gently guides her to a shack casually covered in ripped camouflage netting. Meekly, Orli follows him. While the soldier talks on his cell phone, Orli looks at the crater and rubble left when Aisha's bomb exploded. There are no body parts or blood. The place has been tidied up.

I stand on the rubble and study my sister. She's shaking and tears are spilling down her cheeks. Why did she come here? I wonder if she thinks I'm still hanging around this spot. I put my arm around her and run my fingers down the tiny plaits she's braided into her hair. 'It's okay, Orli,' I say. But it's not true. I am stuck in this Other World with my murderer and it's definitely not okay. Not for me and not for Orli.

Orli's cell phone rings. 'Daddy?' she says. She looks surprised. 'I'm at the checkpoint, where Yigal was killed. Daddy, I'm scared. It's horrible here. Please come and get me.'

Out of the corner of my eye, I see Aisha wandering about the checkpoint. I glare at her. What's she doing here? I didn't invite her and I don't want her gloating at my sister's suffering. But she keeps her distance, moping around, drifting aimlessly through the checkpoint. I stay with Orli, chatting to her, comforting her, until our parents arrive. When they get there, they fling open the car doors and run side by side to where Orli's standing. Mom hugs her but Dad stands apart, shoulders hunched, collapsed in on himself. Orli points to the bomb crater, takes Mom's hand and leads her to the edge. They're both crying.

Dad's jaw juts out and he looks angry and miserable. Facing the crater, he mutters something so softly Orli and Mom can't hear him but it's not meant for their ears. He's talking to me and I hear him loud and clear. 'I'm sorry Yigal,' he says. 'I'm sorry. I wish I'd made more effort. I miss you. I love you.'

I am stunned. I reach out to embrace him. I tell him it's okay, it doesn't matter now, I love him too. Of course, he doesn't hear me. While I'm still talking to him, he turns away and stands stiffly by Mom and Orli. The three of them walk off to the car, leaving me at the bomb crater, alone. But I'm soaring. My dad actually said he loves me. Unbelievable! Why couldn't it be like that when I was alive?

I'm tempted to hop in the back seat of the car and follow them around for the rest of their lives. But on second thought, it wouldn't work for me. I don't want to watch other people getting on with their lives. I want my own life back. Damn that Aisha. Damn her to hell. And with that thought, I'm back in the Other World Checkpoint, back in hell.

From out of the blue, Hassan, the little footballer, appears. He sidles up and stands next to me, looking down at the ground. He cradles a football in his arms, holding it over his stomach like a toddler with his teddy bear. I half expect him to suck his thumb.

'Want to play?' I ask, relieved by the distraction. He nods but doesn't move. Tears trickle along his cheeks and drip off his nose. 'I miss my mother and my father and my brothers,' he says. A dense fog of misery closes in on me and I have a strong urge to run again. 'C'mon Hassan.' I reach down for the football. 'Let's go play ball.'

'I was shot by an Israeli soldier at school,' Hassan looks up at me. I wince but there's no blame or anger in his eyes. 'I was playing football in the school playground. In our morning break.' He goes quiet but doesn't shift his gaze. The silence drags on until I'm sure he's not going to say any more. I open my mouth, intending to change the subject when he starts up again. 'Our teachers came out and yelled at us. 'Go in,' they shouted. 'The soldiers are coming.' You see, they only came during our breaks. The teachers changed the time of our breaks and then the soldiers changed the times they drove by. We didn't want to go in. A lot of the boys picked up stones to throw at the jeeps and hummers. I didn't.'

Hassan studies my face. I wonder what he expects to see. Just as I'm about to speak, he says, 'I used to throw stones at Israeli soldiers. We all did. But since I got into the sports club, all I wanted to do was play football. I was going to play for the Palestine Football Association. My coach said I could get on the team if I kept practising.' His eyes are gleaming, imagining himself making that winning goal.

With his gaze still fixed on my face, he continues, 'I kept kicking the football while everyone else was yelling and running around. Nobody paid any attention to me. Then they all went in. I was on my own in the playground when the soldiers came. They shot me in the stomach. My guts fell out in my hand. There was blood all over the place.' Sweat pours off me. I feel sick. I desperately want to look away but his gaze is locked into mine, holding me prisoner. He knows. And he knows I know.

He snuggles up to Aisha and whispers to her, just loudly enough for me to hear, 'I tried to be brave. But I was scared. The pain was real bad. I lay there a long time. The ambulance didn't come. My teachers didn't come. My friends didn't come. No one came to me.'

I am bouncing on the balls of my feet, ready to bolt. All I can think about is getting away before he comes out with it. But I'm still standing in the same place when he turns to me and says sadly, 'Why? Why did you shoot me?'

That's when I run. I know I can't get away for long. I just need to be by myself for a moment so I can remember how it was for me. But it's like trying to remember a dream. The more you grasp at it, the more quickly it fades. I must have been running in circles because in no time, there they are again, sitting on the ground, waiting for an answer.

Once I kicked Orli in the stomach. She was five. I was
eight. She screamed blue murder. Mom came running in
from another room and scooped her up. Orli clutched her
stomach and wailed as if she were going to die. Snot was
dripping into her mouth. She was even more irritating than
before I kicked her. Mom kept asking, 'What happened?
What happened?' Orli kept crying, milking the last drop
of drama from the situation. Finally she said, 'Yigal kicked
me.' Mom looked at me and asked, 'Why did you kick your
sister? Why would you do something as mean as that?'
Like there's got to be a reason. Like if you give a reason,
then everything will be all right. Yeah, there was a reason.
I kicked her because she bugged me. I kicked her because
I was bigger than she was. I kicked her because Dad wasn't
around. I kicked her because I felt like it and thought I
could get away with it.

Wherever we went in the Territories, there were boys
throwing stones at us and boys climbing on our armoured
personnel carriers trying to dislodge the top-mounted
machine guns. I wasn't frightened or threatened by them.
Why would I be? They weren't armed. It was more like a
game. We cruised around looking for them. I wouldn't say
I did it out of hatred. Some guys in our unit hated Arabs.
Gil, my commanding officer, sure did. But I didn't. I shot at
them because, well, that's what you do in the army. We're
at war. Soldiers do whatever they're told to do.

I don't say that to Hassan though. Somehow it doesn't
seem to be the point now. I don't tell Hassan I shot him
because that's how an army of occupation keeps order. I

think he already knows that. So why the hell does he ask? What's the point? I go up to one of those concrete pillars I can't get away from and smack it, again and again. And then I run.

CHAPTER 21

Ruth

Inside the balaclava, I grew powerful beyond anything I could have imagined. Hours passed as I experimented with the different positions made possible by the possession of a balaclava and a baseball bat. I tried hiding behind the front door with the bat raised high over my head. When that got boring, I crouched low, ready to spring, the bat like a guard dog on the floor next to me. That was OK until my legs cramped. Then I lurked out of sight at the back of the living room, dangling the bat casually by my side. It sent out the wrong message so I arranged myself in a Kung Fu attack stance. When the stance stiffened, I marched up and down the veranda swinging the bat around my head like a drum majorette with her baton. An innocent glass bowl went flying and I gave that one up. With each position, I tried out various facial expressions - a sinister smile, a sardonic sneer, a lion-like roar. I was the Avenging

Wife, lying in wait to deal with my errant husband. It was immensely satisfying.

And then I got hungry. I tucked the bat behind the kitchen door and made myself a peanut butter and jelly sandwich. I opened my mouth to take a bite and discovered the sandwich had wrapped itself round the balaclava. Only then did I realise you have to take a balaclava off if you want to eat. I yanked too vigorously and peanut butter smeared all over my face. I pulled harder, becoming even more firmly entangled. The cloth was covering my eyes and my glasses were somewhere around my ears when I heard the front door slam. I froze. Footsteps pounded across the living room and down the hall. The bathroom door slammed. The toilet flushed. In desperation, I grabbed the mouth hole and ripped the balaclava apart. I was so absorbed in extricating myself from the torn cloth I didn't hear Orli come into the kitchen.

'Mom, where was this photo of Yigal taken?' I flinched, barely managing to stifle a yelp of surprise. Without waiting for an answer, she said, 'Isn't that Vivi and Noah with him? It looks like San Francisco. Do you know where I was today? I went to the cemetery. I miss Yigal so much. You don't know how much I miss him.' Her head dropped onto her arms and sobs shook her body. I wanted to hug her but I was still involved with the balaclava. I jerked it off my head and flung it onto the table. My glasses flew across the room. On my hands and knees, I groped around the floor, finding them over by the sink. When I finally put myself together, Orli had stopped crying and was twisting the balaclava between her hands.

'Don't you wish you could make up with Vivi?' she said, blowing her nose into the ripped black cloth. 'Oh yeah, Mom, d'ya know what? It was really weird. Dad was there at the cemetery. He was with Shlomo. They came together and went away together. They didn't see me. Don't you think that's odd, that he would go with Shlomo and not with you or me?'

'Nothing would surprise me,' I said, wiping peanut butter off my forehead with my sleeve.

'Why didn't you ever tell me about your visit to Shlomo's place? Remember that time you and Dad came to get me from the checkpoint? Dad wanted to take us to Shlomo's but I wouldn't go. I was too upset. So you and Dad went the next week. And the day after that, you two had a big fight and then we went to Baltimore. But you never told me what happened. Yuck! This cloth is disgusting.' She tossed the balaclava onto the floor and looked at me for the first time. 'Mom, you've got peanut butter on your nose. I wish you would tell me things. Since Yigal died, you've gone all spacey, like you're not really here.'

'I'm sorry Orli. Really I am. I wish I could have talked with you. It's been so hard not having Vivi to talk to these last few years and then today, Rena came over. She ..Well. I found out.. What? Why are you looking at me like that?'

Orli shook her head. 'Oh Mom, I thought you knew. I thought that's why you and Dad were ignoring each other all the time.'

'What do you mean? You knew about Rena? Since when?'

'I followed Dad one day when he went out jogging. Months ago. Like last February or March. I wanted to talk to him on his own. I called out to him but he didn't hear me. He was running really fast. He went over to the Israel Trail. You know where I mean? On the dirt road that goes into the Jewish National Fund grove. Rena was waiting for him under the high-tension electricity line. They jogged down the trail to the abandoned Arab village. Then they, uh, held hands and...' Orli looked down at her own hands and rubbed them together.

'Go on,' I said. I couldn't be more hurt than I already was.

'They climbed up to the white domed shrine at the top of the slope. They didn't come down for a long time. I didn't stay. You must have known. I thought that's why you never saw Rena any more.'

'I've been out of it. Really out of it.' I closed my eyes. Oblivion was so tempting. But I was awake now and couldn't go back no matter how much I wanted to. With each breath, pain pierced my body and I felt everything.

'That trip to Shlomo's was some kind of turning point,' I said. 'That's when I knew David and I were heading off in opposite directions. No, I didn't know. I couldn't face it, not then. I blanked out.'

'Tell me what happened that day. Please.'

I went to the sink and washed my face and hands, trying to remember what happened that day David and I visited Shlomo and his family in Gush Etzion. I'd never been in an ultra-orthodox community before. I knew they were trying to put down roots to make sure the settlements stay as part of Israel. I knew they wanted and got Israeli army protection. But I was surprised to see there were still Arab villages there and Shlomo's settlement was nothing more than a ramshackle collection of prefab houses. It seemed as if it had been thrown together recently.

'Shlomo and his wife, Devora, are originally from New Jersey,' I said. 'They've got seven children. So far. The youngest was four.'

'What was Devora like?'

'In some ways, she was nice but we didn't have anything in common and her views were really extreme. She took me into her tiny kitchen and talked to me while she got dinner ready. The children were running about shouting and kicking each other. The noise level was deafening. I had to ask her for an aspirin. She told me her kids were hyper because they'd just got back from Hebron where Shlomo's sister and her family live. Devora's children spend a lot of time with their cousins.'

'Do their cousins live in the Jewish quarter near the Cave of the Patriarchs?' Orli asked.

'Yes, in the Avraham Avinu neighbourhood. They entertain themselves by terrorising the Arabs. The kids go onto the balconies and throw garbage down onto the Arab market. They climb through the road blocks into the Arab market and knock over their stalls, throw their goods into the street, kick people. They're tough kids. Real fighters.

Devora was proud of them. And the younger they are, the better. If they're under twelve, they can't be arrested.'

Orli slammed her fist onto the table and scowled. 'Mom, what did you think of what they get up to? You don't approve, do you?'

'No, of course not, Orli but I didn't get a chance to argue. Devora bombarded me with stories. Like the time an Arab sniper fired into the Avraham Avinu neighbourhood and killed a ten month old baby girl. You must have heard about it on the news.'

Orli nodded. 'Was that the year before last? Before Yigal was killed?'

'I think so. Well, ten minutes after the shooting, Shlomo got a phone call from his friends at the yeshiva in Hebron. He rounded up his family, including the four year old, and they all zoomed over. They had a plan. They sent a group of teenage girls to run wild in the Arab cemetery. While the soldiers were trying to round them up, Shlomo and a group of men broke into the market. They took whatever they could, trashed buildings and set fire to shops. At first, they fought with the soldiers. Usually the soldiers stood by and didn't get involved. But that time, they had a real free-for-all brawl. Shlomo even head-butted one soldier. Eventually the soldiers cleared out. Then Shlomo and the other men had a night of it. They went into the Arab neighbourhood behind the cemetery and smashed windows and broke down their doors. Devora was leaping about the kitchen, all excited, like it was some kind of victory. She said the Arabs got the message. Most have moved out since. That's their aim, to drive the Arabs out of Hebron.'

'It was a pogrom. There's no other word for it,' Orli said. Her voice was tight and angry. 'They are the reason there will never be peace in Israel. They're the ones who should be driven out of Hebron. How many are there in the Jewish quarter? About 500. And there are 120,000 Arabs in Hebron. Anyway, it must have been awful listening to her talk like that. What did you say?' Orli's face was flushed and her hands clenched. I was glad she hadn't been with me that day.

'I didn't get a chance to say much. She talked non-stop. I just remember feeling sick.'

'Really? You let her boast about her terrorist activities and you didn't challenge her?'

'Orli, what could I say? I may have said something like it could have been Yigal that Shlomo head-butted.' Actually, I hadn't said anything. I'd only thought it. I was no match for Devora.

'You don't think she has a valid point, do you?' Orli asked.

'Well, I can see her point of view. They have a right to worship at Abraham's tomb. And yes, the army should protect them.'

'What if Yigal had been on duty there? What if he'd died in Hebron? How would you have felt then?'

I stared out the window. How would I have felt? I probably would have held Shlomo and Devora responsible for his death. But that was too easy. Yigal had died to protect my right to live in Israel. Didn't that make me just as responsible? But I couldn't stay with that thought. Quickly, I changed the subject back.

'Devora said lots of things that disturbed me. She wanted the army to lock up every single Arab in Hebron, all 120,000 of them. Have them under permanent curfew. Really, she wanted all the Arabs out, once and for all. She thought they should be sent to Jordan or Syria. Driven out.'

I fell silent, thinking about the futility of an occupation designed to protect people like Devora and Shlomo, people willing to risk other people's lives and the security of Israel for their selfish ends. No wonder I'd tried to forget about that visit.

'Mom, do you remember when those men from Gush Etzion were caught trying to bomb the Arab girls' school in Jerusalem last year? Weren't they from Shlomo's community?'

'No, but from one nearby. Actually, Devora talked about that. She said she was glad the police caught them before they blew up the school. But the attacks were legitimate. It says so in the Talmud.'

'Oh really!'

'It says, 'the one who comes to kill you, get up early and kill him first."

'Where in the Talmud does it say that?' Orli looked sceptical.

'I don't know. I didn't pay enough attention at Hebrew school.'

'But anyway, what does it mean?'

'She explained at length, though I didn't ask her to. She said it means you shouldn't be stupid and wait until your enemy has an advantage over you. Every day the Arabs are fed anti-semitic lies on their TVs and radios and in their Friday sermons. They believe it's their religious duty to drive every Jew into the sea. And our government, instead of stopping terrorists, stops Shlomo and Devora and those men who planted the bomb from taking legitimate action to defend themselves. So they have no choice. She said she wasn't going to wait passively to be killed in a wave of terror.'

'She's totally around the bend. Were you convinced?'

'Well, there would be no state of Israel if we didn't take matters into our own hands, so yes, there was some truth to what she was saying.'

'But Mom, can't you see where that kind of thinking leads?'

'Oh yes. Her daughter, Maya, spelled it out. She's 14 or 15. She said, 'if I were in the government, I'd send the army to bomb Gaza City to smithereens. That would get rid of Islamic Jihad and Hamas and all the terrorists!' Devora laughed and winked at me, as if I would approve.'

'What did you say?' Orli asked.

'Nothing. I just wanted to get out of there as quick as I could. All that talk about bombing and fighting and head-butting and throwing garbage. I couldn't stand it. It was just weeks after Yigal's death.' Waves of exhaustion swept over me. As I drifted into sleep, I saw Yigal reaching out to me, whispering urgently. I couldn't make out what he was saying.

Orli shook me awake. 'Mom. Mom. Don't pass out like that. Wake up. You've got to stay awake.'

Groggily, I opened my eyes. The balaclava, lying in a tangled heap on the floor, came into view. If I couldn't have Yigal back, at least I wanted to believe he died for a good cause. Suddenly, my head cleared. I knew what I had to do. I picked up the balaclava and the baseball bat and ceremoniously dumped them in the rubbish bin. Then I turned to Orli and said, 'That's enough. No more violence.'

CHAPTER 22

Yigal

'Stop running. You're making me dizzy,' Aisha says, the hundredth time I run past her. She's leaning against a concrete pillar. Hassan is nowhere to be seen. I keep running to show her she can't boss me around. Then I stop and glare at her. She looks me in the eye.

'So you murdered Hassan, huh?' she says, a smug smile on her face. 'You, the brave Israeli soldier armed with nothing but a tank and a Kalashnikov and the backing of a powerful army, fighting for your life against terrorists the size of Hassan, armed with footballs. It's David and Goliath stuff, isn't that so?'

'You don't know what happened so why don't you just shut up?'

'Why don't you tell me another sob story, like the one you told me about your first time at a checkpoint when you had to humiliate the people, making them wait for hours? That nearly broke my heart, hearing how hard it was for you.'

'Shut up,' I say. 'There's no point talking to you. You'll never understand.'

'You may be right. I do find it really, really hard to understand why you came in a tank to murder Hassan. Of all the Palestinians you could have chosen, you go for a little, twelve year old boy whose worst crime is a passion for football. You're right. I guess I'll never understand. And I bet you don't understand why I did what I did.'

'That's easy. It's because you hate Jews. You want to drive us out. You want the land for yourselves, even though we have nowhere else to go and you have plenty of other Arab countries to go to.'

Aisha's shoulders slump and she rolls onto her back, shaking her head in disgust. 'Aargh,' she cries. 'Is that what you're taught in your schools? Don't you learn any history? Are you really only fed propaganda and lies? You should talk to my mother. She could explain it to you. She's big on dialogue with dumb Israelis like you.'

Aisha goes quiet and I guess she's thinking about her mother. I think about her mother, too. I was impressed with Leila. She seemed strong and sensible. We're both thinking so hard about Leila, that the Other World Checkpoint begins to fade out. Soon, we're standing in the middle of a bedroom. Aisha points to the cards on the chest of drawers. 'Look, it's the start of Ramadan. So it's been five weeks.'

It's dark in the room with just a glimmer of dawn light through the curtains. I hear snoring and quiet sleep breathing from the bed. There are three sleepers, two adults and a girl about ten years old. The girl is on the edge of the bed, her long black hair covering her face. The call to prayer crackles over the loud speaker from the minaret. The three sleepers don't wake up.

As the call to prayer trails off, I hear the sound of tanks in the distance. They are travelling fast and coming nearer. Soon the noise of the tanks becomes unbearably loud, intensifying as the vibrations bounce off the cinder block and cement houses lining the narrow lanes of the refugee camp. The room fills with throbbing. The person in the middle sits up suddenly. It's Leila. She scrambles over the little girl and creeps to the window. I join her. She lifts the curtain from the side about an inch. We both gasp and leap back.

There, stopped right in front of the house, no more than six feet away, is a Dooby. The massive bulldozer fills the road. The bullet-proof windows of the cabin are level with the second-storey window where we're standing. Behind the bulldozer, in single file down the road are a Merkava-mark 4 tank and three armoured personnel carriers. I've been in Merkava-mark 3 tanks but this is the first time I've seen the latest model. We were told in the army it's the most advanced of its type in the world. In the cabin, we see the Dooby operator lifting a loud speaker to his mouth. He blasts out a warning first in Hebrew, then Arabic. 'The house of the suicide bomber will be demolished. You have 30 minutes to get out.'

The little girl falls off the bed and scurries to her mother. The father sits up with a jerk. Aisha's brother, Osama, bursts into the bedroom, his hair on end, trousers and shoes in his hands. 'We'll fight them,' he shouts and slams out, the door banging against the bed. We hear him tumbling down the stairs, opening a window in the back of the house and clambering out, knocking things onto the floor as he goes.

'I'm going to fight with him,' Aisha says but she doesn't move. I grab her arm. 'Oh no you don't. You stay right here.'

'Khalid,' says Aisha's mother. Her voice is shaking. Aisha's dad is slumped on the bed. He doesn't speak or move. Leila turns on the light, kneels down and speaks to the little girl.

'What's she saying?' I ask Aisha. I don't expect to be able to understand them since I don't speak Arabic. I couldn't make out what they said last time I came with Aisha. But it suddenly occurs to me I haven't had any problems talking with Aisha and Hassan. In the Other World we communicate with our thoughts rather than through language. I listen to what Aisha's mother is saying. To my surprise, I can understand every word.

'Fazia, get dressed. We've got to leave the house. Be brave, sweetheart.' Fazia's eyes are wide with terror. There's a puddle on the floor under her feet. She clings to her mother's nightdress, staring straight ahead.

Leila turns to her husband. 'Khalid. You must be decisive. Don't make me do this on my own.'

'Leila,' Khalid speaks. His voice is low, as if he doesn't have the strength to speak any louder. His head droops. 'I don't want to live any more. Take Fazia and go. I'll stay.'

'Oh no you won't,' Leila says.

We hear Osama shouting from outside. He and other boys are throwing rocks at the bulldozer and tanks. The soldiers fire back at them. The boys hide behind buildings, leap out and throw more rocks. The noise in the narrow alley is deafening. We are in a sea of noise. If it's possible, Fazia's eyes have grown bigger. She and her father are motionless. Leila frees herself from Fazia's grip and is running frantically between the window and the bed. She picks up a hair brush and smacks Khalid on the head.

The loudspeaker barks. 'You have twenty minutes to get out.'

Leila wraps Fazia in her arms and speaks calmly to her. Aisha also embraces her sister. 'Be brave Fazia. Do what Mommy tells you. Choose what you can carry because everything will be destroyed.'

Fazia remains rooted to the spot. She's shivering. Khalid is no livelier. He slumps leadenly in the bed. The room is pounding with the noise of machine gun fire, kids shouting, rocks thudding against tanks, windows shattering and engines revving up. Aisha is frantically shaking Fazia and her father in turn.

Leila dresses quickly, yanking on black slacks over her nightgown and thrusting her arms into an ankle-length coat. She wraps a white headscarf on her head.

Fazia is standing by the bed, still shaking and staring. Leila runs out of the room and throws a framed photo onto the bed. It's of a younger Yasser Arafat sitting nervously on a chestnut-coloured horse. He's not in his usual ridiculous *kefiyah* but is actually quite handsome, wearing a brown Russian-style woollen hat with some sort of gold insignia on the front. Just as I try to get a closer look, another framed photo lands on top. This one is a wedding photo of Leila and Khalid, both looking happier, younger, and slimmer. Next, a frayed document in English and Arabic. Then, a pile of books.

Khalid is slouched against the pillows, his eyes half shut. His lips are moving but no one can hear him above the sounds of the battle raging outside. 'Leila,' he calls from the bed. There's urgency in his voice and he lifts his head to face his wife. 'Go now,' he says. 'Save yourself and Fazia.'

Leila screams and hits Khalid with her fists. She drags the bedding off him, pulls his legs onto the floor. The photos and documents fly off the bed.

'You have ten minutes to get out.' It's the loudspeaker again.

Leila scoops Fazia up into her arms. She is poised to bolt but takes a deep breath and stands still, studying Khalid in silence. 'All right Khalid,' she says. 'I've decided what I'm going to take with me. I'm not going to take a photo of Arafat. I'm not going to take our wedding photo. I'm not going to take my favourite books of poetry. I'm not going to take the 1929 property deeds to my family's house in Jerusalem. There is nothing more precious to me than my husband and my children.' Aisha is weeping. Her head hangs down. Leila continues, 'I don't want to die but I can't carry you both. If you won't come with me, then I am prepared to die with you and to sacrifice Fazia out of my love for you. My life wouldn't be worth living if I left you behind.'

Leila is calm. She doesn't cry. She sits down on the bed and kisses Fazia's frozen body and Khalid's slumped form. I feel like I'm in a tornado, swirling out of control with terror. She's playing a much more dangerous game now, gambling with her life and Fazia's, risking everything on Khalid's fragile mental state. Is he suicidal enough not to care about Leila and Fazia? I don't know if I can stand the suspense.

Outside, there's a lull in the battle. For a brief moment, there's no gunfire, no rocks are thrown, no shouting. All we can hear is the throbbing of the bulldozer's engine. I kick Aisha. 'Do something,' I shout at her. 'This is all your doing.' Aisha pulls herself up to face her father. Stroking his cheeks, she says, 'Papa, I martyred myself for you. I took revenge on the Zionist enemy for beating and humiliating you when they invaded our house. Don't give up. Life is too precious. I love you.' Khalid tilts his head as if listening to something far in the distance. Then his eyes focus and his face lights up. As if he has all the time in the world, he smiles at Leila.

Gently he lifts Fazia out of Leila's arms and walks carefully out of the room. Leila doesn't hesitate. She runs after, keeping as close as possible behind. Aisha and I follow them down the stairs and watch them as they climb barefoot through the window into the courtyard behind, passing Fazia's inert form from one to the other. They help each other over a low wall and into a neighbour's yard. The neighbours pass down a ladder and pull them through a window. They don't look back.

Aisha and I stay. The Dooby grabs the outer wall and shakes the house violently. Then the Dooby moves in with its heavy blade. It smashes its way to the heart of the family home, ripping down walls, caving in ceilings, collapsing staircases, shattering windows, bursting pipes. The house and all its belongings are crushed. In half an hour, it's no longer a home. It's just a big pile of rubble.

When the troops leave, an eerie quiet settles on the street. Clouds of black dust billow through the site and into the lane. Neighbours creep cautiously from their houses, covering their mouths and noses with their headscarves. They huddle silently a short distance from the demolished building. They peer anxiously into the dust, not knowing whether the family are buried in the house or have managed to escape.

Osama and four other boys emerge from a hiding place in one of the alleys. They are filthy, battle-scarred with dirt and blood and scratches. They stride toward the devastated building in their uniforms of sockless trainers, pyjama tops and jeans. They walk tall. They know themselves to be heroes.

I am shocked and confused by the feelings that engulf me at the sight of these grubby teenage fighters. When I was inside a tank, I felt invincible. I'd been taught all about the tank's immense fire power, its automatic target tracker, its advanced ballistic protection and its extremely high manoeuvrability. I used to look out at rock-throwing kids and see them as the enemy, as targets to shoot, as sport even. But I'm on the other side now. And from here, I feel nothing but respect for the boys. I am overwhelmed by the urge to salute them, to pay homage to their courage. I stand at attention as they march by, heads held high.

'They went out the back. I'm sure of it,' Osama is saying. 'I'll go find them.' He disappears down a lane. Aisha watches her brother with pride.

'Your brother has a lot of guts,' I say shyly.

Aisha looks at me surprised. 'Yes. I'm proud of him.'

'And your mother too. What she did was heroic.'

Aisha looks sad. 'Yes, she's a strong woman.' She wanders off into the rubble.

Hours pass. I sit, wondering about it all, thinking hard. The dust settles and the ruins emerge into the uncaring sunlight. When I can't bear feeling so confused, I go in search of Aisha. She's perched on a shattered section of ceiling gazing down at a doll. The doll isn't broken but its long dress and headscarf are black with dust. It looks like a Muslim version of the Barbie doll Orli was given for

Hanukah when she was six and which she only ever used as a weapon against me.

'My mother is the most heroic person in the world,' Aisha says. 'All my life, she's been campaigning for peace and justice, fighting against the occupation. I was six when she first took me on a demonstration. We'd go out on the streets and bang pots and pans and chant slogans and carry banners. She's been organising women's demonstrations since the first Intifada. Even when she was tear gassed and shot at, she wouldn't give up. She never lost hope. She's always doing something for somebody – putting up people whose homes have been demolished, handing out petitions, intervening on behalf of people whose passes have been taken, documenting human rights violations, taking foreigners on tours of the refugee camp. She works with Israeli peace groups.'

'Did you used to do things with her?'

'I did until a year ago. Then I realised how pointless it all was. None of her actions ever get in the media or have any impact at all. Things have only got worse and worse for us in the camps, especially in the last two years. I wanted to do something that would really make a difference.'

'Well Aisha,' I say looking around pointedly at her ruined home. 'You sure have made a difference.'

'I didn't do this. You were a witness. You know who did it. So why do you say I did it?'

'Aisha, did you seriously think there would be no consequences for your suicide bombing? Of course you're responsible. Think about it.'

'Do you seriously think that I, an 18 year old Palestinian girl, have any control over what the mighty Israeli army does, the fourth largest army in the world? If I had such powers, don't you think I would have used them to order your army not to occupy my home last year? Don't you think I would have stopped you soldiers from locking us in a bedroom for five days without food and water and access to the toilet? If I were that powerful, don't you think I would have prevented them from beating my father until he passed out? Don't you think I would have ordered them to allow an ambulance to take him to the hospital? If I could get the Israeli army to do what I say, don't you think I would have told them not to send my 13 year old brother to an Israeli prison for four months? If I could make all this happen,' she waves her hands at the rubble, 'then don't you think I would have used my amazing powers to drive you out of our land and return us to our rightful homes?'

I don't say anything in response to this tirade. When she finally grinds to a halt, I find I don't have the energy to argue. I know I should point out the error of her thinking but I'm struck dumb by the image of little Fazia, rigid with terror, shivering in her nightie in a puddle of urine while the most advanced tank in the Israeli army fires at her unarmed brother and an armoured bulldozer prepares to demolish her home with her in it. A slight shift in time and place and that same image could be on a photo in Yad VaShem. I shift uncomfortably. I've been on dozens of trips with school and my unit to Yad VaShem. Each time I come away with renewed resolve to defend Israel and make sure the Holocaust never happens again. But right now, I'm struggling to make sense of why we were attacking Fazia and how that helps us prevent another Holocaust.

'Do you want to know what really convinced me to martyr myself for the Palestinian cause?'

'Was it Hamas?' I ask.

'No. It was an American lady. She was on a tour of the refugee camp. My mother gave them a talk, told them about the time the army occupied our house. It had happened only a few months before and it took a lot of courage for my mother to tell the story without breaking down and crying. The American woman jumped right in, no sensitivity at all. She didn't say, 'How terrible what happened to your family. Is there anything we can do to help? We will go to the military authorities and find out where your son is being held. We will get specialist medical care for your husband and trauma counselling for your daughter. We will go to the media and tell the world about this atrocity against innocent people.' No. She said none of that. She said, 'Are you committed to non-violence? Do you condemn suicide bombers?"

'My mother was sharp with her. 'I am sick of war and violence,' she said. 'I condemn the aggression of the Israeli army against innocent people. I have always been committed to peace with justice.' The lady was like a dog with a bone. She said again, 'But do you condemn suicide bombing?' And my mother answered, 'We have a right to resist the occupation. Do you condemn the occupation?' The American was fed up. 'You have to see the other side. The Israelis have suffered too. There was the Nazi Holocaust. They deserve security and peace. You must stop the suicide bombings. Those are the greatest obstacle to peace.' That's when I truly understood the world only pays attention to violence and martyrdom is the only thing the Israelis take seriously.'

I sigh. I try to collect my thoughts which are dashing about in different directions. 'Aisha,' I say. 'I can't agree with you. What you're saying just isn't right.'

She glares at me and opens her mouth to protest. I hold up my hand. 'I don't agree with you. What you did is wrong.' I grope around for a better word to express my feelings but can't be bothered. 'You've caused me, my family and my friends unbearable suffering and you've brought grief and suffering to your family too. And you haven't brought about an end to the occupation. If anything, you've strengthened it. Wait. You've had your say. It's time for you to listen to me.'

She shrugs and holds herself back. The trouble is I don't know what I'm going to say. I reach into the swirling whirlwind of my mind hoping to pick out a thought but they're whizzing by too fast. I concentrate on slowing the whirlwind down but it's too hard. Just when I decide to give up, my mind goes still and I speak thoughts I didn't know I had.

'I guess I can sort of see where you're coming from, Aisha. Yeah, you deserve freedom and security and a chance at a real life. Why not? It seems like you did what you did out of passion, a kind of twisted, screwed up passion but yeah, it's still passion. Passion for justice. And I guess if I'd been in your shoes, well I think I would have done the same as you.'

Aisha looks over at me and nods. We lie back on top of the rubble, our fingertips just touching. Together, we watch the clouds change shape and merge and blow by.

CHAPTER 23

Ruth

'What did you throw in the bin?' Orli asked. She was braiding and unbraiding thin strands of hair while tapping her foot on the floor. I stared at her in silence. Something remarkable had just taken place between us - Orli and I had had an adult conversation. For the first time ever, she didn't keep changing the subject, she listened to what I had to say, she didn't do all the talking and she didn't play with her cell phone. I had a glimpse of the woman Orli was growing into. I threw my arms around her and hugged her tight.

'I love you, Orli,' I said, kissing her hair and ears and nose.

'Mom, what are you doing? Stop! You've gone mad. OK, I love you too. So what did you just throw away?'

I hesitated. For years, I'd defended David to the children, constantly making excuses for his absence, his lack of interest and his disapproval of everything they did. It had become a habit. 'Nothing,' I said. 'Some rubbish I found under Yigal's bed.' I leapt up, avoiding eye contact with Orli. My gut twisted in pain. She's 17, nearly old enough to go into the army. She knew about Rena. Why shouldn't she know about this? I spoke quickly before I changed my mind. 'A balaclava and a baseball bat.'

Orli tutted. 'They're Dad's, aren't they?' I nodded and she said, 'So he was beating up Palestinians with Shlomo and Devora and their charming children. Right?'

'I don't know. I guess so. I know he went after Vivi.'

'Oh my god! Not Vivi?'

'Well, I never knew at the time. I mean I knew Vivi came to Israel because I talked to Claire.'

'Wait a minute! When did Vivi come to Israel?'

'When we were sitting *shiva* a year ago. She came here to see me and I never knew and David got to her first and beat her up and she went away. Then a few weeks later, he and some others vandalised the Arab village she was staying in, somewhere in the Territories.'

'No way!' Orli's eyes were wide and her face pale. 'Dad beat Vivi up! But why didn't you get in touch with her? And what was she doing in the Territories?'

'Orli, please. I only found out this morning. Here, read this email she sent.' I thrust the paper at her and went to make coffee. My hands were shaking and I cringed every time Orli gasped, which was often. Finally, she put the paper down and sat in silence, watching me. I looked away.

'Vivi didn't know about Yigal. That's for sure,' she said. 'She sent you this last December.'

'But I didn't read it until today.'

'So she still doesn't know. Mom, call her right now. You've dragged this quarrel out for years and it's stupid.'

'Orli, I can't. Anyway, it's three in the morning in Portland.'

'But you're going to, aren't you Mom? Tell me, you'll do it later.'

'It's not just up to me, Orli.' God, I sounded pathetic. 'Vivi thinks I've sold out, that I'm like Shlomo and Devora. I don't think she wants anything to do with me. She was always against me coming to live in Israel. And she never liked David.'

'Mom, it wasn't just Vivi he beat up. It was you too. Wasn't it? It was Dad who broke your nose last year. You said you walked into a door. But two days later, you took me to Baltimore. Was that why?'

'Well. Um.' I looked at my lap where my hands were rubbing together as if trying to wash away the shame. 'The thing is, Orli. Well, the thing is, I'd let it get to the point where David lost control.'

'What? It was your fault Dad hit you?' Orli asked, tugging hard at her braids. Red spots of anger appeared on her cheeks and she was breathing heavily.

'Well, no, not exactly.' The fog was closing in again. My head drooped onto the table.

Orli poked me. 'Don't fade out, Mom.' Her voice sounded far away.

'I provoked him. I screamed at him.' The words dribbled slowly out of my mouth, like speech bubbles in a cartoon. 'I didn't stop until his fist slammed into my face.' Orli bent towards me, frowning with the effort of listening. I wondered if the words had even left my mouth. 'David was wound up. He was angry.' Orli pushed her chair back and stood up suddenly. I forced my eyes open. 'Orli, what are you doing?'

'I'm getting that baseball bat out of the bin. For when Dad gets home.'

I woke up then. Sounds fizzled around my head. The fog vanished. 'No. No. What good will that do? It takes two to fight, you know. I have to take my share of the blame.'

'That's what cowards say, Mom. And battered wives.'

'Orli, it's not so straightforward. Anyway, he did apologise. I refused to go back until he apologised.'

'We stayed in Baltimore for three weeks. Are you saying it took him three weeks to apologise?'

'Look, you're only hearing my side of the story. You should listen to his version before you hit him with that baseball bat. Please, put it down. I don't like the way you're waving it around.'

I also didn't like the narrowed eyes and aggressive stance. 'Orli,' I said more calmly. 'David is much more used to violence than we are. He could do more damage to us than we ever could to him.'

'Ah, but we have the element of surprise,' Orli said. 'He'd never imagine we'd go for him using his own methods. Anyway, I'm not afraid of him.'

'I'm sick of violence, Orli. That's not the way. Really, it's not. I don't want anyone to be hurt.'

'So what is the way then? To run? Like when we went to Baltimore last year?' Orli was still waving the bat around, trying out different positions and facial expressions.

'No, of course not,' I said. 'I did think about staying in Baltimore. I was tempted. Well, for a few days. My mother, all of them really, they put a lot of emotional pressure on me to stay.'

Orli laughed. 'Every day we were there, Grandma said, "You've got to come home to Baltimore. It's too dangerous in Israel. It's getting worse and worse. I can't bear to think of you living with suicide bombers and terrorists. Your children go into the army and this is what happens. Ruthie, there's no future for you there. Are you prepared to lose all your children to prove a point? Please come home."'

I sighed. 'She was never happy about me moving to Israel. She always wanted me to live near her, like Shirley and Adele.'

'Huh, they should be grateful you didn't become a Buddhist or a lesbian or a heroin addict. What more do they want?'

'They're frightened, Orli. Every time they hear about a suicide bombing in Israel, they're terrified, thinking it might be one of us. And then of course, it was. So their fears are justified.'

'You always see other people's points of view, Mom. But they're wrong. Grandma said we should live in Baltimore because it's safe there. I looked it up on the

Internet. Baltimore has the fourth highest murder rate in the United States - 37.7 deaths per 100,000 people compared to Israel with 5.2 deaths per 100,000. That's murders from ordinary crime and from terrorism. When I told that to Grandma, she said, 'Facts, shmacts. I know where's safe and it's not Israel."

I laughed at the thought of Orli trying to use rational argument with my mother. Scraps of memory floated out of the fog bank hovering at the edges of mind. It was tempting to drift into the fog but I forced myself to stay alert. 'I'm going for a walk. I need to think,' I said, heading for the door.

Orli grabbed my jacket and hers and followed me. I walked quickly, swinging my arms. I wanted to be on my own but I also didn't want to leave Orli at home with the baseball bat. We turned onto the dirt road leading into the grove. The fog in my brain lifted as I breathed in the scent of soil and pine trees.

I thought back to the day David hit me. When it happened, I was too shocked to think clearly. It was the first time David had ever hit me but not the first time he'd threatened to hit me. From the time the children were little, David and I had argued. I always gave in first. I've never had the staying power or the anger or whatever it is that fuels his rage. But Yigal's death blew everything apart. I let go and the lid flew off.

The trigger was the visit to Shlomo and Devora's. At first, I couldn't summon up what exactly David and I had argued about that day. But then I remembered how we both were when we got home from that visit. David was bubbling over with enthusiasm, excited and approving of his friends' activities while I felt sick with hatred, my mind churning with images of violence - Shlomo head-butting soldiers, Jewish girls rioting in an Arab cemetery, Devora's children throwing garbage onto a market and Yigal blown to pieces at the checkpoint. It wasn't long before David and I were screaming at each other, harsh, violent, blaming words. The argument escalated to physical violence in a matter of minutes. David hit me hard in the face, so hard he broke my nose.

By the time Orli and I reached the terraces of the abandoned Arab village, I'd remembered why I'd fled to Baltimore.

'It was panic,' I said out loud. 'And I forgot.'

'Forgot what?' Orli asked.

I forgot what my family was like. I forgot why I left Baltimore in the first place. I'd moved on but my family still live in the same neighbourhood where I grew up – an area with large detached colonial style houses, landscaped gardens, black cleaning ladies, two cars in the carports, and a *mezuzah* on every doorpost. In that neighbourhood, children grow up, get married and buy houses across the street from their parents' homes. I was the only one who didn't and I've never been forgiven.

Two days after we arrived in Baltimore, I went into Shirley's kitchen at seven o'clock and found my dad and Adele's son, Simon, wrestling with a cappuccino machine. Half an hour later, my mother burst in, their elderly Labrador dog trailing miserably after. 'Would you believe it?' Mom hollered up the stairs. I think she was addressing Shirley though Shirley was in the basement loading clothes into the washing machine. 'There are seven teenagers here and I couldn't get a single one to walk the dog with me this morning. What is it with kids these days? It's 7.30 in the morning and they're all still asleep.'

'I'm awake,' said Isaac, emerging from Shirley's sofa fully dressed and yawning extravagantly. He'd slept there all night, too lazy to walk across the street to his own bed, too lazy to take his shoes off or get a blanket from the closet. 'Where's the coffee?' he asked, stretching his arms above his head.

'I can't get this damned thing to work.' My father tossed the instruction manual on the counter. 'Look how small the words are. How do they expect anyone to read this?'

Adele arrived bellowing. 'Who's for French toast?' Without waiting for a reply, she opened Shirley's walk-in fridge. 'Shirley! Good thing I brought some milk over with me. I thought you went shopping yesterday. How come there's no milk?'

Shirley flew out of the basement, screeching. 'I'm making pancakes. Not French toast. What do you mean there's no milk? There was plenty yesterday.' She turned up the volume another decibel and directed her voice to the floor above. 'Which of you girls drank all the milk? Get down here.' Shirley pounced on Adele. 'Your daughter drinks a gallon of milk at a time. Straight from the carton. Because YOU never have milk in your fridge.'

'At least it's healthy food.' Adele's voice was still in the bellowing range. 'Your daughter's always drinking our coca cola.'

My mother pushed in between her daughters. 'Coca cola!' she said. 'You call that healthy! What are you doing with coca cola in the house? I brought a delicious coffee cake and Danish pastries over for breakfast. I'll whip up some scrambled eggs to go with it.'

'I am making French toast.' Adele planted her solid, matronly figure in front of Shirley's fridge.

'I am making pancakes,' Shirley said, snatching the milk from Adele.

'This cappuccino machine is crap,' my father said. 'Shirley, you're going to have to take it back to the shop. Who wants to come with me to Sid's Deli? My treat. C'mon whoever's coming. Let's go.'

But my mother was already serving coffee cake and Danish pastries, all the while issuing a constant stream of orders at full blast, 'You lazy bones, get up off that couch and find some plates. What happened to the coffee? Bring the milk over. Jacob, I thought you were making coffee. Where are the girls? Breakfast is ready.'

Waving a piece of coffee cake, Shirley said through a full mouth, 'Ruth, there's a house for sale on Sulgrave Avenue. I called the estate agent yesterday. She'll be there at noon to show it to you.'

'I never said I …'

'Grandma,' Susie yelled. 'Your damn dog peed in the kitchen. I nearly stepped in it. I'm not cleaning it up again.' She stepped neatly over the puddle, her nose twitching with disgust.

'Oh no,' my mother said, not moving from her seat. 'That's like Kramer, the shitsu. Do you remember him, Ruthie? His kidneys failed him. We had to put him down. I was really upset. Especially after I'd paid $2000 for the operation. I don't think I could go through that again.' My mother paused to cram a piece of coffee cake in her mouth. Before she could speak, Adele jumped in. 'Orli could go to Morgan State. Simon's there. It's got an excellent undergraduate program. Simon! Where are you? Come here and tell Orli about Morgan.'

Shirley was energetically whipping pancake batter. 'Do you remember Miriam Levine? She was in my grade at Western High School. She went out with a *shvartze* and ended up in Sheppard Pratt.'

'Of course I know Miriam Levine,' my mother said. 'Her mother, Esther, is on the committee at Hadassah with me.'

Shirley slammed the bowl of pancake batter on the table. 'I know you know Miriam Levine, Mom. I was talking to Ruth. Well, anyway, Miriam married a dentist, had two children, both at college now and guess what, her husband's in a rehabilitation program at Sheppard Pratt. For meth-amphetamine addiction. She kicked him out, sold the house and bought herself a condo.'

'It's Esther I feel sorry for. I knew that dentist was no good, right from the beginning. Jacob,' my mother screeched. 'Turn off the TV. You can watch Seinfeld any time. I can't hear myself think.'

My father flapped his hands at her without turning away from the TV. 'Just a minute,' he said. 'It's nearly over. Don't interrupt.'

My mother paused in her distribution of the coffee cake and said, 'Ruthie, you've got to make some definite plans. You're not seriously thinking of staying in Israel and sending Orli to the army, are you? After what happened to Yigal? Just go and look at the house. It's around the corner. They're not asking much for it and I think you should consider it. I would, if I were you. Anyway, let's decide what we're doing today. I've got a few chores to do but what I suggest is when you get back from seeing the house, we all go to the Harborside. I need to go into Victoria's Secret and return a bra I bought last week. There's a Banana Republic nearby and the Gap.'

'Shirley, do you have any painkillers in the house?' I asked. 'Something really strong.'

Shirley jumped up to rummage in a drawer, exchanging a meaningful glance with Adele and muttering loudly about people walking into doors. I took refuge in the bathroom.

'Forgot what?' Orli was saying. I'd been so absorbed in my thoughts I hadn't noticed we'd walked as far as the ruins of the large stone house left by the Crusaders. Orli sat down on a low wall. I sat beside her and put my arm around her. She leaned her head on my shoulder.

'I don't know now, Orli,' I said. 'I forgot what I was thinking about.'

'Did Dad ever apologise for hitting you?'

'He sent me a lot of emails all saying a variation of the same message, 'Don't be so stubborn. Come back home. Why won't you listen to me? You've blown this up out of all proportion. You are my wife."

'Is that what you call an apology?' Orli asked.

'I guess not. But eventually he sent an email that was different. He said he missed me and he couldn't live without me. By that time, I was so fed up being around my family I thought it would be okay to go back to him, that things would be different between us.'

'You were wrong there,' Orli said.

'Orli,' I said. I didn't know how to say this to her. I closed my eyes. 'David is not a monster. And I'm not going to leave him. We can work this out. He needs me.'

'Mom, you're a doormat. You're not sticking up for yourself.'

'We're married. When you sign the *ketubah*, you vow to make your marriage a place of peace, nurturing, respect, and kindness. I have no intention of breaking those vows. I'm as much to blame as David for the state of our marriage. So I didn't have a choice. I had to go back to him. And I have to find a way through this. I'm not going to run away.'

'What are you going to do then, Mom?'

The question followed me home like a stray cat. I kept shooing it away but whenever I glanced behind, it was there. I tried running but it stuck patiently to my side, looking up at me expectantly. I had no answer. I didn't know what I was going to do. Orli trotted silently beside me. If she spoke, I didn't notice. I was absorbed in an endless loop of question followed by blank nothing followed by question. 'What are you going to do?' 'What are you going to do?'

If only I were still on speaking terms with Vivi. She would know what I should do. Even more important than her opinion, she would listen to me. With Vivi, I could talk it over until I found an answer, even if it took hours of crying, whining and saying things I didn't mean. Like the time, Orli ran away to Haifa. One ordinary day when she was 14, she stood at the kitchen door and said casually, 'Do you ever feel like your life's in a rut and you've got to do something dramatic to break out?' I snapped at her, 'Don't be silly. Brush your hair. Hurry up. You'll be late for school.' She shrugged and went off. I didn't think anything of it until I got a call from the school later that morning. Orli and another girl had gone missing. I spent the entire day in a panic. It wasn't until 11 that night that the other girl's mother called to tell me they'd hitch hiked to Haifa and were camping on the beach. David was no help. 'You're too soft on Orli,' he said later that night. 'Why didn't you stop her? You should have paid attention when she told you she was about to do something crazy. You give her everything she wants. No wonder she runs off like this. You're a lousy mother.' But Vivi was wonderfully supportive. She stayed on the phone, listening to me for hours. Not once did she blame or criticise. If only I could talk to Vivi now.

Back in the house, Orli disappeared into her bedroom and turned her music up loud. What was I going to do? I had no idea what time David would come home. I tried to cook dinner but the thought of eating made me feel sick. I picked up the newspaper and stared at it blankly. I spread out my papers intending to prepare tomorrow's lesson plan but no matter how I shuffled them, no plan emerged. I hovered over the phone wondering what time it would be in Portland. I couldn't figure it out. I wandered over to the sofa and fell asleep sitting up.

I dreamed I was running through my parents' home in Baltimore looking for something. The house was well-organised and tidy. I opened a drawer marked socks and was furious to discover pairs of socks folded neatly together. I knew there had to be a secret passageway to a hidden attic where I would find what I was looking for. I searched everywhere for the entrance but I couldn't find it. I accused my mother of hiding it from me. She wept and I knew she was keeping something from me. The scene shifted and I was in the kibbutz Vivi and I had stayed in the summer after leaving college. There were crowds of people in the background, none of whom I recognised. Someone, it may have been Vivi but I couldn't be sure, handed me a metal star with sharp, needle-like points. I pricked my finger and collapsed on the floor. I knew I was dying. As I lay there, the crowd of people surrounded me and sang fantastic tales of a land without people for a people without a land, of blooming deserts, of David and Goliath, of enemies massing to push us into the sea, of triumphant victory. I slept a long and deep sleep and didn't wake up until Vivi kissed me on the lips.

Wide awake now, I jumped up and paced around the living room. My heart was pounding. What right did Vivi have to take advantage of me like that? How dare she give me that dangerous metal star? Why didn't she let me stay in the enchanted sleep where I was safe? And where was David? I kicked the sofa and pulled my hair. I kicked again. I heard grunting and screaming. The baseball bat was in my hand, flying wildly through the room. It crashed into the sofa and the little side table and the lamp. Sounds of wood and glass breaking filled the house. I was awake and my fury was unleashed.

CHAPTER 24

Yigal

'Look up there.' Aisha points vaguely towards the sky. 'That cloud started out as a tiny diamond-shaped blob. Then it annexed another little cloud. The bigger cloud went about grabbing a lot of other small clouds until now it's a monster cloud occupying about a quarter of the sky.'

'They're just clouds,' I say with a laugh. 'Clouds don't annex and grab and occupy.' Aisha shrugs. She doesn't really care. She's a lot calmer these days.

Since the time we saw Aisha's home destroyed, Aisha and I have stayed in the Other World Checkpoint, watching the clouds together. Here the sky is always blue with fluffy white cumulus clouds floating in an immense dazzling brightness. There is no night and day, no rain storms, no mild autumn evenings, no stifling hot summer days, no freezing cold, no sunsets and no sunrises. Nothing changes but the clouds. A distant wind moves the clouds. They drift across the sky. They expand and shrink. They change shape. They bump into each other and merge. Sometimes they bounce apart. They disappear and reappear.

Time must be passing but whether it's minutes or days or weeks, I have no idea. I'm aware of a sense of peace. I don't have to worry where the clouds are going or what shape they might take. I don't have to stop them from bumping into each other or prevent them from merging. I don't have to explain and analyse their movements. All I do is watch them. It's deeply relaxing.

'I better go soon and see how everyone is doing,' Aisha says. But she's still lying here next to me, absorbed in the clouds. More time passes, maybe hours, maybe days. Eventually Aisha pushes herself up to a sitting position. 'Are you coming?' she asks. I nod and wait for her thoughts to conjure up her family. It used to be instantaneous but by the time Aisha and I emerge into the refugee camp, I've watched the monster cloud divide and reform and split again.

We're in a bare meeting room, like a community centre of some sort. Stained and scuffed plastic chairs are arranged in a circle. Aisha's mother is offering tiny cups of coffee from a tray to a group of twelve teenage boys. Leila is the only woman. I see Osama and I think I recognise some of the boys who fought with him. There's one man in the room, about 30 to 35 years old. When he smiles, dimples appear in his cheeks and creases spread out from the corners of his eyes. He smiles a lot. The boys are shy with him, squirming on the hard chairs, poking each other and occasionally making eye contact with the smiling man. A few glance at him, smile quickly and then look away.

Still standing, Leila puts down the tray, looks sternly at the boys and begins speaking. 'Six months ago, my daughter Aisha Awad, martyred herself for the cause of Palestinian liberation. She was 18 years old. She killed an Israeli soldier. I loved my daughter Aisha as I love my son Osama and my younger daughter Fazia. I am proud of Aisha's bravery and her passion, her commitment to our people, her dedication to our struggle for liberation. I am more than proud. I am awed by what she did. She made the ultimate sacrifice. No one can ask more of an individual.'

I watch Osama closely while his mother speaks. He chews the inside of his cheek nervously and screws up his eyes. After all their arguments, I bet he's wondering what she's playing at. Leila speaks slowly and deliberately, as if she's choosing every word with care.

'You Osama. And you Mohammed. And you Walid...' She names them in turn, looking each in the eye. As they're called, the kids sit up straighter in their chairs, square their shoulders, nod sombrely at her acknowledgement. 'Like Aisha, you young men have also shown your bravery, your skill in battle, your heroism. You are our hope. You are the future of Palestine.' Leila's words catch in her throat and she grinds to a halt. If I were her, I guess I'd be feeling bleak about the future of Palestine too. But she rallies and carries on.

'This occupation is evil. The Israelis want to destroy us all - our livelihoods, our homes, our lives. They want to destroy you, our children, our hope for the future.' For an unbearable minute, Leila is silent, staring intently at the floor. As if talking to herself, she continues in a low voice, 'Our very existence is under threat from the Zionist enemy. Our cause is just but we've been abandoned by the world, demonised by the international community. The Arab states are corrupt and cowardly. We're left alone to fight a ruthless and powerful enemy, an enemy committed to driving us from our land. And this enemy is financed and sponsored by America.' She breathes out a loud shuddering breath. She covers her eyes with her hands. Her shoulders sag. The boys scowl and look away.

'I am sick of this war. I'm worn out. I mourn for Aisha with a sorrow so great it may well destroy me.' Leila turns to face the man who smiles at her, a kind, understanding smile. She struggles to compose herself. The minutes tick by. The boys shift uncomfortably. 'I know you're not afraid to die. I know you're brave and you think first of the cause. But we mothers suffer. We cannot take any more of this needless suffering. All of you are too precious to die.' Leila's voice rises. She waves her hands in the air. 'I don't want to lose another child. I don't want to come to your funeral Mohammed or yours Walid or yours or yours or yours.'

Now she's yelling. In a loud, angry voice, she says, 'We cannot win this war by throwing rocks or Molotov cocktails or doing what Aisha did. You are sacrificing yourself for nothing. Every time another Palestinian is martyred, the Israelis and the Americans rejoice. You are playing into their hands. This is what they want. They want an excuse to kill us, to cage us in prisons, to demolish our homes, to steal our land, to drive us out of our homeland. They do to us what the Nazis did to them. It's no different. Just like the Nazis did to the Jews, the Israelis are determined to destroy us Palestinians.'

The air in the room crackles as if an electric current were passing through. I pace up and down. What does Leila know about what the Nazis did to us? How dare she even compare us to the Nazis! I tune Leila out and think about my grandfather, my dad's father. The room with Leila and the boys fades out of my mind and I think myself into my grandparents' apartment. I see Grandpa snoozing in the ripped red armchair, his mouth hanging open, drooling. Because my dad didn't get on with his mother, he only took us to visit them about once a year. When we did go to see them, there was nothing to do. Orli and I were bored and spent the time poking each other. Grandma talked all the time, criticising Mom and complaining that Dad ignored her. Grandpa was like a shadow, a zombie. I didn't pay any attention to him until the one and only time I paid him a visit on my own. It was a few months before I went into the army and I was in Tel Aviv for the night life. It came into my head to drop by and say hello. I hadn't planned it. I just did it on a whim.

Grandpa opened the door. The smell of boiled cabbage and cleaning solution hit me. I regretted coming by. But Grandpa acted as if he expected me.

'Yigal, soon you go into the army, yes?'

'Yes, that's right. In a few months.' I sat down at the kitchen table. 'Where's Grandma?'

He poured me a cup of mint tea and sat down opposite me, eyes glittering. 'Shopping,' he said. 'What you are doing is …it is the most important thing. You defend the State of Israel. You dedicate yourself to the Jewish people. You are willing to sacrifice your life for the Jewish homeland. Our enemies surround us, Yigal. They still try to destroy us. We can't afford to be soft, to make concessions. It is good what you do.'

'Yeah, yeah, Grandpa,' I said, feeling uncomfortable with his intensity. 'I know.'

He leaned back and frowned. 'I tell you something I never even told your father. I don't tell him because he has no respect for me. He doesn't understand what it was like. He thought we were nothing but victims.'

This was way too serious for me and I hoped Grandma would be back soon. He took a deep breath and closed his eyes. 'I was in Buchenwald for two years. You know what that is?'

'Yes, yes, of course I know,' I said. I must have sounded impatient because he looked hurt.

'All right. I won't go on about it. No one wants to hear these days. They didn't want to hear when we came in 1949. All right. I say nothing about being a slave labourer. My story is about what happened when the Americans liberated Buchenwald. Most of the SS guards fled only hours before. The Americans drove their tanks through the fence. You listen, yes?'

I nodded, intrigued not just by the story but by the change in my grandfather. He'd suddenly come alive. He threw his arms wide. His cheeks were flushed. 'The camp was a hell-hole,' he said. 'There were half-burned corpses stacked like firewood in front of the furnaces. Corpses scattered on the ground by the barracks. Everywhere half-dead people lying in their own shit. We were skeletons. Those American soldiers, they were so innocent and healthy. Your age, many were. They were shocked and horrified. They let us out of the camp to hunt down the SS guards. I could barely walk but I went out with the others. We rounded up dozens of SS guards. The cowards were hiding in the woods nearby. The soldiers helped us. We dragged the guards back to the camp. We slit their throats.'

I didn't know what to say. The thought of my weedy little grandfather slitting the throats of SS guards was mind blowing. I nodded. As I was grappling for some words to say how impressed I was, Grandma arrived. The room filled with her unstoppable talking. Grandpa retreated into his chair, back to his zombie state.

What would Leila make of that story? I wondered. I bet she wouldn't equate Israelis with Nazis if she really knew what happened during the Holocaust. I'm back in the room and Leila is still talking to the boys. 'We have to get smart,' she's saying to them. 'We have to resist in a different way. That's why I've asked Fahmi to come talk to you.'

Abruptly Leila sits down. She takes a sip of coffee. The boys look confused. Aisha looks miserable. Only Fahmi is calm, smiling, as if he's really glad to be here with these kids. He takes his time, looks around and asks, 'How many of you have been in prison?' Six of the 12 boys raise their hands. 'How long for?' he asks.

'Five months.'

'Two weeks.'

'Six months.'

'Forty eight days.'

'Three months.'

'Four months, five days, 13 hours and 26 minutes.'

Fahmi and the boys laugh. Leila doesn't find it amusing, judging by her glum face. I wonder how old these boys are. There isn't one who looks older than 15. Yet so many of them have been in prison. When they're finished, Fahmi nods, pleased. 'I was in prison for 12 years,' he says. The statement spreads round the circle, each boy nodding as he takes it in. They are impressed. Aisha is impressed. I have trouble imagining what this mild-mannered, pleasant man has done to get himself locked up for 12 years. I soon find out. He describes his progress from a rock throwing ten year old to a grenade-throwing 13 year old to a knife-carrying 14 year old, willing to risk his life to kill Israelis. Osama and the others are lapping it up, their eyes glistening.

'I went alone into an illegal settlement and attacked the first Israeli I saw,' Fahmi says. 'I didn't even look at him. I didn't care who he was. All I knew was he was an Israeli. My hatred was so strong it carried me right over my fear. I plunged the knife into his shoulder. It was easier than I thought it would be. He went down and I grabbed the knife to pull it out and hit him again but then I was jumped from behind by two other guys. They kicked and beat me until I passed out.'

Fahmi stands up and lifts his shirt. Scars snake along his back and front. The boys edge forward and peer closely. 'When I came to, I was in a police station.'

'Did you kill the man?' one of the boys asks.

'No, he lived. That's why I only got a 15 year sentence. With three years off for good behaviour, I was inside for 12 years.'

'What was it like? I mean, being in prison for so long?' The boy who asks this is hesitant. Probably not one of the kids who'd already been in prison.

'It turned me into a man,' Fahmi says smiling. 'I found out I was made of something strong and something tender. I was beaten and I didn't cry. I was locked up in solitary confinement and I didn't crack. I wasn't allowed to see my parents but I never forgot they loved me. I was under heavy pressure to turn informer and I didn't give in, even though they bribed me and denied me privileges and kept on at me every year. I developed myself. I learned English and Hebrew. I learned a trade. I've become a computer programmer. I read about our history and about the politics of the Middle East. I found out the Palestinian people and the Israeli people are just pawns in the imperialist power games of America and global capitalism. Just as your mother said, Osama, I realised we're up against a power that cannot be defeated militarily.'

'I began to see things differently. When I came out, I knew I wanted peace with justice for all of us living in this region and I would dedicate my life to working towards it. Even if I don't achieve it in my lifetime, I will not give up. I will not take the easy road of despair and martyrdom.'

'I dedicate myself to a more powerful weapon than violent resistance. When we use non-violent tactics, we are a moral threat to Israel. They are always crying they are the ones under attack, they are the victims while all the time they are oppressing us. When we resist through non-violent means, we show the world and them they are not the victims. We are. Then they have to take responsibility for their actions.'

The boys are torn. He's won their respect and admiration but he's confused them with his message of non-violence. Aisha is listening hard. She's gazing at him in a way I don't like. I poke her.

'He doesn't think much of what you did, does he?' I say with a slight sneer in my voice.

'Oh but he's awfully cute,' Aisha says without taking her gaze off him.

I snort. 'He's way too old for you,' I say with a big sneer in my voice. I feel annoyed. He's definitely not Aisha's type. On the other hand, if only she'd met him six months ago, I'd probably still be alive.

My thoughts wander back to the clouds. This isn't my business, not any more. I wish Fahmi luck. I hope he manages to bring the young warriors with him. But right now I feel restless and bored. What can I do about it anyway? It's a matter for those who are still alive. All I want to do is watch the clouds.

CHAPTER 25

Vivi

The meeting started late, as usual. I was dreading it. Bob, a policy geek, had prepared a PowerPoint presentation outlining his proposals for the city's ten-year plan to end homelessness. I always fall asleep during slide shows so I positioned myself in a corner of the room, hoping to slip out unnoticed and get some work done. I had a backlog of homeless clients to sort out and I resented the time wasted in meetings. Let Bob get on with it, I muttered to myself. Actually what I really intended to do was read the email from Jude I'd printed out on my way to work that morning. As Bob set up his equipment, I unfolded the paper and quickly read.

Hey comrade Vivi,

How ya doing, dude? That's with an American accent, if you didn't notice. Well, Carol and I have been playing cowboys and Indians with the Israelis. All good fun, of course. We went back in July and hooked up with an American, a Canadian and a Frenchman. Our task was to demolish the earth roadblocks in Nablus. This totally crazy Palestinian bloke got a bulldozer, I don't know where from. He was wild. Carol and I jumped on board and we tore down two roadblocks. What a high! Beats drugs any day! We were having a go knocking down a third roadblock when Israeli soldiers suddenly appeared from nowhere and drove their jeeps towards us at high speed. And the chase began! Of course, we didn't stand a chance. Five jeeps against one bulldozer. We all got arrested, taken off in handcuffs in a bus to the police station in Ariel which is one enormous illegal settlement....

Bob cleared his throat and tapped his papers on the table. 'OK, folks, let's begin. Vivi, the lights please.' He stood poised for take-off, a proud smile on his face. I reluctantly stuffed Jude's email into my pocket and settled myself in the darkened room. Bob launched his presentation with a decisive click of the pointer but once launched, his voice droned like a fly in summertime. Despite my best efforts, the words swam out of focus. By the time the first graph appeared, my head had collapsed onto my chest. By point number 14, I was snoring. At point number 33, I jerked awake. A dog was licking my hand and Dudley was calling my name.

Dudley was our organization's latest receptionist. He had no high school diploma, no qualifications of any sort and no aptitude for reception work. But he was homeless and a policy of our organisation was to employ homeless receptionists. It was a worthy policy and would have worked if anyone in the organization had had time to train and support Dudley.

'Vivi, phone call for you in the main office,' he said, loudly enough to cause Bob to lose his place. The reek of unwashed clothes penetrated my lungs and stirred me into full consciousness. 'You better come. The chick says it's urgent.'

'I'm in an important meeting,' I said trying not to recoil too obviously. 'Look Dudley, you're not supposed to interrupt us during meetings. Take a message. I'll call her back.'

'Okey, dokey,' Dudley sang out. 'But don't blame me if it doesn't work.' Once he left, I propped my eyes open and tried to concentrate on Bob's presentation. But I was sound asleep when Dudley reappeared with his dog and his aroma.

'Vivi, wake up. She's calling from Israel. She said she's got to talk to you now. She …'

I shot out of the room and was in the office before Dudley had finished talking.

'Hello?' I said, grabbing the handset.

'Vivi, my mom's gone mental. She's flipped.' English, Hebrew and sobs jumbled together in a loud incomprehensible wail. At first I couldn't imagine who it was but gradually the sobs subsided and I recognised Orli's voice. 'She's got a baseball bat,' Orli said. 'She's screaming and shouting. She's smashing up the furniture. Oh my god. She just broke up the table. Now she's hitting the lamp. Vivi, you've got to help.'

'Orli, Orli, calm down. What's going on?' I could hear shouting and smashing in the background but I would never have imagined it to be caused by Ruth. If Orli had told me it was her father, I would have believed her. But not Ruth. I'd never seen Ruth in a rage. Even when she should have been angry, she wasn't. Like the time, Shirley had ruined Ruth's chances at going out with Sam Goldberg back when we were in the tenth grade. When Sam phoned to speak to Ruth at home, Shirley said rude and nasty things to the unsuspecting boy, so rude Sam never rang back. Ruth cried in the privacy of her room and to me but she never even shouted at her sister, let alone hit her. Ruth's temperament was so different from every other member of her family we'd often considered the possibility Ruth had been adopted. However, the evidence did not support this theory, as the physical likeness between Ruth and her sisters was overwhelming.

'Vivi, what should I do?' Orli said. She was still sobbing but I could understand what she was saying. 'I'm afraid she'll hit me with the bat if I try to take it from her.'

I didn't have a clue what Orli should do or what I would do if I were there. I paced around the small office, tripped over the dog and bumped into Dudley who was hovering nearby. 'Just a minute, Orli,' I said. Turning to Dudley, I said, 'I need to use this phone for a few minutes. Why don't you check out the washing machine we've got upstairs. There's a box of spare clothes you can wear while yours are being cleaned.' Dudley slowly unfolded his arms and deliberately walked out of the office, his back bristling. Tapping my fingers impatiently and nodding towards the dog, I said, 'And take Star with you.' Dudley's nose went up in the air and he snapped his fingers once. Star staggered to his feet and reluctantly followed. I let my breath out and sighed. OK, that wasn't the most diplomatic way to handle the situation but it was the best I could do.

'OK Orli, now tell me. Why is Ruth smashing things up?'

'She's really mad. She found a baseball bat under Yigal's bed. Then she read your email, the one you sent last December. That was the first time she knew Dad beat you up and smashed up the house you were staying in. And Dad broke Mom's nose. And we went to Baltimore. And we came back home. Then Mom found out Dad had an affair with Rena. I already knew, a long time ago. And today Dad went to the cemetery without us. And Mom just got madder and madder. I don't know what happened. I was in my room and it was quiet. And then I heard her shouting and smashing things. She's kicking the sofa now. What should I do?'

I crumpled onto the desk. I'd been handed the pieces of a jigsaw puzzle but I couldn't put them together because some pieces were missing and the rest didn't correspond with each other in any logical way. The realisation David was responsible for the attack on Beyt Nattif shook me to the core but the thought of David having an affair with next-door neighbour Rena was equally staggering. And what did Orli mean about the cemetery?

'Vivi, are you there? Listen, she's gone quiet. Hold on.' I held the phone to my ear, my mind whirring with confusion. I was no clearer when Orli returned.

'Mom's fallen asleep. She's, like, passed out on the sofa. I'm really scared. I don't know what to do.' Orli was crying. I made soothing noises into the phone. Suddenly, she shouted. 'Vivi, I forgot. You don't know. Oh no. Oh no.' The crying grew louder. I heard her say Yigal and I felt my heart beat hard and fast in my chest. I closed my eyes. I was clutching the phone so tightly my knuckles were white. 'Let it not be true,' I whispered to myself. 'Not Yigal.' Orli took several deep breaths and then she said it and the saying of it made it real and final and unbearable.

'A year ago, today, Yigal was killed by a suicide bomber. And I don't know what you and Mom fought about all those years ago but Mom needs you, Vivi. You're her best friend. Please come over and make up with her. I can't do this on my own. Please.'

It didn't take more than a second to make up my mind. 'I'll be there,' I said. And without another thought about the plight of the homeless in Portland, I walked out of the office. And so it was on the 7th of October 2003, exactly one year later, I was back on a plane to Israel.

PART THREE
October 2005

CHAPTER 26

Ruth

It was the 2nd of October 2005, the third anniversary of Yigal's death. I lit the *yahrzeit* candle and placed it, flickering gently, on the shelf in the room that used to be Yigal's bedroom but was now a guest room. Behind the candle, I put two photos of Yigal, one at the start of his life, the other near the end. In the baby photo, he was dressed in a brand new yellow baby-grow and was lying on a cushion on the kitchen table. His dark brown eyes gleamed like marbles in his sombre face. He seemed to be studying the world he'd come into, wondering what was in store for him. The other photo was a close-up of his face, taken soon after he went into the army. He had the same sombre expression as when he was one day old.

This anniversary I didn't wait for Yigal to show himself to me. I didn't sit alone in his room searching for a sign of his presence. I'd moved on. Everything was different now. We'd cleared the room a year ago, on David's insistence.

On that day, the second anniversary of Yigal's death, David had been standing in the doorway of Yigal's room, watching as I picked up a shirt, sniffed it and put it back in the drawer exactly where it had been.

'What the hell are you doing?' he asked. His arms were folded across his chest and both feet were planted on the floor. He looked like a sergeant about to discipline an insubordinate.

If he'd asked me, 'why are you sniffing Yigal's shirt?' in an interested tone of voice, I would have told him I was hoping to smell Yigal's presence. If he'd then asked in a kind voice, 'over the last two years, have you ever smelled Yigal's presence in one of his shirts?', I would have admitted that I had not. If he'd then asked me gently and respectfully, 'so why do you keep doing it?' I would have said the thought of not doing it terrifies me. It would be an admission I no longer cared about my son.

Instead David asked me 'what the hell are you doing?' in an irritable, disapproving tone of voice. I shrugged and picked up another shirt. David shook his head in disgust. He half turned, as if to walk away, then suddenly wheeled back and grabbed the shirt out of my hands. 'This room's like a shrine. Everything's been kept as it was since Yigal died. You haven't moved a single book or T shirt. Don't you see Ruth? That's sick. Yigal is gone. When are you going to accept that? You can't keep living in the past. It's been two years.' His face was red and he was gripping the shirt so hard it looked like he was going to rip it to shreds. I cringed, but he didn't hit me. Instead, he threw the shirt on the floor and said firmly, 'Today, we're going to pack up all his belongings and take them to a second-hand shop. This has gone on too long. It's abnormal.'

While he was out of the room gathering cardboard boxes and bags, I stood rooted to the spot stunned. We hardly ever talked, each of us wrapped in our separate cocoons of grief. I didn't know how David felt and he didn't ask me how I felt. But his outburst lit an ember of hope buried deep inside and never completely extinguished – the hope he would notice me and care about me. I picked the shirt off the floor. It was just a shirt, a navy blue cotton T-shirt, soft and stretchy to the touch. I couldn't even remember when Yigal last wore it. There was nothing of Yigal in it. Why was I carrying out this depressing ritual? It left me feeling bleak and empty, every day a failure. It was clear David was right. My daily search for Yigal was sick and abnormal.

Yet, I knew Yigal was not gone. It's true I never felt his presence in his bedroom or in his possessions. But he had come to me often, always unexpectedly, always when my mind was drifting unfocussed, not searching for him. I'd felt him there with me in the smell of frying onions when I was cooking dinner, in a child's high-pitched laughter in the classroom, in a shadow of a tree, in a stranger's face, in a cloud floating by.

When David returned with boxes and bags, his face showed his determination to do it regardless of my views. He yanked open a drawer and swept the shirts up into his arms.

'OK. OK,' I said, relieved the decision had been made for me. 'I won't keep this shrine any more.'

'Here.' He tossed me the shirts and a box. Working together, we packed up Yigal's clothes and books, his guitar and posters. When the last box was loaded in the car, we came back to the empty room. The *yahrzeit* candle was still burning. The occasion seemed to call for some ceremony but neither of us spoke. Instead, without a word or a glance, we held hands and stood in silence. A minute passed, two minutes, five. With each minute, the room seemed less empty and my heart felt lighter.

Since that day, the room had come alive with guests. I believe Yigal invited them. Hardly a week went by without one of Orli's friends sleeping in the guest room. My parents had been over from Baltimore, followed by an unexpectedly pleasant visit from Shirley and her husband. My nephews and nieces came at intervals throughout the year, staying for weeks at a time, sometimes alone, sometimes with each other. Tanya and Susie came twice that year, spending most of their time out and about with Orli; Tom and Simon were with us for most of August, Isaac in July. And Vivi came. She came with her son Noah and her partner Claire for ten days in June before going to stay with her Palestinian friends in Beyt Nattif.

Vivi's visit was hard for David. He refused to stay in the house while she was around but he didn't dare oppose her visit. I'd had the upper hand in our relationship since the shocking revelations that emerged on the first anniversary.

The balance of power had shifted and I wasn't making any concessions for good behaviour.

Nothing stays the same, I thought as I stood in the guest room with David and Orli on this third anniversary of Yigal's death. I picked up the baby photo of Yigal. 'He was such a serious baby,' I said. 'But as soon as you were old enough to play with, he became a real goof ball.'

'Yeah, that's what I remember most about Yigal,' Orli said. 'He was always joking and teasing me. So where was that photo taken?' She addressed her question to me, her back to David but before I could answer, David quickly said, 'In our apartment in Jerusalem.' He stepped closer to stand behind me and look over my shoulder at the photo. I could hear the smile in his voice. 'I was so excited and proud. My newborn son. He was amazing. I got out the camera and took a dozen pictures of him. I couldn't get enough of him.'

'Did you take that many photos of me?' Orli asked, walking over to the window and looking out. 'I've never seen lots of baby pictures of me.'

'For heaven's sake, Orli,' David said. 'We're here now to remember Yigal. You always turn everything back to yourself, don't you?'

It was true we took a lot fewer pictures of Orli as a baby than of Yigal. By the time Orli came along, the novelty of a baby's first bath, first smile, first burp had worn off. And maybe it had made a difference that our firstborn was a son, though it didn't mean Yigal got more attention or affection. David was often disappointed and puzzled by

Yigal. He was not the son David had wanted. But the truth was Orli was not the daughter David wanted. And I guess I wasn't the wife David wanted.

'We loved both of you,' I said quickly and put the photo back on the shelf. To my relief, Orli merely shrugged. 'Let's go,' she said. 'I want to get back to Haifa by six.' As soon as she left the room, David reached over and touched my arm. 'Wait,' he said. 'I want to tell you about something that happened last month.' He paused, his hand still resting lightly on my arm.

My stomach clenched and I turned away. It better not be another revelation about Rena, I thought. David had spent the last two years alternately denying and admitting adultery with Rena. His story was he and Rena had had a brief affair when I was in Baltimore shortly after Yigal's death, initiated by her, but he'd ended it as soon as I returned home. He stuck to this story for the next year. Then, a new story emerged. He hadn't ended the affair when he said he had. He'd tried to but Rena had pursued him, following him when he went out jogging and forcing him to have sex against his will. David swore these encounters were rare and meant nothing.

'Not now, David,' I said. 'Let's just think about Yigal today.'

'That's what I want to tell you about. About Yigal. The strangest thing happened when I went to get Orli from the demonstration.' He stopped and chewed the inside of his cheek.

'I don't know what you were doing, going to get Orli. She's 19. You can't stop her going on demonstrations.'

'Yes, I can and I will do it again if I find out she's on another anti-government demonstration. She was in a closed military zone. She had no right to be there. Ruth, let me finish what I was saying.'

I crossed my arms and held my tongue. I had a lot more to say about that incident. I'd already heard Orli's version of events and it didn't show David or the army in a favourable light. On the other hand, I didn't want another futile argument. We had come to an impasse about certain topics and could do no more than agree to disagree.

David rubbed his bald patch. 'Just listen to me for once. And don't give me any of your psychobabble nonsense.' He looked at me sternly. 'We were in the jeep driving away from Bili'in. Orli was kicking and screaming and swearing. I felt like I was in a storm being bombarded by hail stones. Then one of the soldiers turned from the window to face me. He called my name and when he spoke, it was in Yigal's voice.' David stopped. He gulped and looked away. Amazed by this show of emotion, I let my arms drop to my side and gave him my full attention. After a few shuddering breaths, he said, 'Ruth, I looked at him and saw Yigal. Not just a glimpse of Yigal. It was Yigal. He had Yigal's long narrow face, his curly brown hair, his straight eye brows, his serious brown eyes, the dimple in his chin.'

'What did he say to you?' I asked, trying not to sound too interested in case David clammed up.

'Nothing,' David said. 'How could he say anything? He's dead. It was just a trick of the mind.' He muttered the last sentence while staring at the floor. He fidgeted with his shirt. A thread had come loose. He pulled on it and the hem unravelled. He yanked the thread and more of the hem unravelled. He's lying, I thought. Yigal came to him and told him something and now he won't tell me what it was. A wave of jealousy washed over me. Why would Yigal appear to David and not to me?

'For a few seconds..,' he said, twisting the thread between his fingers, still not looking at me.

'What?' Was he going to deny the vision? I paced the room, unable to stand the suspense.

'For a few seconds, just for that moment, I felt, well, I guess I'd call it, um, happy. Like seeing light at the end of the tunnel. I've had glimpses of it since. Not often but I know it's there.' He smiled at me. 'Shall we go?'

'That's it?' I asked. 'That's what you wanted to tell me? That your mind was playing tricks on you?'

He hesitated. 'He's okay, Ruth. Everything's okay. That's all I wanted to say.'

But everything was not okay and I couldn't believe David thought it was. Orli and David could hardly spend more than ten minutes in each other's company before an argument broke out. And David and I were at an impasse where we could only get on by not sharing anything meaningful with each other. Yet, big changes were bubbling away under the surface. I was contemplating a course of action I knew would threaten the fragile peace between us and might even jeopardise our marriage. Although I'd been thinking about it for more than a year, I hadn't been ready to act. The time was coming soon when I knew I had to.

At the cemetery, Orli dragged me away, leaving an unusually serene and thoughtful David by Yigal's grave.

'Mom,' she said breathlessly. 'I got an email from Vivi. She wants me to come to the States and go on a speaking tour with other refuseniks from Israel. She wants me to talk about the Shminitsim and why we refuse compulsory military service. She organised a tour of the West Coast. We'll be going to Seattle, Portland, and San Francisco. And San Diego. She wants me to speak. Me! She even raised enough money to pay my airplane ticket. Isn't that amazing?'

Yes, it was amazing but it was also confusing and disturbing. I didn't know what to think. Orli was so different from me. She'd always been passionate but when had she become so sure of herself? I could never have done anything like that at the age of 19. I still couldn't. The thought of knowing what to say and saying it in public was terrifying. Even more worrying was the hurt feeling creeping up my spine. Vivi had planned this speaking tour without talking to me about it. 'When is it?' I asked.

'In two weeks. On the 16th of October. What do you think?' She danced on the spot.

'I don't know. It's so public, so exposing. And what would you say? These issues are so complex. How do you know what the solution is.' I paused, aware of how negative

I sounded. I should be more encouraging. 'Still you are particularly good at arguing. I bet you'd be great.'

'Yes, I know I am,' Orli said. 'Would you come with me?'

'To speak?'

'Yes. Or not, if you don't want to.'

'I don't have anything to say. All I know is I've had enough of the violence. I don't want any more. I'm sick of it. So there, I've said it. I could hardly make a speech out of that.'

'You could say how you felt when you learned Yigal killed a Palestinian child and you could say how Dad nearly killed me when I told him I wouldn't join the army.'

'Orli, for heaven's sake. Don't exaggerate. David did not nearly kill you. And I'm not going to travel around the West Coast talking about our family's problems in public. And I hope you're not going to either. That would be embarrassing.'

'Yes, he did too.' Orli stopped in her tracks, her face twitching with outrage. 'And you defended me, Mom.'

'I think what you've done is very brave. I know lots of girls get exemptions from compulsory service in the army on religious grounds. Few refuse on political grounds.'

Orli snorted. 'Do you remember my friend Dorit? She's not religious. She feels the same as me but she didn't want to risk going to jail so she married her boyfriend at 18 and got out of it that way. And Hila applied for exemption on really silly grounds, saying she needed to be around for her sick mother. And that was accepted. But it wasn't the real reason. I think it's important to stand up for what you believe. In our letter to Sharon that we wrote last March, we said, 'Every person is entitled to basic rights: the right to life, equality, dignity and freedom. It is our conscientious and civic duty to act in defence of these rights by refusing to take part in the policy of occupation and repression.' That's what I'm going to say in my speech.'

I sighed. How simple everything is when you're 19 years old. 'That sound's a bit idealistic, Orli.' I took her arm in mine. 'There's reality you have to take account of as well. But listen, I want to tell you about something I'm going to do next. Something I've been meaning to do for more than a year. I think I'm ready now.'

'What is it, Mom? Tell me.'

'I haven't completely decided. It means going into the Occupied Territories. There's a meeting, a joint meeting with Israelis and Palestinians. I've been in touch with a man named Moshe who is one of the organisers. It's for ....'

'Ruth, Orli,' David called. 'Come on. We've got to go.' He came running over to us.

'I don't want to talk about it with David. Not yet,' I said quickly to Orli.

'Why not?' Orli said. 'Why do you let him bully you? Why don't you do whatever you want to do without having to justify it to Dad?'

'Justify what?' David asked, as he arrived next to us.

'When I'm ready to talk about it with you, I will,' I said, glaring at both Orli and David.

'You are such a doormat,' Orli muttered.

'I heard that,' I said. I felt annoyed but stopped myself from snapping at her. She was right and I knew it. 'Yeah, OK. Maybe I used to be a doormat before Yigal was killed. But not any more.' Now I'm a chrysalis, I thought, a chrysalis soon to emerge as a butterfly. I sensed the changes inside my cocoon. Yes, I used to try hard to be a good mother, constantly vigilant to keep my children safe. I'd spent years in a state of anxiety and fear - leaning over their cribs in the middle of the night to see if they were still breathing, worrying about the safety of the house when they were toddlers, fretting over the nutritional status of the meals I prepared, nagging them to do well at school, angsting over their relationship with David, agonising about suicide bombers and car crashes when they went out on their own as teenagers. And what good did it do? Worrying hadn't prevented Yigal's death. All it had done was prevent me from being happy, from treasuring each moment of his short and precious life.

I closed my eyes and imagined stepping out of the cocoon. Would I be a colourful butterfly like the Monarch or one with a striking black and white pattern like the Swallowtail? Whatever the design, I knew I'd be a worry-free butterfly.

'What do you mean, not any more?' David said. 'That's what you are, Ruth, someone who is easily influenced. Especially by Vivi. Is this one of her schemes?'

I laughed. 'Yes, yes it is. Vivi sent me a letter a few days ago with a paper she and I wrote when we were 13 years old. She'd found it when she was visiting her parents. In their attic they'd kept every story, homework assignment and poem Vivi had ever written when she was a kid. I'd forgotten all about that vow but it's a good example of how Vivi influenced me. It was all her idea. I just went along with her because it was easier than arguing with her.'

'Do you have it with you?' Orli asked.

'Yes, I was going to give it to you to read. You asked the other day what my reasons were for coming to live in Israel. Maybe this will make it clear.'

I handed her a piece of notepaper with blue-tinged scalloped edges covered in Vivi's neat, round handwriting. Orli read it aloud.

'Our Resolutions for Life:

We, Vivienne Rubenstein age 13½ and Ruth Shapiro age 13¾ on this day January 19, 1969, solemnly and resolutely and meaningfully have come to the decision that we will go on Aliyah to Israel as soon as we are of age. When we reach Israel, our goal will be to help with the building of the Jewish State which will be based on the enlightened teachings of our religion and the lessons of our history. We will never forget or forsake our religion. For the rest of our life, we will remain true to Judaism. We sign this resolution with G-d as our witness.

Signed Vivienne Rubenstein and Ruth Shapiro

Please dear G-d give us the strength and the determination to follow through our resolution and reach our goals. Thank you for making us come to these decisions. Please help us carry them through. Hear, O Israel, the Lord our G-d, the Lord is One. Amen.

P.S. We will allow for any changes of mind if we agree with them then but please G-d don't let us change our ideas.'

Orli snorted with laughter. 'You two were awfully intense. Typical 13 year olds. I like the P.S. You guys covered all possibilities, just in case. Which of you thought of that one?'

'Actually that was me,' I said. 'The thing is that in a funny kind of way, we've both kept to our resolution, even though we've done it differently.'

'What are you going on about?' David said. 'Vivi didn't make *Aliyah*. And she hasn't remained true to Judaism. She's made clear her opposition to Israel. She's an out and out traitor.'

'Is she?' Orli said, looking hard at David. 'You can remain true to Judaism without belonging to a synagogue and without observing the Sabbath. You're not observant, Dad, so what are you going on about? And Vivi has come to Israel and done her bit towards helping to build the State of Israel and helping its citizens including its non-Jewish citizens by fighting against the lack of democracy here.'

'That's twisting things,' David shouted. 'Vivi turned her back on the vow she made when she was 13. You can't argue with that. Ruth is the one who didn't forsake the religion.'

'Well, maybe I did,' I said. 'I was brought up in a much more observant family. Since I married you, I've only been to *shul* once a year. We don't keep the Sabbath. We don't have a kosher home. I let myself be influenced by you, David.'

'I've had enough of this conversation,' David said and turned to walk away.

'Dad,' Orli called loudly. 'I want you to hear me. You never listen to me. Don't walk away.'

With his back to us, David said, 'Orli, I have heard you. Many times. You've made it clear what you think and what you're going to do. When do you ever listen to me?' He turned to face her.

'I do listen to you. You want me to go into the army to defend Shlomo's right to steal land that belongs to the Palestinians.'

'Shut up, both of you,' I said. 'I don't want you two fighting by Yigal's grave.'

'It's not about Shlomo,' David said. 'Don't you think all of us wish we lived in a time when it wasn't necessary to have an army, where we could live our lives in peace? I wish we weren't surrounded by enemies who want to destroy us.'

'We don't have to occupy the Palestinians' land, Dad. Yigal died to defend the occupation, to defend settlers like Shlomo.'

'It's not that simple, Orli. We have no choice. We can't just pull out. We would be driven into the sea. We can't show weakness like that.'

'Please stop,' I said. 'You're just going round and round in circles, saying the same things.'

But Orli was in full swing and unstoppable. 'So you're happy to sacrifice Yigal and me. For what? So Shlomo can live in the land that was once the ancient kingdom of

Judea? Why should I sacrifice my life for stupid ideas like that?'

'It's not for the settlers, Orli. It's for all of us, for all the Jews of the world.'

'What did Yigal get out of it?' Orli said. 'He didn't deserve to die. You don't even know how beautiful a person he was. You didn't even care about him. You don't care about me. Can't you just listen to me for once?' She stood with her hands on her hips.

David sighed. 'OK, I'm listening. Say it and get it over with once and for all.'

Orli took a breath and launched in. 'After what happened to Yigal, I'm determined not to go into the army. And it's because I do love Israel. Not the distorted, paranoid Israel where only Jews count. The Israel I love is the one which has Wahid and Habiba and the people of Beyt Nattif in it as well as all of us. I want to live in an Israel where people don't blow themselves and us up because they're so angry at the way we treat them. I want to live in a country where we do our Jewish thing next door to the people doing their Muslim thing while down the road the Christians do their Christian thing and the people who aren't religious do their secular thing. That's what I want.'

'We all want that, Orli,' David said, shaking his head wearily. 'We all want peace. But we can't afford to be naïve and idealistic. Wherever Jews are a minority, we are oppressed and persecuted. That's the lesson we learned from our history. Can we drop it now?'

It was a long walk to the car. I was the buffer in the middle, the two of them sniping at each other around me. But they were listening to each other. I smiled at David to show him I noticed and appreciated the effort he was making with Orli. Maybe the appearance of Yigal in the jeep had softened him. He did seem calmer. Encouraged by David's openness, Orli seized her chance and said, 'Dad, Mom's family in America aren't persecuted. They're openly Jewish and nothing bad happens to them. You are so paranoid.'

That did it. David's calm evaporated. 'Paranoid?' he said, his voice rising several octaves. 'How can you say I'm paranoid after Yigal was killed by an Arab suicide bomber? My parents lived through the Holocaust. It's not safe in the Diaspora. Jews are vulnerable. We can't rely on any other country in the world. If everyone refused to go into the army, where do you think we'd be? We'd be driven into the sea. That's where. This is what we have to do to keep Israel going.' He pounded his fists in the air. 'It's just the way it is. How can you even question it? There's no other way to look at it. The Arabs say they want to eliminate us. I'm not making that up. I'm not paranoid. I wish it were different. I really do. But for the moment, we have to have our own state where Jews are in the majority.'

Orli was not fazed. 'Dad, it's not about numbers. Everyone deserves equal rights whether they're in the majority or the minority. There are nine million of us living between the Mediterranean and the Jordan. Can't we find a better way to live together? Why do we have to occupy and oppress people so we can pretend we have an exclusively Jewish state?'

'Because we can't trust them. We have no partners for peace. Do you know there's no word in Arabic for negotiation? We can't afford to believe their lies. The stakes are too high.'

The volume had reached unbearable levels and was beginning to affect my breathing. I stopped and closed my eyes. Orli and David walked on still shouting, not even noticing I was no longer there. I considered yelling at them to shut up, then decided against. Let them work it out for themselves, I thought. I looked around me at the cemetery we were walking through. That's when I saw the butterfly lying on the path. It was solid black with white dots on the tips of its wings and a vivid red border running along the widths and bottom of the wings. It was stunning. I held my breath in an infinite moment of joy. Seconds later, it lifted its wings and flew away.

'Thank you Yigal,' I said and with a light heart, joined my still quarrelling family.

CHAPTER 27
Vivi

The ringing of the phone seeped into my consciousness. I knew I was supposed to do something in response but I was paralysed by sleep. With great effort, I cracked one eye open. It was night-dark, time to be asleep. My brain registered this fact and closed the eye. The phone kept ringing. I knew somebody was at the other end and my brain considered the possibilities - Noah in a car crash, my father in the hospital with a stroke, a woman in labour needing Claire's midwifery help, a wrong number, a hoax call. I didn't like any of the possibilities. I drifted back to sleep. The phone kept ringing. Who was it then? Curiosity penetrated the fog of sleep. I dragged myself to a sitting position and picked up the receiver.

'Unh,' I said.

'Shalom. Shalom. Vivi, is that you? I'm coming. Definitely. I really want to do it.'

'Orli?'

I glanced at Claire lying under the duvet. She had one eye open and it was pointing accusingly at me.

'Orli, it's the middle of the night here.'

'I told my mom. She's OK about it. Well, I think she is. She won't be coming with me. But I definitely am coming.'

'Orli, hold on. I'll call you back in a few hours.'

'Yeah, awesome. You really mean it that you're going to pay for my ticket?'

'Yes, yes. Of course. I'll call you back later. Then we can talk more.'

'I didn't tell my dad yet. I'm going to tell him tomorrow.'

'Do you think he'll try to stop you?'

'Probably. He won't like it. I want him to listen to me, to try to understand the way I see things.'

'Vivi,' Claire said, poking me hard. 'It's four in the morning. Go downstairs and talk.'

'Orli, I'll call you later. Goodbye.' Orli was still talking as I hung up.

I snuggled under the duvet, knowing my sleep for the night was over. My mind was locked in wide awake mode. I sighed and tossed from side to side.

'Go back to sleep,' Claire mumbled.

'I'm sorry. Orli's not the most considerate, is she, calling at this time? She's used to calculating the time difference to Baltimore, not to Portland.'

'So, is she coming?'

'Yes, she is. She's really matured in the last two years. She'll be great. Now, I've got to confirm the speakers from Yesh Gvul and find a venue in San Francisco and start the publicity and raise money and ..'

'Not now, Vivi. Go back to sleep.'

Claire rolled over and closed her eyes. Within minutes, she was snoring gently. It always amazed me how easily Claire could let herself fall asleep. I lay as still as I could and tried to disengage my brain from planning mode. Instead, I thought back to the trip I took to Israel in October 2003, that time after Orli told me about Yigal's death and Ruth's violent outburst.

It was Ruth's idea to meet in Jerusalem at the YMCA Three Arches hotel. She said it was not yet a good time for me to come to Tsur Hadassah and risk an encounter with David. When she'd confronted David with the baseball bat and the balaclava, he hadn't been at all remorseful. In fact, he'd expressed a strong desire to inflict more damage on me and the village of Beyt Nattif if I were ever to appear in Israel again.

At the agreed time, I was in the lobby, pretending to be interested in an exhibition of paintings displayed on the wall. Ruth was always late and I didn't expect her for another hour. But it was my nature to be punctual. I couldn't do anything else but wait and worry which I did with my usual intensity. What if I got the time or the date wrong? What if David found out I was in Israel and was planning to kidnap me? What if David stopped Ruth from seeing me? What if Ruth changed her mind and decided she didn't want to see me? What if our friendship was over and we didn't have anything to say to each other?

By the time, Ruth and Orli arrived, only half an hour late, I had worked myself into a stomach-clenching, hand-wringing state. Orli bounded across the lobby, shouting my name. She threw her arms around me and we hugged, rocking vigorously from side to side. Behind her, Ruth walked slowly towards me, biting her lip. She looked like she'd aged 40 years. I noticed with alarm how fragile and beaten she was. The spark was gone.

'Hey Ruth,' I said, disentangling myself from Orli's grip. 'At last we meet.' We embraced, both of us awkward and shy with each other. I buried my face in her shoulder, not daring to look her in the eye, shocked by the change in her. When I tried to end the hug, Ruth held me tightly. Her shoulders shook. Next to me, Orli tutted. 'See what I mean, Vivi,' she said, her arms folded across her chest and her face twisted with anxiety. 'She keeps falling apart. She wasn't like this until a few weeks ago. It all started on the first anniversary of Yigal's death.'

Ruth straightened up. 'She? Who's she?' she said. 'You're talking about me as if I'm not here. And I'm not falling apart. I'm pulling myself together for the first time in a year.'

I stroked Ruth's hand. 'What a tragedy you've had. I still can't believe it.' Tears trickled down Ruth's cheeks.

'I can't deal with this,' Orli said. 'Let's go eat.' She turned and raced across the lobby to the restaurant. We followed. Halfway there, Ruth stopped. 'Look at this place,

Vivi. I love it. It's amazing. It's 1930s art deco Byzantine-Islamic style. It's by the same architect as did the Empire State Building. Did you know that?' Her eyes lit up and her voice bubbled with enthusiasm. This was the Ruth I knew. Relief flooded through me. We were friends again. As we sat down at the table Orli had chosen, I took her hand and said, 'I'm so glad we've made up, Ruth. I couldn't bear having all that tension between us.'

'Vivi, I needed you so much. All this last year, since Yigal died, I've been a zombie. I didn't feel safe with anyone. I wish we hadn't had that fight. It was so stupid. I can't even remember what it was about now.'

'I remember and what was stupid was we couldn't talk it through. Ever since we were on the kibbutz, almost 25 years ago, Israel has been a taboo subject between us. I haven't been true to myself with you. And when I did try to say what I felt that Thanksgiving three years ago, it came out all wrong and aggressive. I'm sorry. Really sorry because it meant when Yigal was killed, I couldn't be here for you. And that's what matters. Not our positions and opinions and who's right and who's wrong. What matters is our friendship and being real with each other and and well, that's it.'

Ruth burst into tears and ran outside. I smacked my forehead in frustration. I was so clumsy with words. Once again, I'd managed to wound her. I stood up to go after her.

'Let her go,' Orli said, grabbing my arm. 'She needs to be by herself to calm down. Let's order some food.'

'I didn't handle that very well, did I?' I said, staring blankly at the menu. I no longer felt like eating.

'It's not what you said,' Orli said. 'She cries if I say hi to her. The food here is really good. Why don't you get the shrimp pie?' I nodded absentmindedly, trying not to cry.

'Hey, Vivi,' Orli said. 'Chill. Mom's totally emotional since she found the balaclava and the baseball bat under Yigal's bed and had that little talk with Rena. She keeps crying and having these weird dreams she tells me about.'

'That only makes me feel worse, Orli,' I said.

'Vivi, tell me about Beyt Nattif and about what's really happening here in Israel. It's something I've been thinking about a lot, especially since Yigal died. But even before. Next year, I'm supposed to go into the army. I need to hear another side of the story, not the propaganda I've been brought up with.'

'I'm going to Beyt Nattif next week. Why don't you come with me? We can talk on the way and you can hear the Palestinian story direct from them.'

'Awesome,' Orli said. She leaned towards me, her eyes gleaming. 'Yes. Yes. I really want that. Thank you Vivi.'

If I weren't distracted by worry about Ruth, I would have enjoyed talking with Orli. She was intelligent and knowledgeable and thoughtful, reminding me of her mother as a teenager. But I couldn't concentrate and Orli's phone kept ringing. 'It's Dorit,' she mouthed at me. Next it was Tirza, then Hila. Each time, she shot rapid fire Hebrew into her little phone. It seemed to me Orli did all the talking. I never noticed her pause even to take a breath, let alone give her caller a chance to speak. My Hebrew wasn't fluent enough to follow the conversation and I soon got bored. I went to sit in the lobby and wait for Ruth.

When Ruth returned, Orli had already left to meet her friends. Ruth was beside me before I even noticed her come in. She sat down, her head held high, a determined tilt to her chin. My legs were shaking and my heart pounded in my chest. I took a deep breath. Recklessly I grabbed her hand. 'Ruth. I'm sorry for upsetting you. It's just that I want to talk to you about something. Something important to me. Important to our friendship.' Ruth's eyes widened. She withdrew her hand.

'Vivi, you said it all in your email. I know what you think.' Ruth took a breath. 'This isn't a good time for me to hear your views on Israel.' She paused, her composure draining away. 'I'm in such a state.' She stared at the ground. 'I can't take things in.' Her hands fluttered in front of her face. 'I'm so angry. Can't make sense of things.' She rubbed her eyes. 'I'm not in a very good space right now.' Still, she wouldn't look at me. 'And all this craziness from David. It's like he's flipped. I'm so ashamed for what he did to you and shocked.'

'I'm not carrying any anger towards you about what David did, Ruth. It's not about that. It's more about what's going on for you and for me and why I decided to come to Beyt Nattif last year. I need to talk to you about all that.'

'I need you to listen to me, not to tell me things.' Ruth glared at me, then quickly looked away.

'I always listen to you,' I said. 'But you don't listen to me, not about really important things.' Talking to Ruth was like walking around lost in a fog. I couldn't figure out what the truth was.

'Don't be so dramatic,' Ruth said, scowling. 'You always exaggerate everything.'

I felt like yelling at her but held myself back. It would just confirm Ruth's accusation. Slowly and deliberately, I said, 'One of the things we argued about was Barak's so-called generous offer. Well, while Barak was prime minister and during the time of the Oslo Peace Process, the number of Israeli settlers doubled and the land area of the settlements tripled in the West Bank. So..'

'Don't dump facts and figures on me,' Ruth said. 'I don't want to be lectured by you. You shouted at me and called me names. You picked up a chair and waved it around, like you were going to smash it up or hit me with it. That's when I left the house.'

I frowned. Did I really wave a chair around? I didn't remember that at all. 'You said some unforgivable things too. But okay. Fair enough. You're right. I didn't behave very well. Anyway, let's forget about all that. The argument started when you said I had no right to an opinion because I don't live in Israel and don't know what it's like living here. Do you remember?'

'Yes, and maybe I still think that,' Ruth said. She crossed her arms. 'And I don't want to hear your opinions right now. I told you I'm just not up for it at the moment.'

'The thing is Ruth, I do have an opinion. Well more than that really. What I have are passionate feelings. You've made it impossible for me to share with you what I feel. It's like I'm being dishonest when I'm with you. It's such a big part of my life I've got to talk to you.'

Ruth shot an exasperated glance at me. 'Do you know why I block you? It's because I don't want to have you going on and on at me. You put me down. You make me feel stupid. You always have the complete analysis, the answers. You know the right way to do things, to think about things.' Ruth wrapped her arms around her knees. Tears trickled down her cheeks.

'What are you talking about?' I asked. I felt out of my depth. It was impossible to have a straightforward conversation with Ruth.

'When I need your support, you're not here for me.' The trickle became a flow. Ruth lowered her head and hid behind her sobs.

I scowled at the top of Ruth's head. I wanted to slap her. Instead I sputtered, 'What do you mean, I'm not here for you? As soon as Orli phoned and told me Yigal had been killed, I dropped everything and flew to Israel to be with you. Do you think I don't have a life? That I can leave my work, Claire, Noah, just like that. And the cost of the flight! There were no flights from Portland. I had to go to Seattle. And last year, I did come to see you. David wasn't exactly welcoming. Was he? In fact, he beat me up. And you have the *chutzpah* to say I'm not here for you.' I stood up suddenly. I felt an overwhelming urge to run away and cry.

'At least Noah's alive. Do you have any idea what it's like for me?' Ruth jumped up, blazing with anger.

'But that's why I came here. I didn't come because …because I wanted to argue with you about politics.'

'You don't know what it's like. You don't know. You can't know.' She was sobbing again. I bit my lip. I glanced at Ruth's face and saw the sad, beaten-down expression. Fighting back my irritation, I sat down.

'Let's start again,' I said. I hesitated, then spoke slowly, carefully weighing each word. 'Ruth, I'm struggling. I don't know how to show you I care about you. I don't know any other way than what I'm doing. You're my best friend. My best friend in the whole world.' Ruth gave no sign of acknowledgement. 'Ruth I love you. I mean, I love you like family. When I heard Yigal had been killed, I had to be with you. I knew you'd be devastated. I know how I'd feel if Noah were killed.'

Still no sign from Ruth. 'I came because I want to be here with you, to comfort you. I imagined we'd cry together and talk about your beautiful Yigal. But you seem angry with me, bringing up things from the past.'

With that, I ground to a halt. The sound of my voice, warbling into the silence, unnerved me. I knew if I kept talking I'd end up in another embarrassing poor-me tirade. I glanced at Ruth but she was staring at the tiled floor. I waited. Confronted with Ruth's wall of pain, I realised further explanation would not work. I counted to 100 in my head. Silently I named the letters of the Hebrew alphabet and practised the few words of Arabic I'd learned from Wahid.

Ruth's jaw was clenched. Her body swayed back and forth. Her breathing was ragged. As if it were an effort to get the words out, she asked, 'The people you stayed with, they lost a son, didn't they? How old was he?'

Surprised, I looked closely at her. 'Ahmed was sixteen.'

'When did he die?'

'In May 2002, about five months before Yigal was killed.'

'They're still together, aren't they? They're carrying on living their lives. It's not like that for me.' At that, Ruth held out her arms to me, like a child in need of a cuddle.

'Oh, everything's falling apart. I can't do it. I can't go on,' she cried. I pulled her into my arms and rocked her back and forth, tears pouring down my own cheeks. On the bench in the public lobby of the hotel, I felt we were in a row boat on a stormy sea with the safety of land just out of reach.

But storms eventually subside and row boats come in to shore. I led Ruth to my room. I ran a bath for her and left her to soak while I sat on the end of the bed. When Ruth emerged from the bathroom, she was wearing my light cotton kimono bathrobe. Her hair was wrapped turban like in a white hotel towel. She plumped the pillows, threw the bedding back and sat at the head of the bed. Her movements were deliberate. My turn to speak had not yet come.

'Vivi,' Ruth said. 'I need to talk to you. I am in a mess but it's not just about Yigal being killed and David acting out. At the *shiva*, a year ago, I overheard Yigal's commanding officer saying Yigal ... Yigal...' She tried to speak through her sobs. 'Yigal (sob) shot (sob) he shot (sniff) a little boy (gulp) a kid (sob) and killed him.' The last words came out in a wail. My heart missed a beat. I felt icy cold. I paced around the room rubbing my arms to warm myself. My teeth chattered. My mind went numb. I didn't know what to say. I sank down on the floor and buried my head in my arms.

Ruth brought herself under control. 'Vivi, please just listen to me. Don't say anything. I'm so confused and I'm easily thrown off course. But I've been having these disturbing thoughts and you're the only one I can share them with.' She gave me a pleading look.

I nodded. I was too overwhelmed to argue. I closed my eyes and waited for her to speak. She was silent. The silence drifted from Ruth to me. Gently but persistently, it sought the corners of my mind, gathering up my thoughts and feelings and sensations and bringing them into the space between us. It collected Ruth's and nudged all of her into the space. The silence filled the room. When I opened my eyes, Ruth took a deep breath and spoke.

'I know the boy's mother, the boy that Yigal killed. I don't know her name or how many of her children are still alive. I don't know where she lives or what her favourite food is. I don't know how old she is or whether she's a morning person or a night owl. But I know there's a raw, gaping hole in her heart. I know there's a tight, clenched feeling in her chest. I know her pillow is wet with her tears, her mind is racing with bitterness and grief and the unfairness of it all. I know her son's smile and his boy-presence lingers around the edges of her mind. I know her first thought in the morning is of her son and the last thought she has before she falls asleep is of her son. I know that missing him is like a physical ache. I know she understands now, what she didn't truly understand before, that he was precious beyond words. I know she cannot believe she will never see him ever again.'

In the silence that followed, I closed my eyes and let my thoughts come and go. The silence stretched comfortably into the evening. Twenty minutes passed before Ruth spoke once more.

'A few nights ago, I dreamed I was walking along on a clearly marked concrete path on solid ground. Without my noticing it, the path became a bed of quicksand. Before I could call for help, I'd sunk up to my neck. I knew I wouldn't survive. It was all over.'

To my surprise, Ruth looked peaceful and calm. She said dreamily, her eyes closed. 'When I first came to live in Israel, I went all over. Exploring, hiking, discovering Israel. I went by bus, I hitch-hiked, I got lifts with friends. Most of the time I went with David. I was in love. I felt wonderful. I thought I was in love with David. Well, yes, I was in love with David.' Ruth smiled at me. 'But it was more than that. I was in love with Israel. I was madly, passionately in love with this land. This sky. These hills. This air. The way the sunlight caresses the land. The way every cell of my body comes alive in this place. The magic that twinkles at me from every rock and bush and hill. I felt as if I'd come home. As if I'd been waiting for thousands of years and now I was home. It felt right. It was meant to be.'

'But now Yigal is dead and the magic is gone. And I see things differently. But in between the grief and the pain and the disbelief and the rage and the numbness and the confusion, I get these moments of joy, of love. Like I'm waking up. It's so strange. And I don't know where it's taking me.'

It was certainly strange and I didn't have an answer to any of it. Before I could think of the right thing to say, we heard hammering on the door and a babble of over-excited teenage voices. Ruth laughed and leapt out of the bed. On the way to the door, she hugged me tightly and said, 'Thank you Vivi. That's just what I needed. You really helped me.'

'I didn't do anything,' I said to her back. 'How did I help you?' But there was no point arguing. Orli and her friends crowded into the room, talking loudly, filling the space with their wild energy. Before I stepped into the bubbling stream, I had a fleeting thought. Maybe, just maybe, I didn't have to do anything to help Ruth. Maybe it was enough just to be with her and not say a word.

Remembering that visit two years ago cheered me up but it didn't help me back to sleep. It was still dark. The sun wouldn't rise for another hour. Claire was lying on her side, breathing evenly, deeply asleep. I crept out of bed quietly so as not to wake her and tiptoed downstairs. I wanted to be with Ruth, to hear her voice, to find out where her journey was taking her, two years later. I phoned her home number in Tsur Hadassah, my heart beating fast with anticipation. David answered the phone and in his usual curt manner, told me Ruth was out. Did I believe him? No, but I let it go. He'd lost his power to keep us apart. I would be in touch with Ruth another time.

CHAPTER 28

Yigal

After Fahmi's talk to the young fighters, Aisha and I went back to the Other World Checkpoint. There we hung out in timeless space, watching clouds. We marked the passage of the months and years by occasional forays to the world of the living. Neither of us enjoyed these trips. We did them out of a sense of duty. I went because I needed to know my mom was all right while Aisha went to check on her dad and her little sister. We knew we couldn't do anything practical to help but we couldn't move on until we were satisfied they would be okay.

Aisha was particularly torn up about her sister. Fazia had started wetting the bed soon after Aisha died and hadn't spoken a word since their house was demolished. In the last year, the bed-wetting stopped but the muteness carried on, causing Aisha agonies of guilt. Aisha's dad was still moping about the house though she was less bothered about him. He'd been depressed for as long as Aisha could remember and she had come to accept he probably always would be, no matter what was going on around him.

And my mom was sure hard to reach. No matter how often I was with her and no matter what I did to comfort her, she couldn't sense my presence. She was so caught up in her head, in her guilt and her grief, she couldn't allow me in. Even when I was singing her favourite songs in her ear or stroking her hair or reminding her of the fun times we had together when I was little, even then she blocked me out. I badly wanted a sign from her, a sign that let me know she heard me. There had been nothing at all during the first two years and only the most fleeting and haphazard signs over the last year. Still I kept going back and I kept hoping.

The last trip to my family was hard for a different reason. My cousins, Tom and Simon, were visiting my parents and staying in my old bedroom. By listening in on their conversations, I figured out it was August 2005. Tom has a job in his father's real estate business and Simon's in law school. Both are planning their weddings. Hearing about their lives was painful. It isn't that I'm into real estate or law but I still want all the things you do in life, like getting married and making a living and travelling and everything Tom and Simon are doing which are all the things I will never do.

Since my return to the Other World Checkpoint, I've been feeling fed up. I don't feel like watching the clouds or talking to Aisha. I drift along the dusty pathways, absorbed in my jealousy.

'Things are changing,' Aisha says. 'But I can't figure out what's different.'

Reluctant to let go of my misery, I glance quickly around me. The barbed wire is still here and the concrete barriers, as is the watch tower on the rocky mound and the concrete pyramids. But I sense it too. Something is different. It bothers me I can't pinpoint the change. I stare at a fence post. Was it always tilting at such an absurd angle? Why did I never notice the huge gaps in the pathways?

Clouds still float across the sky but now they're embossed with grey smudges instead of dazzling me with their whiteness. Before, I watched individual clouds moving about on their own fascinating but mysterious business. Now there's a single unbroken cloud pockmarked with patches of blue, like eyes to another world. As I watch, wisps of cloud plaster over the blue. When the eyes are shut, I am seized with unease and anticipation. Aisha, too, is restless and moody. She paces nearby and often looks over at me but rarely speaks.

'Maybe it's going to rain,' I say, more to break the silence than because I think it will rain.

Aisha nods distractedly and chews her lips. In a whisper, she says, 'Where's Hassan? We haven't seen him for …for ages.'

'You're right,' I say, turning in circles and looking in all directions. 'Hassan and his football. I wonder where he is.'

The heavy grey cloud hangs over us. It's so close I can reach up and touch it. Will Aisha vanish like Hassan? Or for that matter, will I? Whatever is in store for us, I sense it will happen soon.

'Yigal,' Aisha says. She's looking at me with a strange expression. 'I wish…' She clams up.

'What?' I ask, irritable that she doesn't say any more. The cloud is pressing down on my head.

'I wish…. well, I guess I wish I'd met Fahmi before I decided, you know…before I decided to become a martyr.'

The cloud is no longer grey but black and menacing. I try to lighten the atmosphere. 'You unfaithful woman!' I say, clutching my heart and moaning. 'After one meeting with the grinning Fahmi, you want to elope. Girl, he's too old for you. And to think all along, I believed you were in love with me. I'm devastated.' Aisha stares at me perplexed. She does not know how to take a joke.

'Maybe…' she says, looking at me with such seriousness I shudder. 'Maybe martyrdom wasn't…' Aisha frowns and chews her lips.

'Maybe your mother could have told you better ways of getting a boyfriend,' I say. In the distance, lightning streaks through the gloom. There's an electric excitement in the air. Aisha makes a half-hearted attempt at a smile. 'You're right. Maybe I should have listened to my mother.' She traces a pattern in the dust with her foot. Without looking at me, she says, 'If I had, then you would still be alive.'

There's a flash of lightning and I see Hassan in the distance kicking his football. 'Hassan,' I shout. But he's gone. I turn to Aisha. 'That's right,' I say, 'I would have been alive.' Another flash of lightning lights up the sky, this one so close it leaves me tingling. I would have been alive but not awake, I think to myself.

A gust of wind erases Aisha's dust drawing. The slanting fence post falls over. The gaps in the pathway open wider. Hail stones fall, dissolving the concrete barriers and demolishing the pyramids. The Other World Checkpoint is breaking up.

I reach for Aisha's hand. 'It's happening. Come with me,' I say urgently. 'It may be the last time I see my family.'

As I concentrate my thoughts on Orli, the watch tower slides down the rocky mound and fragments into a spectacular dust cloud. For a moment, I'm in both worlds at once. I can hear the crashing of the wind and the hailstones in the Other World Checkpoint at the same time as I hear shouting in the world of the living. The shouting is accompanied by a chorus of cheering and singing. I hear Arabic, Hebrew and English. Out of the blur, the only words I recognize are the frequently repeated phrase, 'leave our land'. Snatches of song mingle with clapping and cheering. A solitary chant in a language I'm not familiar with rises above the babble of voices. Beneath the tumult, a bulldozer engine throbs heavily.

I'm struggling to bring the scene into focus. There's something odd about my vision. Instead of the usual things I expect to see in the world of the living, like people and trees and cars, I see waves and lines in sharp, vivid colours, all in constant, rapid motion. When I squint a certain way, I can make out ghost-like human shapes moving about within the field of colour. The waves seem to link the ghosts to each other and to radiate from within the ghosts but there's so much movement it's hard to see how they're related. Except for one straight blue line coming out of an orange ghost, there are no distinguishable, separate beings. There is just a single unified mass. I watch as the mass surges forwards and backwards, scattering and reforming. Within the field of colour, some of the ghosts beat others with batons. They point guns and shout. A black spray penetrates the space and I recognise tear gas. The waves explode and billow in all directions as a sound bomb is detonated. From the edges of the field, ghosts threw rocks into the centre. As I watch, the ghosts disperse in small groups. They are still connected by waves of colour but with less intensity and movement.

Aisha and I are drawn to a group of people getting into a jeep. They are still insubstantial but are more easily recognisable as separate beings. One of them is my dad, another my sister. Three soldiers are with them. Dad and a soldier are shoving Orli into the jeep. She kicks and screams but they soon overpower her. Dad sits on one side of Orli and the soldier on the other. The two soldiers in the front seat are embarrassed and drive off quickly.

Black clouds cover the sky. A gale force wind is blowing. 'Hurry,' Aisha says.

'Orli, Dad, I've got to say good-bye now.' Panicking, I look to Aisha for help. I don't know what to say. A few heavy hail stones fall on the windscreen. Aisha gives me an agonised look. 'Quick. Say it now,' she says.

'Dad. Orli. I want you to hear me.' I am shouting now above the din of the hail stones and the wind. 'I love you both. I don't know how to say this but it's not what you think. Just love each other. We're all part of the same big family. We can't get away from each other. There's no way out.'

The jeep is dissolving around me under the force of the storm. I shout good-bye one last time and then it's all gone. No jeep. No hail. No Israelis. No Palestinians. No Aisha. No me. Just pure light.

CHAPTER 29

Ruth

She was short and plump and waved her arms in the air when she talked. She wore an ankle-length black leather coat over a pink tunic top and black trousers. I guessed she was about ten years younger than me. Under her loose white head scarf, her black hair was tied back in a pony tail. She spoke good English with a strong accent and a quick energy. Like an actor, she commanded my total attention. This woman had presence.

'My name is Leila Habibi,' she said when it was her turn to introduce herself. 'It is not easy for me to get here. I do not enjoy the support of my family to come to this meeting. My twelve year old daughter, Fazia, she clings to me and she sobs. My heart is breaking to see her so frightened. My husband, he suffers from depression. Today was a bad day. Today he could not get out of bed. My heart is breaking to see him so beaten, so sad. My 17 year old son, Osama, he is a fighter. He is angry I meet with Israelis. He yells at me. 'Mama this Forum you go to, it is disloyal to our people. Only traitors go. You are stupid. You are naïve. You bring dishonour to our family.' My heart is breaking to see him so bitter, so quick to seek violence.' She took a breath and slowly scanned the group of twelve Israelis and Palestinians. When she looked at me, something clicked. I felt a jolt of surprise, as if some understanding had passed between us. Embarrassed and confused, I looked down at my lap. She hesitated before she spoke again.

'I tell my family I have enough of suffering with the death of my daughter Aisha. My hope for peace, for an end to war, is here with you. My heart is happy to be with all of you. I want to tell you about Aisha. I want you to know her as I knew her. As she really was. Aisha was 18. She is never going to come back to throw her arms around me, to sing at the top of her lungs, to dance, to play with her little sister, to fight with her brother, to defy me, to argue with me, to be a young girl about to become an adult, a girl with promise and hope and everything before her. I cannot accept she is gone forever. No, it is not believable.'

She ended on a whisper, shaking her head in disbelief. Yes, yes, I feel that too, I thought. Again, she looked around the group. People nodded and smiled at her. When she looked at me, I felt a tremor run through me. The tears hovering on the edges of my eyes spilled over. This time, I did not look away.

'Aisha was a passionate girl, even as a little child,' Leila continued. 'When she was six years old, I brought her on her first demonstration. She was a leader even then. She would bang a saucepan with a wooden spoon. She would lead the children. She would sing and shout slogans. She did it with energy, with enthusiasm. Aisha had no fear. She would walk right up to the Israeli soldiers in their tanks with their machine guns pointing at her and she would shout at them and tell them off. It was terrifying to be Aisha's mother. Everyday I am sick in my stomach with fear worrying will she arrive home from school safely. Worrying, worrying, worrying.' Everyone in the group, Israelis and Palestinians, nodded at this. We all knew worry.

'Aisha has, she had a generous spirit, a big heart. She would go out of her way to help other children or anyone she saw in trouble. She cared about justice, about a Palestinian state, about our rights. If she had lived, I think she would have been a politician, like Hanan Ashrawi. She would have travelled to America and Europe to speak on our behalf. You see, she was bright. She did well at school and she was a hard worker. Whatever she set her mind to, she achieved. She would have gone to university. I think she would have studied law or politics. She had a purpose in life. She was not depressed. She was a happy girl.'

When Leila stopped speaking, there was silence in the room. Not a lonely silence but a shared one. Minutes passed until Moshe gently asked if Leila wanted to say anything more.

'Yes, but I am finding it hard to say it,' Leila said. We all nodded, encouraging her. 'No you don't understand. All I have said about Aisha is true. But she had a dark side. I knew about it and I hoped it was an adolescent phase, that she would grow out of it. She sometimes got carried away with extreme ideas, ideas about violence and revenge. The heroes she worshipped were freedom fighters, martyrs, suicide bombers, people who died for a cause. She made a scrap book of Palestinian women who martyred themselves. I found it after her death. I ripped it to pieces, I am so angry with it. I am angry that an impressionable, idealistic, beautiful girl would be attracted to such terrible, violent ideas. And I am overcome with hatred for those people in our society who took advantage of her passion and her idealism, who exploited her for their own ends. But I do have to accept that my Aisha, my beautiful, happy daughter, was attracted to violence. I want to see her as pure, like she was when she was born, but the truth is she had her own views, and many were different from mine. I taught her to stick up for herself, to be a fighter and she was. But she didn't follow my teachings about non-violence and peace and justice. She didn't respect my philosophy. She went her own way.'

'And now she is dead. She will never have the chance to grow out of her silly, adolescent ideas. She will never be the leader of our people I know she could have been. She will never have a family and children of her own. She will never come running in and say 'I love you Mama.''

'My heart is broken by her death. I am in pieces. I come to the Forum in pieces. I come because I hope our work, Israelis and Palestinians together, will make me whole again. I hope together we will create a future where our children can grow up to be all they were meant to be when we brought them into the world.'

Leila looked straight at me as she finished speaking. She smiled, a sad, desperate smile. I wanted to hug her. I wondered what kind of crowd Aisha had got involved with and whether her silly, dangerous ideas had anything to do with her death. I wondered if Leila had managed to say all she wanted to say to us. It was on the tip of my tongue to ask her how Aisha had died but before I could speak, Moshe asked me to introduce myself.

Tongue-tied, I bent my head and stammered, 'My name is Ruth.' Tears choked me and the words stuck in my throat. Moshe, sitting on my right, patted my arm. A woman on my left with a black head scarf tied tightly around her head squeezed my left hand. Everyone waited patiently for me to pull myself together. Embarrassed, I twisted my shirt into a knot trying desperately to stop snivelling. I looked at Leila. She smiled at me, a kind smile. Encouraged, I spoke to her, the words tumbling out in a rush, gasping as if I were running uphill.

'Yigal was killed. He was 19. He was a corporal in the army. He was my first born son.'

Leila closed her eyes in pain. She nodded slowly. I pushed myself to keep talking and soon the sobbing eased off. 'Before Yigal was killed, I closed my eyes to what was happening in Israel, to the reality of the occupation. I didn't know. I didn't try to find out. And when he was killed, I was able to see for the first time.'

'What I need to share with you, well it's hard for me to talk about it.' My face turned hot. I forced myself to continue. Leila kept nodding supportively. 'Like you, Leila, I am in pieces. I am in pieces because Yigal is dead. And I am in pieces because of what I learned about him after his death. My beautiful, funny, charming, sweet, loving boy. He too had a dark side.'

I wondered how Leila would react. Would she be shocked and outraged? Would she shun me? But the need to unburden myself was greater than my fear. I ploughed on.

'When he was patrolling with his unit, he shot and killed a 13 year old boy.' There, I said it. Leila still kept nodding at me. Moshe and the woman on my left kept patting my arms. The rest of the group continued to look at me with sympathy and sadness. I breathed a sigh of relief. Perhaps, it wasn't such a surprise to them as it had been to me. Oh, I had been in denial!

'He never told me about it. As if it was a normal thing to do. As if that's what you do when you're in the army. That's what my husband said and my neighbour and my husband's friend. But no, I can't accept that. I can't come to terms with it. That is not the Jewish state I came here to build.'

'I am filled with anger at the army who gave him a gun and sent him into places where he would be attacked and have to make impossible decisions about whether to shoot or not. And I feel hatred for those politicians who used him to hold down another people and keep them from having their own state. And I curse the settlers who force us to send our children to defend them. And I wonder what part I played. I wanted my comfortable life in a Jewish state and I never questioned the cost of having that until Yigal's death.'

'So I come here for the same reasons as you do. I want a different vision of Israel so none of our children are faced with these inhuman situations. So all of our children can grow up to be the best they can be instead of being turned into murderers.'

To my surprise, Leila rushed across the room and grabbed my hands in hers. 'Yes. Yes,' she said. 'Thank you. You said what is in my heart. But I am not as brave as you. I could not bring myself to say what I wanted to say.'

Moshe interrupted. 'Ruth, I'm sorry. We have to go. I just heard there are tanks on the road and we need to be out of here right now.'

'Ruth,' Leila said with urgency. 'I want to stay in touch with you. Here is my phone number.' She scribbled her phone number on a scrap of paper and handed it to me.

'Where do you live, Leila?' I asked.

'For the moment, we're living with my cousin in the al-Aroub Refugee Camp. You will call me, won't you?'

I nodded, hardly taking in what she was saying. Then I ran to catch up with Moshe. As I squeezed through the concrete rubble at the road block, I felt my finger tips tingling. But this time it wasn't an anxiety attack. This time, I was tingling with hope.

CHAPTER 30

Vivi

One week after Orli's pre-dawn wake-up call, she woke me again with another early morning phone call. This time, I answered after the second ring.

'Vivi I know it's six your time and I waited two hours to phone you and I can't wait any more and I've got to tell you what happened I escaped I got away and Mom helped me.'

'Wait a minute, Orli.' I rummaged on the shelf above my bed for my glasses. A hair brush clattered to the floor and papers and books rained onto Claire's side of the bed, fortunately empty since Claire was on an early shift at the hospital. Once I'd found my glasses and looked at my watch, I was ready to listen. 'OK. Go on. What did Ruth help you with?'

'I escaped Dad kidnapped me he and Shlomo grabbed me when I was leaving work it was yesterday God it seems like a week ago I was at work at the cafe I finished at three I came out I was walking along thinking about the speaking tour and what I need to do and suddenly Dad was next to me saying I want to talk to you in an angry voice we'd already had …'

'Orli. Whoa. Slow down. Take a breath, will you?'

'… blow up last week when I told him you'd invited me on the tour it's a good thing you're so far away Vivi because he sure hates you if you were here he'd probably break every bone in your body I said No way there's no point talking to you You never listen to me You just yell at me Like what's the point? We've already said everything we're going to say to each other and then Shlomo appeared I don't know where from and he starts on at me as if I'm going to listen to him what an idiot and I said no go away Except I was starting to…'

'You're talking too fast. What were David and Shlomo doing in Haifa?'

'..a bit scared I don't get scared well hardly ever but there was something about the way they were talking to me like they had a plan and I was all alone and I got out my phone I was going to call Mom or Hila she's my friend I'm staying with in Haifa and Dad snatched it off me then they tied me up and pushed me into the back of Shlomo's car and put tape ..'

'Orli. Slow down. I can't follow what you're saying.'

'over my mouth and tied my hands behind my back and tied my ankles together and drove me all the way like that from Haifa to Shlomo's place in Gush Etzion and …'

'What are you saying? That David and Shlomo tied you up and kidnapped you?' I sat down on the bed, gripping the phone with one hand and clutching my throat with the other.

Orli took a deep breath and spoke slowly. 'Yes, that is exactly what happened. Really.'

'And they did this because?'

'Why do you think? Because Dad doesn't want me to come on this speaking tour. He's, like, totally opposed to it. Did you think he would agree to it? After what he did last year when I told him I wouldn't serve in the army? That's why I left home and went to live in Haifa with Hila and her mother.'

'What happened when you got to Shlomo's place?' I retreated under the duvet. Any thoughts of getting ready for work had vanished.

'They just yelled at me for hours and hours. They took it in turns. They are so stupid, Vivi. They really thought if they argued with me and told me how wrong I was, that I would change my mind and see things from their point of view. They never asked me what I think or why.'

'Who did the yelling?'

'Shlomo and his wife Devora and Dad and some other people I didn't know. Ilana, that's Shlomo's sister, she was there and her husband. Their tactics were crude. I actually got bored. You see, they think you brainwashed me so what they're doing is like cult deprogramming. I saw a programme on TV about it so I know what they're up to.'

'Cult deprogramming? What are you talking about? What cult?'

'You, Vivi,' Orli said, laughing. 'They think you're the cult and you've got me under your influence. It's all your fault.'

'Oh for Heaven's sake! What is the matter with them? How did I become a cult?'

'Oh, cult's not the right word. This is what they said.' Orli made her voice deep and menacing. 'Vivi is a poisoning, self-hating Jew, a predatory lesbian, a twisted evil personality who's got her clutches in you because she wants to control you and destroy Israel. Do you think she cares about you? No. She came to Israel to aid terrorists. Do you know where she was when Yigal was killed by a suicide bomber? With Arabs! Your so-called friend is an enemy. She stands with those people who want us all dead. She has betrayed the Jewish people. At a time when Israel is isolated and under attack, when anti-semitism is on the increase, when Jews need to pull together and support Israel, that's when Vivi goes and backs the terrorists. What she's done is unforgivable. She's poisoned your mind.' There was a silence while Orli caught her breath.

Once I had a chance to digest this information, I said, 'Well, I haven't made a good impression on your dad and his friends, have I?' My tone was light but inside I was shaking with rage. Predatory lesbian, indeed! What *chutzpah*! 'What did you do, Orli?'

'I didn't pay any attention to what they said about you. I thought it was funny. It was what they said about justifying the occupation of our ancestral homeland that wound me up. And when they said the Arabs are scum, Islam is a religion of evil and all the Arabs should be driven out of our land, by force if necessary. Then I couldn't help it. I argued back but there was no point. They had a lot to say in reply but none of it made any sense. Basically they believe there's no moral equivalence. Like, what's a few demolished houses or dead Palestinian children compared to thousands of years of anti-semitic violence and the Holocaust?'

'You can't get anywhere arguing with extremists,' I said, knowing from experience how frustrating and futile such arguments were.

'You're right,' Orli said. 'So then, I tried going on the offensive. Whenever they stopped ranting long enough to ask me whether I agreed with them yet, I shouted, 'I hold you responsible for the murder of my brother."

'What did they say to that?' I asked.

'They didn't know what to say. They changed tactics. That's probably when they got into slandering you. I can't remember. But most of the time, I tuned them out. I let their shouting become background noise, like the roar of traffic. I closed my eyes and pictured sweet little Habiba and her sisters in Beyt Nattif who you took me to visit two years ago. They were so friendly and welcoming to me, an Israeli girl, even though their brother had been killed by settlers like Shlomo. And I looked at the picture that's always in my mind, the one about Yigal shooting a boy playing football in his school playground. And when I opened my eyes and saw these bullies holding me hostage, I realised they're nothing more than scared, desperate people. And what they're doing is begging me, a 19 year old girl, not to tell the world their cause is unjust. Then I felt sorry for them.'

'You feel sorry for the people who kidnapped you and held you prisoner and intimidated you?'

'Yes, I do. Like Shlomo said, they feel misunderstood because most people in the civilised world see us Jews as the perpetrators of the violence instead of its victims. Well the way I see it, if you want to be seen as a victim, then you want people to feel sorry for you. So I feel sorry for them. They're victims of their fear and of their distorted thinking and of wanting to be victims.'

'That's a profound insight, Orli,' I said. 'Certainly, they're driven by fear. So tell me, how did you escape?'

'Well, finally they let me go to sleep. They put me in a bedroom with three of Devora's daughters, a girl called Maya who's 14 and two younger girls. Devora stood guard outside the room. I got up about five times pretending to need the toilet. Each time, Maya followed me and Devora had to wake up and watch me. I made a lot of noise, shouting and banging things, trying to annoy everyone in the house. It was like a game we were playing, except I was the only one having fun. In the morning, I kept pounding on the bedroom door. I demanded to be taken back to Haifa or I'd call the police. Shlomo shouted at me. He was angry in a scary way. He threatened to tie me up and keep me prisoner for a week so I wouldn't be able to come on the speaking tour. I decided to cooperate, in case he really meant it. Then Ilana, Shlomo's sister, arrived with about ten children and asked me to come with her to Hebron. She was nice to me, said she'd been a rebellious teenager herself. She even told Shlomo off for being so aggressive to me. I knew it was an act but I agreed to go with her. I thought it would be a lot easier to get away from her than from Shlomo. And it was.'

'What's it like in Hebron?' I'd never been there myself but I knew that a small group of hard line Jews lived in a settlement right in the middle of the large Arab city. The Jewish settlement was guarded by soldiers, at least one for each settler. It was surrounded by more than 100 unmanned roadblocks and 18 manned checkpoints. And it was the site of two horrific massacres – the murder of 66 Jews by Arab nationalists in 1929 and the 1994 murder of 29 Muslims at prayer by the Jewish nationalist, Baruch Goldstein.

'It's bad, like the worst you could imagine. Ilana lives on the Shuhada Road, which used to be a main commercial street. It's a wide street, with palm trees in the middle. Now it's totally off-limits to Palestinians. All their shops and homes are boarded up. They've all left. There were soldiers in full combat uniform jogging up and down the road and military posts with camouflage netting. You wouldn't believe the graffiti I saw on the boarded up buildings. 'Death to the Arabs' on one and 'Rabin is waiting for Arik' on another.'

'I guess Sharon's not too popular with the Hebron settlers after disengaging from Gaza.' I said.

'Vivi, I'm fading out. I haven't eaten since yesterday and I didn't get any sleep last night.' Her voice suddenly turned groggy.

'Why don't you get something to eat and call me back later?'

'It's Ramadan, Vivi. Sunset's not for another half hour. Then we can eat.'

'Hang on, Orli. A minute ago, you were walking along Shuhada Road with Shlomo's sister and her children. Now you're observing Ramadan, presumably not with Shlomo's sister. What happened in between then and now?'

'OK. So we were walking along and I peeked around a corner and saw a narrow doorway. I couldn't tell where it led to. There was rubble around it but it wasn't completely blocked. I asked one of the children about it and he said it went to the Arab market. This kid then boasted how he and his brothers and sisters and cousins go through that doorway and cause havoc in the market. So I said, 'I don't believe you're brave enough to do that.' And he said, 'Oh yes I am.' And I said, 'How old are you? You look like you're not even nine years old.' He said he was ten. Anyway, I dared him to take me through the doorway. Not with his millions of brothers and sisters. Just him and me. He got scared then but I kept goading him until all of a sudden, he nodded and ran for it. I ran after him. I could hear his mother screaming at us to come back. When we got to the doorway, he stopped and said that was far enough. I went through and kept going.'

'Did the doorway take you out of the Jewish settlement into the Arab part of the city?'

'Yes but I didn't know where I was at first. I was walking through a closed up market. There weren't any people about. It was like the old city of Jerusalem - cobbled roads and arches, dark narrow streets. The street was covered by a wire mesh running from one side to the other. As I kept walking, I came across a few open stalls. There was a butcher shop with a skinned camel hanging in front of it. I only know it was a camel because its head was still on. I noticed the wire mesh above the street was covered in garbage. It was disgusting. I saw dirty diapers, bones, broken bottles, what looked like toilet paper, rotten food. In one place, the wire mesh was about to collapse under the weight of all the garbage. The further I got from the Jewish settlement, the more lively the market was and the more stalls were open.'

'Didn't you get any funny looks, a Jewish woman walking around on her own?' I asked, trying to imagine Orli in the Arab market.

'How would anyone know I'm Jewish? They think Jewish women wear long skirts and run through their market in gangs, carrying guns and knocking over their stalls. I was on my own wearing a head scarf and greeting people in Arabic.'

'I didn't know you spoke Arabic, Orli.'

'I've been studying it for the last year and a half. I took Arabic at school since the 7th grade but we only learned formal literary Arabic. When I left school, I had to take classes in spoken Arabic. Since I've been living in Haifa, I've met Arabs so I've had lots of chance to speak. And now I can speak fluently.'

'What about the head scarf? Where did you get that?'

'I bought it at the first clothing stall I found. I had to wade through racks of bras and jackets to find the scarves.'

'That was brave, Orli. Didn't you feel uneasy being in a strange city on your own?'

'No. They're not my enemies. They're just people, same as you and me. You taught me that, Vivi. Anyway, I'd escaped from my dad and the people who were holding me prisoner. So I was feeling good or I was until I saw four soldiers down the road, kicking a kid, a boy about 12 years old. Everyone melted away. No one went to his rescue. I was mad. I marched towards them. I don't know what I was going to do. Then all of a sudden, an old woman, no more than five feet tall, wearing a red baseball cap and a purple track suit rushed past me right up to the soldiers. She spoke to them in English with a New York accent and persuaded them to hand the boy over to her. Which they did. Then she and the boy scooted down a side street. I followed.'

'Orli, I'm glad you didn't have a confrontation with the soldiers. They might have shot you. They would have thought you're a Palestinian.'

'I know. Anita pointed that out to me later. At the time, I didn't think.'

'Anita?'

'Yeah, she's the old woman who rescued the boy from the soldiers. She's with the Christian Peacemaker Team. I went with her to her office and she told me about their work in Hebron. And then she helped me get to Mom.'

'How did she do that?'

'First I used her cell phone to call Mom because Dad had stolen my phone. I told Mom what had happened. When Mom stopped hyperventilating and freaking out, she said she knew a Palestinian woman in a nearby refugee camp she wanted to visit.'

'Ruth knows a Palestinian woman?'

'Well, she only just met her last week but they're already best friends. Anita sneaked me out. That was exciting. She didn't think it was safe to go through the checkpoint with an Israeli passport so she took me a secret way, through a tunnel between the houses. Then she got me a taxi.'

'Where are you now, Orli?'

'I'm in the al-Aroub Refugee Camp. Mom's here too. We're with a woman named Leila and her family. I collapsed as soon as I got here. They fast for a whole month. I couldn't do it. I'd die after one day. I slept for about an hour and then I woke up all buzzy and called you on Mom's phone. Hey, here's Mom. You talk to her. I've got to say goodbye. I'm passing out again. Bye.'

'It's Vivi.' I heard Orli say and then Ruth was on the phone. 'Oh Vivi, this is more than I can bear,' she said. Her voice was faint and tearful.

'It's unbelievable,' I said. 'I'm shocked. Surely even David wouldn't treat his own daughter like that. What is the matter with him?'

'Vivi I can't talk now. I'm in shock, not about the kidnapping. I've just found out something so shocking I don't know how to think about it. I'll call you in a few days.'

Sobbing, she hung up. I pulled the duvet over my head and lay there, shivering. What am I supposed to do about all this? I wondered. Did I put Orli in danger by inviting her to come on the speaking tour? Should I have known David would go to such lengths to stop her? Should I call it off? Would David and the extremists he hangs out with take out their anger against me on Ruth and Orli? What is Ruth in shock about? Oh God, what should I do now?

Just then Buber landed on top of me. Purring like a well-tuned motorbike, he pounded rhythmically on my head. I sat up and hugged him to me. 'Oh Buber, what should I do?' He wriggled indignantly, squirmed out of my grip, darted to the end of the bed and stared pointedly at the door, his tail swishing from side to side.

'Don't leave me. I need your advice, Buber. What should I do?' I stretched out my arms to him. But Buber did not come back to me. Instead, he turned his head, looked me straight in the eye and walked out of the door, his tail an exclamation mark of amazement at my ignorance. I burst out laughing. Of course, there's only one thing to do in these circumstances. Feed the cat now!

CHAPTER 31

Ruth

'Stop. Here it is,' I shouted. We were driving along a main road through open countryside. Trees, low shrubs and dry, brown fields covered the Judean hills in all directions. Just before the road turned sharply to the right, I saw Leila. She was standing by the side of the road, her hand shielding her eyes from the glare of the sun. A burly man with close cropped grey hair and a moustache stood beside her. There was no sign indicating the existence of the camp and the narrow road into it was blocked with concrete barriers.

'You want me to let you off here?' the taxi driver asked incredulously, without slowing down.

'Yes. Please. Look there are people waiting for me.' I waved frantically to Leila as we drove by.

'Lady, what is this place? I can't leave you here.'

'Turn around. I told you to take me to al-Aroub and this is it.'

'Are you nuts? This is a Palestinian refugee camp. It's not safe for you to be here.'

'Just stop the car,' I shouted. With an angry squealing of tires, the taxi driver screeched to a halt, took my money and drove off, leaving me to walk back along the dusty, busy road. Leila ran towards me.

'Welcome,' she said, hugging me warmly. She laughed when I told her about the taxi driver.

'But he's right, Ruth. It isn't safe for you here. There are extremists in this camp, people who have carried out terrorist acts. I think they would harm you if they knew you were here.'

'Even though you invited me?' I asked. I had convinced myself there could be no problems if I were Leila's guest and wore the headscarf she suggested I bring.

'Oh yes,' Leila said, nodding her head energetically. 'But don't worry. This man is the director of the camp. He will guarantee your safety while you are here.'

'No one would dare harm you while you are under my protection,' he said. He was a heavy-set, large man with an air of authority about him that instantly reassured me. 'I would like to show you around. We are building a new playground and park for the children.'

Leila interrupted. 'When Ruth's daughter arrives, then you can show them around. Until then, I think Ruth is too worried to concentrate. Isn't that so, Ruth?'

I gulped, not wanting to offend either one. But my opinion turned out not to be necessary. Leila was the more powerful party. She whisked me through the narrow streets, past the chaotic jumble of concrete houses and into her cousin's home where she was living. I hesitated at the entrance, suddenly overwhelmed by the fact I was the only Jew among many Palestinians. There were at least 20 people in the room, sitting on chairs and sofas with children on their laps or on the floor. Except for two old women, I was relieved to see that none of the women or girls had their heads covered. I wiped my sweaty hands on my trousers and took a deep breath. Leila did the introductions. I nodded and smiled at each member of her family, not taking in either their names or their relationship to Leila. But I did pay attention to three people.

'This is my husband Khalid,' Leila said, placing a protective hand on his shoulder. He nodded to me, a fleeting smile on his face, then withdrew into himself. I wondered what kind of relationship they had and whether Leila was the stronger of the two.

'And this is my 17 year old son Osama.' Osama did not grace me with even a glimmer of a smile but looked me straight in the eye, cold and hostile. He had his arms folded across his chest and his feet plant solidly on the floor. If anyone fit the description of a terrorist, Osama was the one. I grimaced uneasily at him.

'And here is my beautiful baby, my youngest daughter, Fazia.' Leila stroked the girl's head tenderly. 'She isn't a baby, of course. She is 12 years old.' Fazia was indeed beautiful with her long black hair and big brown eyes. Like her brother, she did not smile at me but instead of hostility, she seemed timid and fearful. Tears welled up in my eyes. I wanted to scoop her into my arms and cuddle her. To my surprise, Fazia took my hand and held it tight. Then she led me to a hastily cleared spot on the sofa and sat at my feet.

As soon as I sat down, my phone rang. Orli was in a taxi at the entrance to the camp. Leila, Fazia and I went to meet her. Though she impatiently said she was fine, Orli was clearly on edge. She gabbled non-stop, her story spilling out in a breathless torrent of words. Leila and I looked at each other in alarm. As soon as we were at the house, Leila bypassed the introductions and led Orli into a small bedroom. She lay on the bed and fell asleep with her shoes on. I pulled them off and Leila covered her with a blanket.

'Did you bring any photos of your son, Ruth?' Leila asked when we were settled back in the living room. I handed her a photo of Yigal taken two years before he died when he was visiting Noah and Vivi in California. In the photo, he looked relaxed and cheerful, as if he had his whole life ahead of him. I wondered what he would think of us mixing with Palestinians in a refugee camp in the Occupied Territories.

'What a handsome boy,' Leila said, smiling at me. 'My Aisha would have liked him. I wish I had a photo of Aisha to show you. But we have nothing left.'

Osama said something in Arabic and ran out of the room. Leila shouted la, la at him but he took no notice. He returned holding a rolled-up poster. Leila tried to intercept it but Osama stood between his mother and me.

He unrolled the paper and held it up for me to see. Then he said, 'Aisha. *Fii shahida.*' There was unmistakeable pride in his voice and defiance in his look. I caught my breath at the sight of his sister. Though Aisha was a strikingly beautiful young woman, it was the determined expression on her face and the machine gun in her arms that made me shudder. This was not a picture of a victim.

I looked questioningly at Leila. 'What is this?'

Leila sighed and closed her eyes. When she spoke, it was with reluctance. 'At the Forum meeting, I told you Aisha had a dark side, that she worshipped those people who martyr themselves for the cause. Violence is not my way nor is it what anyone else in my family want. Like you, we want peace. We want an end to violence. I am horrified, ashamed even, of what she did, Ruth.'

'What did she do?' I had to whisper the question. I could hardly get the words out.

Leila opened her mouth but didn't speak. Osama did. He spoke in Arabic, looking directly at me, and indicating with his head that his mother should translate. With her arms hanging limply by her side, Leila said softly, 'She strapped explosives to her body and blew up herself and an Israeli soldier at a checkpoint.'

'When?' I whispered.

'2002. The 2nd of October.'

A date. That's all she said. Yet the speaking of that date caused a whirlwind to enter the room and suck out every molecule of air. Movement, sound, words, even thoughts, all came to a standstill. I was aware of nothing but my desperate gasping for breath. We remained like that, in a vacuum, for what seemed like forever.

Then everyone came to life at once. Leila stepped towards me, arms outstretched, a look of agony on her face. I leaned back, raising my arms in front of me. The air rushed into my lungs and I shouted, 'No. No. Stay away from me.' Osama jumped back, clutching the poster to his chest, his eyes wide. Fazia hid behind Leila. Khalid, who up till then had disappeared into the background, emerged to stand beside Leila. The rest of the family shouted at Leila, filling the space with their alarm and confusion. I ran.

I ran to the room where Orli had gone to sleep. Only she wasn't sleeping. She was on the phone. Seeing me enter, she said, 'It's Vivi' and handed me the phone. But it wasn't Vivi I needed at that moment. I needed Orli.

'Mom. What?' Orli asked when I hung up. 'What's so shocking you can't talk to Vivi about it?'

I paced until the sobbing subsided and my breathing became even. 'Leila's daughter, Aisha. She's the suicide bomber who killed Yigal. I just found out.'

'No way,' Orli said breathlessly, staring at me wide-eyed. 'Do they, like, approve of what she did?'

'I don't think so. Well, probably Osama does.'

'Who's Osama?'

'He's her brother. He's 17.'

'But Leila doesn't, does she, Mom? She wouldn't have come to the Forum meeting if she supported suicide bombing, would she?'

279

'No, I guess not. No. I'm sure not.'

Orli stretched out on the bed and closed her eyes. I listened to the argument coming from the living room and glanced uneasily at Orli. She was deep in thought and didn't appear to have noticed. Were we safe here? What if the rest of Leila's family were extremists like Aisha? Leila was a strong woman but she was just one. The director of the camp wasn't here to protect us. My finger tips tingled and it was becoming harder to breathe. I knew I had to stop these scary thoughts or I would trigger a full scale panic attack.

'I'm so hungry I could eat a camel,' Orli said, stretching her arms above her head. 'I saw one in the *souk* in Hebron. Are you okay, Mom?'

I didn't answer. My body was flooded with feelings. The current flowed so swift and in such a frenzy I couldn't pick out any particular feelings and hold onto them. Just at that moment, the call to prayer began and the sound of shouting came to an abrupt halt. I focused on the blanket Orli was lying on. It felt soft and warm to my touch. The smell of cooking caught my attention. I'm okay right now in this moment, I told myself. Air came in through my nose, into my lungs, down to my feet and out again. No matter what else was going on, I was still breathing. I followed my breath, in and out, in and out, until I felt calmer.

'This is a nightmare, Orli,' I said when I could speak.

'It would be if Dad were here. Can you imagine what he would do?'

'He would find some way to take revenge. And it would only make things a hundred times worse.'

'Mom, listen to me.' Orli propped herself up on one elbow. She looked exhausted. 'I've thought about this a lot. Yigal killed that Palestinian boy. Aisha killed Yigal. It's sort of like we're even. What else can we do? I don't have the heart for revenge or any more bad feeling. Let's make our peace with these people and get on with our lives. It's what Yigal would have wanted. I know that. He wasn't like Dad. Come on.' She dragged herself to her feet. We embraced, a long comforting hug. I'd never felt Yigal's presence any stronger than at that moment.

'I know you're right, Orli. But it's not that easy to let go of my feelings just like that.'

'Yeah, yeah, but isn't it harder and more painful to hold onto them? Come on, let's go in.'

Just before we entered the living room, Orli stopped behind the door and listened intently. The shouting had begun again. 'Oh God no,' she said, shaking her head. 'We've got to explain. No, that can't happen.'

She flung open the door and without introduction, spoke rapidly in Arabic. Since I couldn't understand the words, I listened to the tune, taking it all in, as if I were observing a scene in a play. I saw Orli waving her arms in the air, speaking passionately, without anger, pouring her soul out to the people in the room. Shocked into silence by the sudden appearance of an Arabic-speaking Israeli, the family, adults and children all, listened intently. Finally, Leila said something in a flat voice, her arms wrapped protectively across her belly, her head hanging down. An older, white-haired man interrupted Leila in a rude and angry tone. He then turned his back on her, hunched his shoulders submissively, and addressed himself to me and Orli, his voice low and pleading. I kept a close eye on Osama. When Orli burst into the room, Osama moved away from the wall he'd been leaning against and stood upright, feet apart, his hands in tight fists at his side, like a boxer getting ready for the fight. He scowled and stared fiercely at her, not saying a word. As she continued to speak, his position shifted. He tilted his head to one side, his fists uncoiled and his face softened. When Orli finished speaking half an hour later, Osama nodded, a slow thoughtful nod. Leila rushed over to hug Orli, tears streaming down her cheeks. The submissive man straightened his shoulders and took a breath, looking at the rest of the family with a satisfied expression. Whatever Orli had said, she'd succeeded in putting a stop to the argument.

Leila cleared two children off the sofa and squeezed in beside me. She started to say something but I shook my head. I wasn't ready for words. Trays of food appeared, brought by the girls of the family, Fazia as well. My spirits lifted at the sight of plate after plate of hummus, falafel, baba ganoush, spinach pastries, rice with pine nuts, fried chicken, cauliflower pickled salad, and mounds of flat bread.

'Leila,' I said as I filled my plate. 'Don't you feel sick eating such huge quantities of food after fasting?'

She laughed. 'Yes, I do. Often. And what's worse, I never lose weight during Ramadan. Every year, I think I will but every year, I do it all wrong. I eat a large meal after the call to prayer, I have too many sweet foods and way too much bread. I drink more coffee and I do less exercise. So I actually put on weight during Ramadan, even though I'm fasting for a month.' She patted her ample belly, pointed to her thighs and smiled shyly at me.

'I've given up trying to lose weight,' I said, noting my belly was no flatter than Leila's. 'I like food too much.' Was I really chatting about losing weight with the woman whose daughter murdered my son? Across the room, Orli and Osama were deep in conversation, surrounded by other members of the family. 'Leila, what was all that about, that argument and what Orli said?'

'As soon as we realised who you are, my cousins wanted us to leave tonight. They are frightened. They worried you would tell the army where we are and then the army would come and demolish their house and make them homeless. We put them in danger by moving in with them two years ago. You can see why they were scared.'

'No, that's ridiculous. The Israeli army wouldn't do something like that. That's unfair.'

Leila stared at me, open mouthed. Then she blinked, shook her head and shrugged. 'Anyway, your daughter convinced us neither of you would tell the army where we are living. She told us she refuses to serve in the military and is on her way to speak in the United States about it. What she said filled me with hope. I am so glad to have met you and Orli. Are you going with her?'

'No, no, no. That's Orli's thing, not mine. She is going with two soldiers who refuse to serve in the Occupied Territories and have been in prison for refusing. The tour is organised by a friend of mine in the United States. She's an active campaigner for the Palestinian cause.'

'This friend, is she Jewish?'

'Yes. Now Leila, did Orli say anything about her father, my husband David?'

'A little bit. I understand he tried to prevent her going. She said he would not approve of you being here.'

'That's for sure,' I said. 'I haven't even told him I came to the Forum meeting last week. If he knew who you were, he would certainly take revenge.'

'Ruth, we must break the cycle of violence before it destroys us all. I hope you can help your husband to understand this. I failed with Aisha despite all my efforts. I am deeply, deeply sorry for what she has done. It is not what I would have wanted. I ask your forgiveness. I don't know what else I can say.'

'I can't forgive you. Forgiveness is not part of the Jewish way of thinking.' I took her hand and held it in mine. Tears trickled down her cheeks and she bowed her head. 'I can't forgive you.' We sat in silence. Fazia offered me walnut pastries and coffee. I savoured the sweet crunchiness of the pastries and thought that anyone who could produce such delicious food must be all right. When I'd finished the last morsel of pastry and the last drop of coffee, I nudged Leila and said, 'I can only forgive you for something you yourself did to me. You didn't take my son from me. Aisha did. Look at Orli over there. She's my daughter. I gave birth to her. I raised her but she's her own person with her own views. She chose not to go into the army. Am I responsible for her choices? And Yigal, he chose to go into the army where he killed a child. Am I responsible for his choices? No, I can't forgive you for something you didn't do.'

That was the truth but only part of it. The real reason I couldn't forgive Leila was because I wasn't ready to forgive myself. The decisions I made and the decisions I should have made but didn't were all tangled up in a knot. I would have to disentangle them and see which ones contributed to this tragedy. Should I forgive myself for leaving my family in Baltimore and choosing to live in Israel? Or the decision to marry David – why didn't I listen to Vivi who warned me about him before we married? Or once married, why did I become a doormat instead of a strong partner able to stand up to him? And most confusing, did I have a part to play in Israel's trend towards militarism and aggressive policies by staying away from the political process, by not acting as a consistent voice for peace? Maybe, it would all begin to make sense someday.

'I don't claim to understand how it ended up this way, Leila. I do know we can't change the past and if we don't let go of whatever's holding us back, we won't have anything worth living for. I want us to create a vision together of the kind of world we do want to live in. What do you say?'

Leila dabbed her eyes and smiled. 'I say yes. At least we can agree on what we don't want. We don't want to lose any more of our children.'

'That's a start,' I said.

'Ruth, you must go with Orli on the speaking tour. There are so few voices like yours. Tell the world. People will listen to you. They have written us off but you, they will listen to.'

'Leila, I'm not anybody important or famous. No one's interested in what I have to say. I've never even spoken in public before.'

'Ruth, we are in prison here. I cannot even leave al-Aroub, let alone travel to the United States. It is America who is keeping this region in conflict and the American people are fed lies about us. You must tell them the truth. Tell them what Israel is really about. For my sake, Ruth, and Fazia's and Osama's. We don't deserve to live like this. And they will listen to you. You are the mother of a martyred soldier who died in the service of his country. For you to speak, that is really something.'

'I think I have a more important task to do here.'

'Of course, of course. When you return, we will work together to create a new society. But now, promise me you'll go. You have more power than you think.'

'I can't be your voice, you know. I don't know what I can do. I'm still finding my own voice and my own way. Anyway, I have confidence in Orli.'

'Don't just leave it to your children to sort out. There are no bystanders in this conflict. No one is innocent.'

'God, Leila, you and Vivi are so alike.'

Orli and Osama snaked their way through the people in the room to stand in front of us. 'Mom,' Orli said. 'There are a few people Osama wants me to meet. We'll be back in about an hour.' The meal had brought the sparkle back to her eyes. She no longer seemed on the edge of collapse.

'Oh no, you won't.' Leila and I shouted the words in unison and then looked at each other in surprise. Orli rolled her eyes and Osama made a dismissive gesture. We all opened our mouths and drew breath but before any of the four of us took the next step in the authoritative parent-wilful teenager dance, I was suddenly struck by the absurdity of the situation. A giggle bubbled beneath the surface of my stern parental expression. It gained momentum and burst out, catching Leila by the throat. Soon Leila and I were laughing so hard tears were pouring down our cheeks and we were clutching each other and gasping for breath. Our teenagers looked down their noses at us, glanced at one another with obvious concern for our sanity and then diplomatically exited from the room without further argument. Whatever they were up to was clearly none of our business.

Two days later, I sat at my kitchen table putting the finishing touches on my letter to David. The house was clean, the laundry done, my suitcase packed with sweaters and a raincoat for the colder weather in Portland and San Francisco. I reread the letter one last time.

David,

There's a casserole in the fridge for tonight's dinner and more in the freezer for the next few nights. I will be away for three weeks. I think you know why. I won't bother to spell out how I feel about what you did. If you don't know already, then I hope you will use the three weeks without me to start thinking about the consequences of your actions on our marriage. You obviously didn't do that kind of thinking before, so here's your chance. If you do know how I'm feeling, then I sincerely hope you will use these three weeks to come up with a plan of what you are prepared to do to save our marriage. That is, if you want our marriage to continue. If you don't, then say so and get out. I won't stop you, though it's not what I want or even believe is possible. We've been through too much together. We're stuck with each other but not at any price.

David, we're into final status negotiations now. If you are willing to treat me with respect, to accept me as I am and not to resort to violence, then I'm willing to find a way to be with you. The thing is, despite everything you've done, I still love you and have hope for our marriage.

Ruth

Well, that couldn't be clearer, I thought, as I taped it on the fridge door. Then I walked out of the house and made my way to Ben Gurion airport.

PART FOUR
October 2006

CHAPTER 32

Yigal

I throw my head back and push with my legs. That's better. Now I can see snatches of blue sky. No clouds today. Just solid blue sky. In between me and sky is a makeshift wire mesh ceiling running from one side of the street to the other. I'm in a market at a stall with open boxes of nuts and dates and grains and brightly coloured candies. Piles of powdered spices are arranged in neat pyramids and shelves are crammed with jars and cans. A forest of thickly padded children's jackets, pink, blue, green, black and red, hang from the wire mesh alongside racks of white bras with polka-dot hearts. Past an arch of ancient stone, I catch a glimpse of a camel carcase, its head intact, hanging from a hook above a table where piles of meat lie unwrapped on a tray and scrawny chickens look out of a tiny cage.

In this part of the market, the sunlight doesn't reach through the wire mesh as far as the narrow cobbled street. Here, the wire mesh is covered in garbage - dirty diapers, bones, broken bottles, toilet paper, bits of wood, discarded packaging, rotten food. In one spot, the wire mesh bulges precariously under the weight of the garbage. It won't be long before the mesh collapses, spewing garbage onto the market.

A few yards further, shouts rain down from high above me. Craning my neck, I see women and children leaning over the roof of the building. They're jeering and screaming and throwing more garbage onto the wire mesh. A woman with a white scarf over her head and a baby under one arm flings a paper diaper onto the mesh. Wet, green shit bursts out of the diaper and drips through onto the street beside me. The woman screams in Hebrew, 'Get out, you filthy Arabs. This is our land. Run away. Run, you scum.'

'You should be ashamed of yourselves,' the woman holding me screams in Arabic. She shakes her fist in the air. I can feel her body vibrating. 'You don't deserve this land. You've violated the covenant with Abraham. We'll drive you out. Just you wait.' She plants herself on the spot and carries on screaming. The women and children on the roof scream back. I add my voice to the symphony of screams, bellowing as loud as my little lungs allow. Which even to my ears, is impressively loud.

I'm gathering breath for my next contribution when I hear a familiar voice calling me. 'Yigal! Is that you? Hey, up here. On the roof. It's me, Aisha.'

I squirm until I can see that the person calling my name is the baby in the arms of the diaper-throwing woman.

Aisha's face is rounder and her hair curlier and shorter but nevertheless, she's unmistakably Aisha.

'*Assalamu 'Alaikum*, Aisha. I didn't expect to see you for another twenty years.' I'm so excited I can't stop wiggling. 'Hey, what did they name you?'

'Same as before. Life. I'm called Chava. What about you?'

'Adil. Justice. I like it. It suits me. So Aisha Chava, how was your journey?'

'Great!' she says. 'It only took four hours. It was really smooth. When I got in, I had a few days rest in a deluxe, state-of-the-art, clean hospital. All mod cons. What about you?'

'All right. All right,' I say. 'You don't have to rub it in.'

Aisha laughs and I note she has the same sense of humour. 'You weren't stuck at a checkpoint, were you?' she calls.

'Yes, we're always stuck at checkpoints.' I have to shout to be heard above the clamour of voices. 'I wasn't expected for another four weeks so it was a surprise when labour started. We were three hours at the checkpoint. That was scary. My mother was lying on the ground, groaning and screaming. I've got a three year old brother and a two year old sister. They were there crying their heads off. Eventually we were allowed through and I was born soon after we got to the hospital. It was clean but I needed an incubator and there weren't enough so I had to share with someone else. I thought I'd have to go back to the Other World Checkpoint and start again. Anyway I got through all that and I'm here now.'

'Hush, hush, my darling.' My mother lifts me onto her shoulder and pats me. 'Don't cry. Shh Shh.' I stop shouting and hiccup a few times to encourage her to focus on me instead of arguing with the Jews on the roof. Out of the corner of my eye, I notice Aisha's mother has her free hand on a plastic bucket balanced on the edge of the roof.

'There's pee in the bucket,' Aisha shouts. She's dangling from her mother's other hand and doesn't look too comfortable. 'You better tell your mother to get away quick.'

I try to communicate this to my mother but without success. Instead of leaving, she lifts me into the air and waves me at the people on the roof. 'You see this baby,' she shrieks. 'This is my son. As soon as he's old enough, he will redeem us. He'll drive you out with guns and bombs. He'll fight your army. You won't stand a chance. You'll see.'

But I know otherwise. I've had enough of guns and bombs. No way, Mama, I think to myself. That is not what I will be doing. But she's not ready to listen to me yet so I don't try to explain. I have to be patient. Many years will pass before I'm ready to tell her of my dreams and to live the life I've planned with Aisha.

'Yigal Adil. Remember our pact. You won't forget, will you? We'll find each other as soon as we're old enough. We'll tear down these walls and these cages. We'll find a way to live together in peace and justice, all of us.'

'To life,' I shout, raising my hand in what I intend to be a clenched fist salute but with my infant co-ordination, is nothing more than a smack on my mother's nose. Still, it focuses her attention onto me. She hugs me tight to her chest and sprints away. The shower of urine splashes onto the street, missing us by inches.

About the Author

Lisa Saffron was born in 1952 in the United States and grew up in a non-religious, Zionist-sympathising Jewish family. She moved to England in her twenties where she raised her family and worked in parenting support, health research and feminist women's health information. She belongs to a progressive synagogue and hosts a weekly programme on Radio Salaam Shalom, an internet radio station for Jewish-Muslim dialogue. She travelled to Israel and the Occupied Territories several times since her first visit in 1968. Her latest trip with the Compassionate Listening Project was the inspiration for Checkpoint. This is her first novel. She has published non-fiction and autobiographical books and articles.